"Fran Metzman knows how to bring to life an important subject in a way that promises to frighten and provoke her readership. You will feel captivated by the situation, challenged by the decisions, and in the end feel a part of something much larger than yourself."

– Ken Bingham, author of over 25 novels, twenty plays, Professor, Drexel University

Design and composition by:
Tim Ogline / Ogline Design

ISBN: 979-8-9866188-7-6

Publisher's Cataloging-In-Publication Data
Metzman, Frances
    The Cha Cha Babes: Dance with the Devil

Categories: Fiction, Thriller, Mystery

Published by Tributaries Press
102 Sandy Ridge-Mt Airy Road
Stockton, NJ 08559

Printed in the United States of America

First Edition

"*The Cha Cha Babes Dance with the Devil* is a follow-up to *The Cha Cha Babes of Pelican Way*. After being abducted into the dark realm of sex trafficking, the women break free and aid other women who are ensnared in this brutal industry. These ladies are determined to seek justice. This gripping tale is a true testament to their bravery in taking on the Mafia. It's a novel you can't put down and keeps you on the edge of your seat. A must read."

– Gloria Mindock, editor of Červená Barva Press,
author of award-winning *Ash*

"In the aptly titled, *Cha Cha Babes Dance With the Devil*, Fran Metzman's indomitable Celia Ewing and cheeky sidekick Marcy, a pair of baby boomers with attitudes, become trapped in the ugly underworld of human trafficking, quickly learning firsthand the hellish reality that millions of individuals from all over the world face on a daily basis, a hope-crushing, abuse-filled nonexistence. But as readers of Metzman's much-praised *The Cha Cha Babes of Pelican Way* know, you can't keep a Cha Cha Babe down. Equally ready to use a firearm and do a mean Google Search, plucky and fearless Celia seeks more than personal survival. There are women to free and bastards to take down. Breathlessly paced, the novel's surprising twists and turns make this an exhilarating read, as plucky Celia and her still-ready-for-the-fashion-runway pal push the Cha Cha 'I'll do it my way' code to the limit. This adventure tale may do more for awareness about one of the world's truly insidious practices than a shelf of nonfiction books on the subject. Read it and look forward to the third Cha Cha book in the series."

– Ned Bachus, author of *City of Brotherly Love*
(winner, IPPY Gold Medal in Literary Fiction, 2013),
Open Admissions (nonfiction, 2017), and *Mortal Things* (novel, 2022)

A Novel

by Frances Metzman

Tributaries
Press

*My love goes to my children, grandchildren,
in-law children, step-grandchildren, and all
girlfriends—both theirs and mine.
And to Jay, of course.*

*They unconditionally support my endeavors
and give me so much comfort. They have my heart
and that puts it in the best hands.*

Chapter 1

Fritzie's II Rendezvous Bar at the Devonshire Hotel had a strange vibe. Something odd about the atmosphere struck Celia as soon as she walked in. On the surface the modern, upscale space appealed to those with chic, sophisticated taste. But woven into the air, the hushed buzz of the crowd hinted at frenetic secrets. Marcy, her dearest friend, sashayed in front of Celia. Marcy had insisted that they stop by Fritzie's tonight to cheer themselves up. They both missed their dear friend Deb, part of their once inseparable trio. Deb had moved away from their condominium complex in Boca Pelicano Palms, in Boca Pelicano, Florida, a year ago. It seemed to Celia that Deb had performed a magic trick that had gone awry and disappeared into a puff of smoke.

She and Marcy parked their carry-on suitcases beside the black leather bar chairs they slipped onto. They'd stopped at Fritzie's in Philadelphia on the recommendation of the bartender who worked at Fritzie's in Boca Raton not far from their condominium complex. He'd overheard them say they were going to Philadelphia to visit Celia's daughter. She and Marcy had gone to Fritzie's a few times. They'd never minded the seedy appearance with barn-wood walls and a scratched dance floor. They loved to do the twist to all the oldies, Elvis, and Chubby Checkers. And, of course, the cha-cha. Dancing sent shivers of delight from Celia's skin into the depths of her bones. In those moments, all her problems dissipated.

Now, for the next two weeks they'd forgone the warmth and sunshine of Florida for a chilly fall in Philadelphia. Celia's daughter, Allison, had offered her and Marcy the guest room in her Center City apartment, and was waiting for them. Lots of tension remained between Celia and Allison for past missteps, mostly by Celia. Stopping for one drink would help with her jitters.

"I'm glad we stopped," Celia said. "My nerves need preparation to meet Allie."

"Stop," Marcy said in a subdued tone. "Allie's issues had nothing to do with what needed to be done. Never mind what happened between you two. That dopy husband of yours cut you out of parenting and took control of Allie." Marcy narrowed her eyes. "For selfish reasons."

"I allowed it." Celia tried to lighten her spirits. "I'm slowly getting my confidence back."

"Ha! We make mistakes. Last year was the worst when I convinced you and Deb to help move Melvy. His weight," she huffed, "unbearable when he died on top in me, in the midst of lovemaking. Things changed after that."

"At least he died having hot sex with the hottest looking babe at Boca Pelicano Palms." Celia smiled, but looked around to make sure no one was listening. The suits talked among themselves as though making business deals.

"But, damn," winced Marcy. "Did it have to be on his office desk?"

"He died in the throes of ecstasy. It made sense to move him to his own bed."

"You saved my ass. Otherwise, eviction awaited me—my third infraction. Three strikes, you're out."

"I knew what we did was illegal," Celia said. "Evidence tampering? Obstruction of justice? Whatever. You were innocent and what could we do for a dead Melvy? I'd help you all over again." Celia grimaced at Marcy's stricken face. "We have each other's backs—always."

Marcy ran her hand down the side of her red knit dress. "This body is designed to attract men. It's made for love." She laughed.

"Darling, truer words were never said." Celia's mention of love always cheered Marcy up.

"Life goes on and so should we. Remember that disgusting guy I danced with at Fritzie's? We had barely reached the dance floor before he asked if I'd sleep with him."

Celia gave a thin smile. "I saw him edge his hands up the side of your boobs on the dance floor, the creep. Deb gave me a lesson about elderly guys loving boobs that night. What'd she say? 'Intelligence is a low priority in Florida. Big ones win every time.'"

Marcy rounded her hands in front of her. "Can't deny I have big boobs, but I hate when men don't appreciate me for my intelligence."

They broke out laughing.

"You are intelligent, Marcy," Celia said. "The deal is, you don't care if men ignore that about you."

"How about the sarcastic remarks of those biddies at Boca Pelicano Palms who wanted to see us in jail? Maybe it's funny now because we broke up that scam," Marcy said. The eerie, pale blue neon light reflecting from the mirrors above gave Marcy's eyes a dazzling turquoise haze.

"I miss Stanton but don't have the energy to see him as often," said Celia, smiling at the thought of later in life love. "He wants to move to another level in our relationship. For me? Not now. Painting gives me all the pleasure I need."

"Well, we'll have fun with Allie," smiled Marcy. "Nice she invited us."

"Got my fingers crossed. I wish Allie called me more often." Celia sighed. "We were on a great path to patching things up, and then she shied away, saying I stirred up trouble wherever I went."

"Allie will come around. We promised no downers tonight," Marcy said.

"The good news is she got promoted," Celia said. "They've added another department for her to direct. Gerontology at Rudrow Hospital." Celia set her elbows on the bar and her chin in her hands. "She's a remarkable woman. Just that her love life has been a mess. One divorce, and a bunch of broken romances. She comes by it honestly, given the kind of parents she had."

Marcy drooped her arm over Celia's shoulder. "Once she gets her shit together, she'll be fine. Look, she's got a man in her life now. A doctor, yet."

"Allie tells me this guy is nice. Still, she's spooked about relationships. They work in the same hospital." Celia's face softened as she gripped Marcy's hand. "Maybe we should start to smoke pot again to forget the bad times, like we used to."

"Now you're talking. We're not over-the-hill at, ahem, fiftyish."

Celia pointed upward with her thumb. "Go up a few years."

"Just a couple." Marcy gave a high-pitched laugh, more like a yelp. People sitting next to them stared. Marcy brought her voice down an octave. "I insist you make it up to Stanton. You guys love each other. Are we cool?"

Celia smiled. "Stanton once said that in war there is friendly fire that kills your compatriots. And that's what humans do in relationships."

"Smart guy. That's life, babe."

"I do love the guy. I've been so moody lately."

"I can't believe the man hangs in there. You put him off so many times, I'd dump you myself."

The mirror behind the bar gave a full view of the room. No dance floor, just smooth, white marble not meant for dancing. Celia took in the vibe of the room, as it absorbed into ice blue walls. The space was gorgeous in a cool, calculated way. A few middle-aged and older men, dressed in pristine chalk-striped suits, blinding white shirts, and red or purple ties, sat at black granite tables that matched the bar top. Beautiful, much younger women accompanied them. Some men sported the trendy, tight, tapered suits that made them look as though they'd outgrown their Bar Mitzvah outfits. The men seemed clear-eyed. The women sitting with them in short dresses revealing shapely, long legs mostly stared into space.

Why would they be interested in men so much older? They look as though they want to be elsewhere. "Those women seem out of it."

Seeing men her age with women thirty to forty years younger put her on edge. Age differences didn't bother her, but the room looked like a freeze-frame from a movie set, filled with cut-off, fashionable mannequins pre-arranged by a set designer.

Marcy ordered two martinis. The bartender, Willy, nodded then scanned the crowd with an arched eyebrow as he delivered the icy stemmed glasses filled to the top. He put olives on the side in a little white dish.

"Maybe I'll meet one of those old geezers." Marcy elbowed Celia to look at a man in a black silk suit looking in their direction.

"He's only about fifty. You're too old for all of them."

"Those young babes have nothing on me. I've still got it." Marcy tossed her red curls back over her shoulder.

"These guys go for girls who look like models."

"Well, don't I fit that bill?"

"Yes, for the Medicare set." They both laughed. "Learn to take care of yourself first, and then look for a nice guy," Celia said.

Celia recognized Marcy hadn't had a man in her life for over a year—a long time for Marcy. She had been abused by parents through her childhood and needed love like an addict needed drugs. This didn't seem like the right place to find it. She started to rise.

"Leaving so soon?" Willy said. "How about one more?"

Marcy tugged on Celia's sleeve to stay seated.

Chapter 2

Celia noticed several men slipping Willy money by way of a secret handshake.

"These men usually have big expense accounts," Celia whispered. "Why not write tips on bills rather than surreptitiously hand a bartender money?"

"Don't get paranoid."

"Why hide the fact you're tipping?"

A man, standing close to Celia, stopped Willy. She heard him say softly, "Thanks for Lorraine's number. She's hot but a little too old. None older than twenty-five. I made it clear to the d'yavol sitting over there."

Willy shushed him. "Oh, our resident devil," he whispered.

"I think d'yavol is Russian. And is Willy pimping girls?" Celia whispered to Marcy.

Marcy whirled her stool in Celia's direction, her dress mid-thigh, legs crossed. "Now, Miss Marple, nothing wrong with paid escorts. It doesn't necessarily mean sex. Some guys need companions." Marcy made a biting motion, imitating a vampire. "This place is loaded with men."

"Stop frothing at the mouth. Look around you."

The air in the room bore heavily on Celia.

"Take a look at that." Celia nodded at a very young woman, legs up to her neck, with her much older date. He half-dragged her as she stumbled glaze-eyed to the elevator that led to hotel rooms. Soon another suit brought his date to the elevator just before she nodded off into her soup.

"This place does seem like it's a fancy cat house," Marcy stretched her neck to look over Celia's shoulder.

The young woman, barely standing, caught Celia's eye with such sadness, she wanted to grab her away. Why does that escort look so out of focus? Wobbly. It gives me the heebie-jeebies.

Willy wiped a cocktail glass and tilted his head in Marcy's direction. "I see you and that guy in the black suit making eye contact."

"I don't ask for men to flirt with me. It's just my dazzling personality that entrances everyone. And these boobs." She gave Willy a look that spelled trouble to Celia.

"So, Willy." Marcy thrust her head forward. "What's with the tips passing back and forth between you and the suits?"

Willy eyes grew wide. "What the hell you talkin' about?"

Celia pinched Marcy's thigh under the counter.

Marcy shrugged her shoulders. "Don't bullshit a bullshitter. You're taking bucks from guys, using the secret handshake. What're you up to?"

"Dumb nonsense," he said. "But you sure got an imagination." He looked upset.

"Marcy, we have to leave now." Celia finished her drink and stood up.

Marcy swung around. "Look who's coming over."

"Oh, don't go," the man's deep baritone voice rang out as he walked up to them. "I want to buy these lovely ladies a drink." The man loosened his black and gray striped tie. His ink-black hair with touches of gray at the temples had not one strand out of place. He looked like the CEO of a rip-off company. Celia sensed something slimy about him. He motioned to Willy. "Another round, for beautiful ladies." He took a seat next to Marcy.

He had an odd accent. His lips moved as if he were trying to imitate the way Americans spoke. It was his phrasing that was off.

Marcy beckoned Willy closer. "You know we're drinking dirty martinis."

"Thanks, but we really have to run." Celia grasped Marcy's arm. Marcy pressed Celia's toes with the heel of her shoe—a sign to sit down.

"You ladies the best-looking here, and smart. Young ones drink too much." He grinned, teeth so white the lights pinged off of them. He made a sniffing motion. "Do drugs."

The man touched Celia's shoulder gently urging her to be seated.

"Come on, Celia. Don't be a party pooper." The words sounded like a plea. "Well…just one quick drink."

"Peter is my best customer and a great guy." Willy chuckled as he shook a chrome shaker. "You gals got it all over those young ones." Willy looked calmer since this man came over.

"Please, join me. You see, Willy can vouch for me."

"You married?" Marcy asked as drinks were served. Icy glasses contained a pale blueish liquid, reflecting the lights overhead.

"Divorced. Am here on business often. Please forgive my English. I live abroad. What are your names?"

"Marcy and Celia." Marcy gave him a big grin. Celia enjoyed the iciness of the martini cooling her flushed face.

"I'm Peter. What are lovelies doing here?"

"Here for a visit. We live in Florida." Marcy batted her eyes at him.

Peter raised his glass of beer and clicked their glasses. "To Willy. Good man."

Marcy crossed her legs to better show off her thighs.

Celia worried Marcy might flirt till the wee hours. Peter was so slick he looked dipped in Vaseline. She wanted to go, the sooner the better, but the martini was fogging her brain. Too strong.

She took a big sip of her cocktail figuring she would drink half and they could leave. Celia nudged Marcy to finish and stop chatting up Peter. I haven't been to Philly in a dog's age and want to see all the sights. First, I'll report this place to the police.

She wished Stanton was here. She thought about a painting she'd done of him, silver streaks shooting across his face across a black background. She'd been trying to capture his mercurial moods. I'm sorry I spent so little time with him this past year. Can't always be scared of being hurt.

Suddenly, the room spun at a dizzying speed. Celia could see Marcy's chin hit her chest before clunking her head on the bar top. She tried reaching out to her, but her arms were glued to her sides.

I've had two martinis before. This feels…different. A black wall with a pinhole light blocked her vision. She tried to see through the pinhole, but blue and red flashes blocked it. Then moonless darkness descended. She tried to raise a nonexistent window shade to let light in. Her legs trembled, then turned to rubber.

"My God," Celia heard her voice as though in an echo chamber. "I'm…"

Her tongue trapped words in her throat. She could hardly breathe. Peter's loud laugh thundered in her ears as he told the patrons nearby, "Just drunken ladies who should know better at their age."

Chapter 3

A fog shrouded Celia's sight as she came out of what felt like a nightmarish sleep that left her fatigued. Her temples squeezed against her skull causing pain to explode in her head. She banged against something hard. Irritated that her eyes stuck together, she tried blinking.

How did we get to Allie's? Did we stagger in? Can't remember a thing except being at the bar. She tried to get up. Something held her back. Panic seized her chest. She worked her eyes open and realized she sat in a rough, splintered chair, in a dimly lit, very large room. Her legs were tied together and hands tied to the armrests. Her stiff neck agitated an already raging headache.

She rotated her head as much as the pain allowed and saw Marcy in the same position next to her, her head drooping to the side.

"What the hell? This has to be a joke. Christ. Marcy," she shouted, "Wake up!"

Marcy opened her dazed eyes and stared straight ahead, a blank expression on her face. "Where are we? Why can't I move?"

Through her haze Celia saw they were in a shadowed echo of a once resplendent ballroom. It looked gritty and seedy; three massive crystal chandeliers, covered in dust, hung from the ceiling. A light, barely audible tinkling drifted downward as a slight breeze brushed crystals together. Faded and peeling, dark purple and red-flowered silk wallpaper reached from the ceiling to the wainscoting. Beneath that, nicked, scratched, dark oak paneling stretched to the floor. Hardly any furniture except for the chairs they were tied to. No windows. The room looked eerie and out of a horror novel.

Celia narrowed her eyes at the amateurish, faded copy of the Sistine Chapel ceiling. God's giant, gnarled finger reached out to a stringy armed Adam. Celia thought the finger pointed to her. Rushing gusts of air slammed in her ears. The out-of-proportion drawing reminded her of a howling clown. The mildew smell in the room overpowered. What was this place? Where were they? Some dilapidated mansion? Italy? Romania? Spain?

"Ach," Marcy groaned. "My head's pounding. What happened? Why the hell are we tied up? This is not funny."

"I don't know. Hey," Celia yelled, her face contorted. "Anyone out there? Yo, come get us." Her voice echoed throughout the room. No response.

"Help us for Christ's sake," Marcy shouted as she tugged her bound hands. "Where the hell are we?"

A woozy memory snapped into Celia's mind; the bartender's thumbs-up and the metallic laugh from Peter, probably not his name. She almost laughed to think they were imprisoned or kidnapped. Who'd want two old ladies with little money? This had to be a bad joke.

"We passed out last night right after those drinks," Celia said. "I saw your head hit the bar top." There was a red lump on Marcy's forehead. "Oh, shit. That's why we have headaches. Those men at the bar drugged us." She huffed. "Damn, Marcy. You accused Willy of pimping those young women to the older men. You scared the hell out of him."

"I didn't call him a pimp," Marcy snapped. "Well, maybe I suggested it. Listen, um, they can't kidnap us just for that. It's against the law."

The reality hit Celia. "Those young women might be just that—escorts without sex. The men paid bartenders to drug them—a date-rape drug—just what they gave us. Willy's on the take. It means a hundred times more than a bartender's salary. You hit Willy where he lives, and I'm pissed at you. It's not the first time you've gotten us into trouble."

"My brain doesn't know how to keep my mouth shut. I'm sorry."

"Sorry doesn't cut it. We've got to get out of here. But these ropes look strong enough to hold anchors on a cruise ship."

Celia shifted, pulled, and yanked as best she could to no avail. Then she stamped her feet and tried to lift herself. The chair lifted three inches but the ties held strong. She slammed back down on the oak floor. "My God. We're prisoners."

"They have to release us. Kidnapping is a federal offense," Marcy cried.

"Don't be ridiculous. They don't give a damn." Celia turned her head in the direction of heavy footsteps. A large, wide-shouldered man in army fatigue pants and an olive tank top appeared. He moved to the side of the door, saying nothing. An overhead light reflected off his shaved, tan scalp.

"Let us go," Marcy shouted. "Yo, you. I'm talking to you." Marcy pointed her chin at him.

The man focused on the wall across from him. His bulging biceps rippled. A holster at his waist held an ominous, thick knife. He guarded the only door in the room.

Footsteps again but more delicate; flexible, leather-soled shoes tap-tapping on a marble floor. A tall, slender man stepped inside, wearing a black silk suit, blood-red shirt, and matching red tie. Celia blinked to get the fog out of her eyes. It wasn't the man who drugged them. Leaning over, he said something to the large man in what sounded like an Eastern European language—Russian? Her grandmother had come from Russia, but she wasn't sure.

He looked over at Celia and Marcy and gave them a dazzling white smile. As he walked toward them, he stuck out his arms as though welcoming long-lost friends.

"Good morning, my lovelies. Even after bad night, you both beautiful." He ran his hands over brown hair that looked like it had been super-glued to his scalp.

Why didn't I haul Marcy out of the bar and leave sooner? Maybe they'd have kidnapped us outside anyway.

"We're just quiet ladies who live in a retirement community," Celia said. "We won't tell anything. We didn't see anything. Let us go, please. Why do you want of two old ladies?" Celia's voice diminished to a whimper.

"I wouldn't say old." Marcy stuttered.

Celia shot Marcy a penetrating look. "Stop that. This is seriously weird."

"Ahh," he said. He clasped his hands behind his back. "Have for you most important job. My boss likes you very much."

Celia could swear she saw the guard snicker. *Are they drug runners? Do they want us to be mules?* "Please, let us go." Her voice cracked. "We know nothing about your business and care less."

"They say you make big talk about business last night in bar." He looked directly at Marcy. "Yes, good business. Our women like. All make money."

Then it hit her. Drugging escorts took on a new meaning. Was this straight-out sex trafficking? Did they kidnap those women?

Or, have I read too much about what the papers say is an epidemic? She had seen posters at the airport about watching out for men with younger women or children that looked frightened or acted strangely.

Why can't Marcy recognize red flags? This can't be good. Is my will up-to-date? Allie gets my apartment but there's only a little bit of money.

"You know about girls," he said, his voice bouncing off the walls.

Marcy put on her most innocent face, the one that looked angelic as though she'd never heard a bad word in her life. "The girlfriends of the nice men, you mean?"

He sneered. "You tell Willy he take dirty money."

"Uh, just a big, fat joke. Just teasing. We don't know anything." Marcy gulped.

"Maybe you think go to police. All over this country we have police in—right here" He patted his pocket and howled with laughter. "So, you do what I tell. Not be harmed if obey."

"Please let us go." Tears rolled down Marcy's cheeks.

"You good for job. We feed you, take care, but not free." He looked pleased with himself. "You are thinking escape maybe?" His grin turned hard, and he stared at Marcy. "We find where you go." He turned to Celia. "One bad move and you die." His face tightened. He bent toward Celia. "We be happy family. You work for us now, for the girls. You groom."

"No," Celia screamed. She tugged her fists against the ropes, wanting to slap the man, pound his chest. Groom? Groom them for sex? They had to get out. Allison would be beside herself when she realized her mother had disappeared into the clouds. *Don't mention that we have children. Why in the world did we go to that bar?*

"One more loud noise, I gag you." He nodded at the guard, who waved an olive-green hankie.

"Please, please, please," Marcy begged. "What do you want? House cleaning? Cooking? We can do that, but let us out."

"Please. We'll do anything you want." Her husband, Gabe, would say how she'd gotten herself into doing the wrong thing—again. Was Allie worried? Had she called the police? No one at Boca Pelicano Palms would know she was gone. Maybe Allie would call Stanton.

"You cooperate, no hurt."

He found a folding chair against the wall, brought it over, and sat on it backwards. He smiled, displaying crooked bottom teeth, and eye teeth wolfishly prominent. He sat as though they all were enjoying a friendly conversation.

He gave a fake grin, but his eyes scrutinized them. "You ladies be good teachers to girls. Make girls feel safe. No run away. You tell how prevent babies." He reached into his jacket pocket and held up a compact of birth control pills. "No babies. Especially young ones."

Celia's stomach crunched. "What do you mean by young ones?"

His half-smile matched his one arched eyebrow on the same side of his face. "You find troublemakers. Tell who want escape. You say to them they are illegal here with no passports, no papers. Police will arrest for prostitution and they deported. Then they come back to us."

"Where are we?" Marcy asked.

He cleared his throat, stared at them with his black bushy eyebrows meeting over the bridge of his nose. "You make sure girls not frightened. They not good with men when scared. Be mothers to them."

"Where are the girls from?" Marcy asked.

"We bring girls from many countries. Americans like many

different. They scared. You make nice." He fluttered his hand from the wrist. "The Italian and Slavic Mafias kiss my ass to get these girls. Pay plenty."

Celia tasted bile in the back of her throat. "You damned, stupid, son-of-a-bitch coward."

He jumped up and slapped Celia across the face so hard fragments sliced into her brain. She screamed and rubbed her cheek against her shoulder.

"Son of bitch, yes, but not stupid." He sneered. "Good business-man. You nothing. You be nice to girls and tell us who good or bad." He sniggered. "We need know."

His face broke into a grin, then reassembled into a forbidding expression. "We know you have kids. We know where they live and work." He laughed. "And you," he said to Marcy, "Have grandchild, no? You love, huh?"

"I'll kill you first." Marcy cried.

"Drop dead and rot in hell. You dirty pigs," Celia shouted, turning her face away, waiting for the slap.

The man jumped up with fisted hands, stepped closer to her and punched downward, stopping just before her cheek. She cringed. The next instant, he smacked her hard across the face. She felt a pop as her head snapped back further than muscles allowed. Hot pain shot through her neck and skull.

"Stop it! Don't you dare hit her," Marcy shouted, tugging at the ropes.

"You curse me? Then you will be dead with families, too." He pointed two fingers at the them. "You cooperate, you live." He grinned. "You make all good."

Celia didn't answer. Face stinging, neck muscles stiff, she pressed her lips together. Tears rolled down her cheeks and burned the deep scratch he'd made across her cheek with his ring.

"I want answer." He waited and no answer came. He raised his fist over Marcy's head. "She die first if say no. I kill with fists. You watch."

"Yes. We got it," Celia said in a hoarse voice.

His oversized front teeth pressed down on his bottom lip. "Talk later." He turned to the guard. "Jerzy, untie but watch. Feed. They are clever, old bitches. Any funny business, beat shit out of them."

Jerzy nodded and grinned. Celia wondered why they didn't speak their native language to each other. Was it so she and Marcy could understand the threats? He padded out in his shiny crocodile shoes. The room closed in on her. She wheezed, trying to catch her breath.

Chapter 4

Six months ago, back in lovely, warm Florida, Celia and Marcy had read an article about an Indonesian gang that had been arrested in a sting operation for forcing captive children and young women to become sex slaves. The article had gone on to say the United States ranked as a country involved in human sex trafficking and the US Department of State estimated that approximately 15,000 to 18,000 people are trafficked into the United States each year. Of course, since it is illicit, it is hard to estimate the actual number. Trafficked victims are terribly abused physically, sexually, and mentally. They are prisoners who produce billions of dollars worldwide and are subjected to the whims of brutal masters. The article had shocked them at the time, but they hadn't given it much thought after that.

The guard whose name was Jerzy lumbered up to Celia and Marcy, his boots thumping on the sooty terrazzo floor. With methodical precision, he untied their hands and feet. Celia could see that he'd done this before. She massaged her chaffed and bloodied wrists and ankles where the ropes sliced her skin. As he untied Marcy's ankles, he peeked up her dress and laid his hand on her thigh.

She pushed his hand away. "Stop that you dirty shit."

Jerzy grinned sideways.

He pulled a cell phone from his pocket. "Food!" he shouted,

and walked back to his post, tapping his hand on the handle of the knife.

Celia tried taking a step, but felt woozy and sat back down. Marcy remained in the chair.

"We've got to get our hands on his phone," Celia whispered to Marcy. "Got to call our kids to tell them to hide."

"Exactly how do you propose to do that?"

"When he falls asleep, we can do it and then run for our lives."

Marcy gave her a doubtful stare.

She's right, Celia thought. What and who were in the other rooms? How long had they been unconscious? Celia scratched her upper arm but it hurt. *Look at that, a tiny red needle mark. That's what kept us unconscious. Supposing we're in some foreign country, how do we make sense of street signs? And how do we know the first person we try to talk to won't turn us back to our captors?*

We have to reach Allie, and Marcy's son, Lionel, to let them know what happened and to tell them to go into hiding immediately. But why would they believe us? We have to get his phone…

Jerzy stepped aside for an elderly, stooped woman, her wooly white hair pulled back in a loose bun. She held a large tray and her hefty body rolled side to side with each step. She wore a cotton housedress like the one Celia's own mother had worn—yellow and blue flowered pattern, a belt that slid through a slit at the waist and tied in front. The woman's eyes were ringed with dark circles and bloodshot.

At first Celia thought the woman looked older than she and Marcy. Deep wrinkles surrounded her mouth and crow's feet fanned out from the corners of her eyes. But, up close, the skin on her forehead and cheeks were smooth. Celia tried to signal but, stone-faced, the woman set the tray on the floor and stood.

"Do you speak English? Where are we? Who the hell are these people?" Marcy asked, looking across the room. "Jerzy. Hey, you." He didn't move.

Celia looked at the bowl of soup at her feet. She was so hungry she felt she might swoon. "We've got to eat no matter what's in that soup," said Marcy, lifting the bowl and gobbling noisily with the large tablespoon the woman handed her. "Hey, it's good. Yummy beef and cabbage borscht."

"I make good soup," the woman said.

So, she does speak English. Celia noticed a questioning look that the woman speared at her.

"Maybe they're drugging us again," Celia said.

"No, no. It's good," the woman said.

"It's either die from starvation or be drugged." Marcy said, and kept eating. "So hungry."

"Zutka. Out," Jerzy shouted. The woman backed away, turned, and lumbered out.

"Zutka is trying to tell us something," Celia whispered. Her stomach growled as she pulled her bowl onto her lap and began eating with caution. *How long since we ate?*

Then she said loud enough for Jerzy to hear, "It's good." Celia liked the dish more than she expected. She'd thought about refusing to eat, but knew they needed energy to try for an escape. Obviously, the house they were in was involved in the sex trade. That meant guards all over.

Is Zutka also a madam? Or was she putting out vibes for help? Can she even be trusted?

Marcy put her empty bowl down and approached Jerzy. He held his hand out to signal her to stop.

"We need a change of clothes, toothbrush, and toothpaste."

Jerzy pulled out his phone and mumbled indecipherable words. Within minutes, Zutka rolled in a small cart that contained two wrinkled yellow dresses, used oxfords, and a large bowl of water that splashed on the dresses when she pushed the cart over broken floorboards. Two toothbrushes slipped toward the edge. Two thin, worn towels and a bar of gray soap stopped them from rolling off the cart.

"No toothpaste?" Marcy asked.

"Nyet." Zutka shook her head. "Use soap. Shoes good."

"Can you help us?" Celia mouthed, risking that she might be a spy.

In a whisper, so soft Celia hardly heard her, she said, "You help. I help."

The woman looked over her shoulder at Jerzy who stared at her. She spun on the heel of a rubber backless shoe and hurried toward the door, her thick body tottering with panic.

When she passed him, Jerzy grabbed her arm. "Bring me food."

The woman kept her eyes down and nodded.

"Zutka is terrified of him," Celia whispered. "We have to make contact with her before they tie us up again."

"I don't think she'll defy them." Marcy wrinkled her nose. "I'm thinking we just pop him over the head with a chair. I'll distract him like I'm offering to have sex with him and you do it." She flung her head back.

"You think he'll fall for it?"

"Never met a man who didn't find me sexually attractive. Young or old, doesn't matter."

"Okay. I'll wait for your signal, but you have to get him away from the wall so I can sneak up on him." Celia looked at the tired wooden chair she sat on. It had heft. She'd have to be sure she could lift it and then slam him hard. *Can I do this? Hurt another person?*

Marcy stood, flipped her hair back and beckoned Jerzy to her. He met her halfway and   again held out his hand to stop her. Marcy stepped a few paces to the side so Jerzy had his back to Celia.

He pointed at the bowl. "Wash. Sleep."

"On that filthy straw mattress? Oh, Jerzy, sweetie. Don't make us do that. Do you have a more comfy, cleaner bed for us? Hmmm, you're so handsome. How about your bed? Huh?"

Without a word he knocked Marcy down. Celia ripped off a loose armrest, unable to lift the whole chair. *Is he going to rape her?* Celia gripped the armrest, but Jerzy whirled and knocked it away. He pressed Marcy's wrists to the ground with his knee. She yelped as though an eighteen-wheeler parked on her.

Jerzy pulled a rope out of his pocket, tied Celia's and Marcy's hands and feet, and pushed them onto the straw beds. Celia gagged from the stench of dirt and sweat.

"Sleep," he said, walking back to the door.

"I must be losing my touch." Marcy whispered.

"What are you talking about? These are killers. Women are just dollars to them."

Just as Jerzy returned to his post, Zutka walked in with a tray that held a bowl of borscht, boiled beef, and potatoes. She handed the tray to Jerzy and reached outside the door to pull in a folding table and chair into which he promptly sat down. Jerzy stabbed a piece of meat and stuffed it into his mouth. Zutka peeked over at Celia and Marcy. Celia showed Zutka her tied wrists. Zutka looked away. *We're done for.*

Jerzy raised his fork and knife as though about to stab someone. Once he devoured the meat and potatoes, he attacked the bowl of borscht, drinking it as though it were a cup of tea.

Celia watched, hoping the enormous amount of food would put him to sleep. They had to risk trying to knock him out even if they had to crawl like worms. *Maybe find a way to cut the ropes. That knife…*

She tried making eye contact with Zutka who hung about the threshold watching Jerzy. The guard's head was inches from the bowl, sopping up remnants with a slice of bread. Zutka furtively nodded at the women, and turned back to Jerzy. With one movement she disappeared.

What did Zutka mean by her nod? Did she commiserate with them? Did she want to cooperate? How? Celia looked over at Marcy who was curled in a fetal position on the crude mattress, eyes wide and breathing hard. The guard finished every morsel, patted his stomach, and let out an enormous burp. He laughed, stood, and returned to his post close to the door.

"What the hell are we going to do?" Marcy whispered. "No self-respecting animal would sleep in this filth."

Celia shushed her. It seemed like nothing would save them. What had happened over a year ago and the accusations of murder looked like a piece of cake now.

A loud crash of plates and cutlery made her struggle to sit up.

Jerzy had slumped to the floor, overturning the empty dishes. Celia watched with horror as his body shuddered violently, the overhead lights causing his faint shadow to dance on the floor, imitating a boxer. Within a minute he stretched out his legs and his body went still.

Chapter 5

Zutka stepped inside and stood over Jerzy's body. She tiptoed over to Celia and Marcy, her hands fluttering. *Is Zutka going to call someone, and say we did something to him? We're dead in the water.*

"He die from rat poison."

Marcy started to cry. "Oh, please don't hurt us."

"I do to him. These pigs have Svetlana, my daughter. So, I forced to cook for them. I spit into the food and mix in different sheet every day. If I leave, they kill my Svetlana."

Marcy hunched her shoulders.

"These pigs take Svetlana when sixteen, three years ago. I need you to look. The d'yavol takes her."

"Oh, Zutka. My heart goes out to you," Celia said. "Isn't d'yavol the name for devil?"

"Da, he devil." Zutka took out scissors from her pocket, and used it to cut the ropes.

And he must be a very, very evil devil!

"If you tell who are bad girls, they beat them. You do that, you be pimp too. Make girls work all time till no breathe." Zutka finished untying Celia. "You be groom for make young girls be whores."

"Why did they want us? There are younger ones," Celia said in a hushed voice.

"Want women who look like American mamas. You tell girls all is good. Women work night and day—some die." She choked back a sob. "I take chance now for save daughter. You look for her. All work for bastards."

"Will you help us get out?" Marcy asked.

"Promise to look for my daughter. If I leave, they kill her and me. If they know I let you go, they kill me and Svetlana."

Marcy and Celia looked at each other and nodded. "Of course, we'll do it. Do you know where we can look?" Celia said.

"New York, maybe. Maybe Philadelphia. That is where Jerzy say you are from."

Marcy hummed, "Not exactly, but…"

"I sneak into boss's office. He keeps lists by hand, no computer for proof. My daughter speaks English real good. Went school in US. Teached me English. Name is Svetlana Chesinski." She handed Celia a picture of a young, olive-skinned, wavy-haired young woman with wide-set almond eyes. "Bastard who take her, Vladimir Stompovich. He tell her he love her then make her prostitute." She placed the picture in Celia's hand. "Keep."

Celia and Marcy stood, free of the ropes. Celia tucked Svetlana's picture into her bra.

"Can we get Jerzy's cell phone, too?" Marcy asked.

"Boss can't know I did." She spit. "When d'yavol comes here, rapes young girls." Zutka pushed back damp, flat curls on her sweating forehead. "Make like you knock him out and kill with knife. And then knock me out. Yes? They no care what kill him. They bury him, then look for you. You run fast."

Zutka walked over to Jerzy, found the cell phone, and gave it to Celia.

"Do not go police," Zutka said. "Some friendly with them."

Zutka slipped the knife from Jerzy's holster, handing it, glinting, to Celia who held it gingerly. The light twinkling on the blade made it look playful. *Playful, no. Frightening, yes.*

"Do."

Celia and Marcy stood open-mouthed. Celia raised the knife, and trembled so badly it fell from her hands.

Without a word, Zutka raised the chair and hit the corpse. Then she grabbed the knife and plunged it deep into Jerzy's back. Blood spattered on the floor and wall, soaking the strip of carpet under him. She turned toward the other room, leaving the knife stuck inside Jerzy.

Marcy sucked in her breath.

Celia's knees buckled.

"Kitchen." Zutka walked quickly.

Celia stumbled as she followed Zutka.

"Oh, God." Marcy's body convulsed like she'd been struck by lightning. "We'll never get out of here. They'll torture and kill us and our children."

Zutka reached into her pocket and pulled out a jangling key chain. Bits of tissue floated off the keys to the floor. She pulled off one key. "This is for small window in basement high up. Only one in house with no bars." She jiggled the keys. "Unlock and pull out. Small. Make wider. Work. Hard to see."

Marcy stared at Celia. "How the hell can we do that?"

"No choices now, Marcy."

Zutka's eyes teared and her shoulders shook. "You find my baby... she is good girl. They make her whore." She hung her head. "Looks like you kill Jerzy and try to kill me." She handed the women housedresses and aprons, hanging behind a door. "Go out like kitchen help. Carry tray. No speak."

"Wait. Where do we go if we make it out? What country are we in?" Marcy asked.

Zutka looked puzzled and wrinkled her brow. "You not know?"

Celia shook her head.

"This Pittsburgh, Pennsylvania. Did I say right? Much sex trafficking in cities in US. Much in California, Texas, Florida, New York. Much all over the world. Every country do it."

Celia blinked in disbelief, trying to see out of dirt encrusted windows. *Pittsburgh? Thought we were somewhere in Asia.* Smears of sunshine struck the blurry glass like oil stains.

"What?" Marcy shouted.

"Shh," Zutka said, putting her finger against her lips. "They want you help kidnap girls on streets. Kids no homes. You become, how do you say, um, scouts. They make you be kind and help girls then grab and make sex slaves. Fool them like my..." Zutka groaned. "We came for better life to US. I am slave in kitchen and don't know what happened to Svetlana."

"Maybe we should call the police now. After all, we're in the USA." Marcy's indignant voice hissed.

Zutka backed away. "Not matter. USA much money and men pay for young things. If bad police comes, you be dead. No proof. One mole tell them and they hide women. Men out." She zipped her finger over her throat. "They tell girls if run away, get arrested for prostitution and deported. They listen to men."

Celia suspected that organized crime, worldwide, ran their illicit businesses with the help of sizable payoffs to police and politicos.

"You must do." Zutka turned her back, pointing to her head. Then she picked up a large wooden rolling pin and handed it to Celia over her shoulder.

Celia gritted her teeth, knowing they had to do this so Zutka wasn't blamed for Jerzy's murder. She and Marcy held onto the end and brought it down on Zutka's head with as little pressure as they could manage to inflict damage. Zutka lurched forward. A trickle of blood covered a line of hair. "Again."

Celia directed the edge of the roller to hit Zutka's head again, but in a sliding motion where the greatest impact hit her shoulder. Still, Celia felt flesh torn open as Zutka's forehead smacked the floor and, this time, didn't lift up again. Celia dropped the roller, ran to the sink and threw up. Marcy seemed frozen, staring down at Zutka as though viewing a horror film.

After running the water, Celia pressed against the sink. "God help us. I hope she's okay."

Marcy turned, knelt, and put her fingers on Zutka's wrist. "She has a strong pulse. Learned how to do that as a candy striper when I was a kid. That's how I knew Melvy had died on top of me." She stood erect. "I hope these freakin' animals don't kill her. Let's go."

Celia wiped her mouth on the apron. They dressed in housedresses and aprons, and picked up two trays that held plates with butter, cheese slices, black bread, and salt and pepper shakers.

Celia looked back. Zutka grimaced. "Go."

Chapter 6

They stepped out of the kitchen and looked for the front door. The furniture was arranged, in no particular order, around a brick fireplace. Small, skimpy tables were littered with junktique vases and three pink threadbare loveseats accompanied them. Obviously, people living in the house didn't congregate for fireside chats. A guard appeared from the doorway of the foyer and stopped them. They held up the trays, indicating that they were servers. He pushed them against the wall.

"Who hire you, Vladimir Stompovich?"

They both nodded.

"Then you good for me." He reached for Marcy's breasts, but Marcy sidestepped. Celia's stomach flipped as he next reached for her. She prayed for self-control to keep from throwing the tray in his face. He looked back at Marcy, made a beeline for her crotch, and she made a frightened mouselike noise. As he reached for his zipper, Celia held the tray up and pointed to the stairs. He must have gotten the hint that someone above him in rank wanted service. His waving hand motion indicated they should come back as soon as they finished.

Marcy nodded. He returned to the front door foyer from where he had emerged and closed the door.

When they were out of earshot, Marcy said, "Over my dead body. I'll cut off his thingie first."

Celia turned and slinked over to a side door under a carved and dusty staircase. She ushered Marcy in. It had a locked bolt. They were on a landing for another staircase that reached into a black hole. She heard footsteps overhead that sounded like they were on the stairs. Celia shut the door quietly with her elbow. A loud male voice rammed through the door. Celia trembled. Marcy closed her eyes. Soon the voice drifted away.

Celia dialed Allie, hoping she wouldn't think the call was spam.

Allie picked up on the second ring. "Who is this?"

"Allie," whispered Celia. "Don't ask questions. But you have to get out of town."

"Mom? Where the hell are you? I was scared to death when you didn't show up! I called the police, but they said it was too early to declare you a missing person. I thought you were back on antidepressants and loopy again."

"Just listen, please. You must get away. Something awful happened."

"What are you talking about? What the hell's going on?"

"I've been kidnapped along with Marcy and can't explain now."

"Kidnapped? How is that possible? Do they want a ransom? Do you know where you are? Mexico?"

"Pittsburgh, I think. We're getting out." *I can only hope.*

"Mom, you have a phone. Call the damned police. Now."

"Can't. Don't worry. I'll explain later." *If we get out.* "But you're in serious danger. Go somewhere safe for a while. Please. Promise you'll do it. And call Marcy's son, Lionel, and tell him to do the same." Celia gave her the telephone number.

"Holy shit. How do I know this isn't your normal hysterics? I can't just go away. They're giving me a promotion. And Justin is wonderful.

We're engaged. I can't leave him." Celia heard a snort. "Are you sure, Mother? Are you smoking pot again?"

"I am sober as anything. This is no joke. Please listen to me. Take off for a few days. Please do it!" Celia's voice broke and she let out a sob.

"Okay, I believe you. After what happened to us in Florida, I'm not taking chances. Please, keep calling so I know you're safe. I will pray my head off to whomever out there will listen." Allison hesitated. "Once this latest crisis is over, don't expect help from me." Allison groaned. "You are back to being a major screwup."

Dear God, I am.

"Come, here little brat. Drink," a man's baritone voice carried into the landing.

"Please let me go home," a childish voice pleaded.

"Shut your mouth. You want me to kill your parents?"

Celia took a step forward, scowling, as though to crash through the door with her shoulder, but Marcy gave her a body check, pulling her back. Celia thought about Allie and the danger they all faced. Then she heard the heavy footsteps stomp up the stair treads above them and another pair of reluctant footsteps trailing.

"Move faster, you brat," the deep voice said.

Marcy said, "We've got to find the basement. I think it's right down these stairs. We need to start working on that window."

"Not till we help that child."

Marcy looked aghast in the dim light. "We'll get caught. Let's try to get out, first."

"We have to do this."

Celia peeked out the door, tray in hand, and saw no one. The living room was empty. She and Marcy entered the hall, pushed the door closed, and went up the staircase. When they reached the top, she saw a tall man, shirt straining over a potbelly, holding the child's hand in his grip. He yanked her into a room and slammed the door shut. Celia followed and knocked. He came to the door. "What the hell do you want?"

"Sir, I'm the new madam. I brought you a snack."

His leathery face grinned, deepening the crow's feet at the corners of his eyes as he opened the door wider. Celia walked in and set the tray on the bureau. The sparse room looked weary with empty liquor bottles on the night table.

"Just leave it there."

"Can I get your bath ready?" She didn't know where that came from.

Now the man laughed. "Fucking right. Wait for me to piss."

The man poured a half glass of vodka, left it on the nightstand and turned his back to Celia as he walked into the bathroom. A girl about twelve years old lay on the bed, trembling, long, auburn hair in disarray and her clothes disheveled. Celia put one hand on the child and with the other quietly pulled open the drawer. There was an open package of condoms. *That pervert.* More disturbing was a bottle of Rohypnol. Celia knew that as a date rape drug. She plunked two into his vodka glass. Mixed the liquid with her finger till they dissolved. Then she put a dose of salt inside a loose condom. She heard the sound of running water.

Urging the child up, Celia put two pillows under the covers and pulled the blanket up. She took the child's hand and tiptoed out. She heard the man yell for the child to sit up. She placed a sturdy chair under the door handle. Together they ran down the stairs.

They reached the landing where Marcy waited wide-eyed. She whispered to the child, "What's your name, sweetheart?"

"Mary," the girl whispered.

"Mary, we only have minutes, but we're going to try to escape. Okay?"

"Now let's go downstairs." Celia said, looking at Marcy. She flipped the wooden bar to lock the door and looked around for the light switch and flicked it on.

Marcy put the tray down and patted the quaking girl's head. "Let's go."

At the bottom of the steps, they were surrounded by darkness and the stench of rancid garbage. She felt around till her fingers ran over a cracked plastic plate and a light flipped on. Celia stumbled backward at the sight of a dozen or so women, dressed mostly in ragged clothing, some with blankets over their heads, huddled against a cinder block wall smeared with years of black, oily dust. Celia guessed the average age of the women to be about fifteen or sixteen.

Celia gazed at the group, which consisted of all races and nationalities. The women stared back, many with a vacant look in their eyes. An adolescent child moved forward, dragging a blanket that smelled like wet dog hair. She might have been pretty, only now with a head full of greasy, bedraggled hair, gaunt face, and dark rings under her blue eyes, she looked sickly. Behind her another woman stepped aside. Unlike the other women, she wore a sexy, very short red dress, dirt spots along the hemline.

Celia stared. The woman in the red dress looked vaguely familiar. "Were you …?"

"Name is Nikki. I saw you two at the bar/hotel in Philadelphia. I was there only as an escort, not a prostitute. Then I wake up in this place, two, maybe three days later. What the hell are you two doing here?"

"We got kidnapped. They want us to be madams to the women. More like spies." Celia still thought she had walked into a nightmare and might awaken soon.

Marcy gasped. "We saw you going up in the elevator. You looked so sad."

"I was drugged. I've been doing this work for a while, since after I aged out of the foster system, I was living on the street. This escort service gave me a job. Promised only lonely men. No sex. I had enough unwanted sex in the system."

"We thought this mostly happens in foreign countries." Marcy looked flustered.

"Welcome to the real world." Nikki tried to straighten her wrinkled skirt and wiggled her butt. "Mafia mobs from different countries work together. I got a quick education from these women. Counselors warned us, but we leave the system with no skills. What are we supposed to do? The men romance or dupe us with promises for better jobs. Lies!"

How ironic! These enslavers of women were demanding that Marcy and I monitor women and girls. They have the wrong women.

"Are you two giving out birth control pills?" Another bedraggled woman asked. "We don't want those assholes getting us pregnant—us or kids. So, give 'em out ... come on." She held her hand out. "How many kiddies did you, ahem, ladies recruit this time?"

Celia shook her head. "No, no. We're not doing that. We just want to free you all. We need to get started."

Mary broke away from Marcy and stood next to a girl about her age.

"Do they make you work in these conditions?" Marcy asked.

"We clean up real good when it's our shift. That's when they let us shower and eat better. We almost beg for our shift so we can have a decent meal," the bedraggled woman said.

The very youngest, maybe ten, stared at Celia with dull, black eyes that bore the tiniest gleam of optimism. "Do you know my momma?"

"No darling, we don't know her. We're trying to find a way out." No one moved.

A hiccough of a sob came from the child. "Is the bad man coming down again? I hate him."

Celia's knees turned to liquid at the thought of this twig-thin child being raped. "Do you all speak English?" The child reached out to Celia and wrapped her arms around her knees.

"Many are taught English for American men," Nikki said. "A lot are Russian. My mother spoke it. I learned it before she abandoned me, and stuck me into the foster system." She swung her hand around the dingy room with rows of battered, thin mattresses on the floor. "Many are promised better jobs in this country of golden streets. Does this look like Bloomingdales?"

"We have to leave this place now," Celia insisted. "Let's get to work."

At once, the women stepped forward. They all looked malnourished. *And that guard, Jerzy, pigging out. Hate to say that I'm glad he's dead.*

According to Zutka the only way out was through a small window. Celia saw a splinter of light up high and figured it was the window. She told Nikki what they intended to do. Celia almost lost heart when she saw that the window was near totally blocked.

"Ladies, are there any shovels, ladders, or tools around here?" Marcy asked.

"Small ones and lots of wire. There are a bunch of milk crates. They're our leisure chairs when we drink our evening margaritas," Nikki said, her voice dripping sarcasm.

Some women sniggered. Celia fingered her phone. *Has Allie found a safe place?*

"Hey, don't use that phone. Some police and neighbors are customers," Nikki said. "Most of these ladies are illegals. And, if they step out of line, their families will be killed back home. Some think the outside world is against them, and only these men will protect them."

Above their heads, feet thumped like thunder on the ceiling. "Let's get to that window."

Without another word, the women ran in all directions finding trowels, small shovels, and thick dowels. They stood on the crates and began digging. Some used their hands.

"They mostly ignore us unless we're doing men," Nikki said. "They sneak us out the back into four black Cadillac SUVs when it's time to work. This is the only room in the manger for us." She hesitated.

"They must be looking for us," Marcy croaked.

"If we're lucky, they'll look in the other rooms first," Nikki said.

Celia stacked more milk crates while several women steadied them and helped her climb. She reached up to the window. The women, digging fast and furious, had dumped a large pile of dirt on the floor. She brushed layers of loose dirt away and ground the key into the window lock. It clicked open. The window frame fell apart, but not even the smallest child could get through. Tapping around the window, she hoped to find hollow spots in the dirt.

Marcy said in a hoarse whisper, "Look at this."

Following Marcy's finger, Celia saw a long, narrow crack in the wall leading down from the bottom ledge of the window. It became noticeable as they removed more dirt. One of the women pulled over a chair and stood on it. Another woman handed her a shovel. Using it, she tugged out the dirt along the crack. Celia reached over to trickles of muddy water seeping through the widened crack, and began digging with a trowel.

Then they hit more concrete. A muffled groan came from the group. "Can you guys handle the beam?" asked Celia. "We'll try to ram it through the crack. The concrete is soaked and mushy."

Four other women loaded rags on the end to muffle sound. Then they held the beam over their heads and heaved it into the concrete barrier. The thin wall of concrete collapsed under the pounding. The space became bigger, but just barely large enough to escape.

Slivers of sunlight poured through the enlarged space. The smell of earth outside wafted in. Celia had always loved it, but never more than now.

The women kept hammering at the crack. The light hurt Celia's eyes as the decrepit concrete kept widening. One by one, women lifted their dirt-encrusted faces and sniffed the air.

"How do we move everyone out?" Marcy asked.

The strongest-looking woman volunteered to go out first, to make sure no guards were out there and help lift the others out. A couple of women dug into the dirt with their hands.

First went some able-bodied women to provide more help. Hands plunged through the hole, fingers wiggling. The children went next as they were pulled through. They communally knew what had to be done. Celia stared in amazement at the almost rhythmic organization.

"We'll push from here," Celia said. "They can't stop all of us." *I hope.* Celia spoke with a strong voice, but inside she was shaking.

"Go, Nikki," someone said.

Nikki tried to get Celia to go next, but she refused. "If you get caught, they'll slam your ass into a shipping container and you don't know where you'll land," Nikki said.

Celia pointed up. She hated hearing yet another horror.

Nikki stood on the crate, stretched her arms till her fingertips gripped the waiting hands. They lifted her up and out.

Celia said. "Go, Marcy."

Marcy stepped up. Four pairs of arms reached in and hauled her out. Marcy stuck her head in the opening. "Come on, Celia. You heard what Nikki said. We can wind up in Moscow."

Celia rotated her head, the room now illuminated by the stray strands of sunlight. The child she'd rescued, Mary, sat hidden in a corner. A pounding on the door startled her.

Marcy looked in. "Now, woman. Grab our hands."

The pounding turned into a thumping against the door to break it down. Lunging for Mary, she lifted her to the waiting arms. Celia, in her weakened state, felt like a hundred-pound weight lay on her shoulders. The women hauled her out just as the door banged open. They huddled together on their knees and agreed to each take different paths, hoping to divert the men. Then the women began their exit as quickly as a dog chasing cats. Celia marveled at how they grouped together to wait till everyone managed to get out.

Chapter 7

Celia heard a horn blast behind her as she ran across the street, just behind Marcy. Two black Cadillac SUVs trailed behind. She saw the driver look at her, then at a large group of women running down the street. They made a beeline for the group that had panicked and stayed together. Celia's heart felt like it stopped.

"Split up," Nikki yelled and swerved away from the pack with Mary in tow.

One SUV bore down on them, jumping the curb, and then squealed to an abrupt stop to avoid hitting a tree. Celia whirled. Six women stood in front of the vehicle with their hands up as though holding an imaginary white flag. *Why don't they run?* Two men jumped out and hustled them into the SUV. The women went with no resistance. Some even smiled at the men. The SUV took off, tires screeching.

Nikki, her arms around Mary, turned to look at them before rounding a corner. This is what brainwashing looked like, thought Celia. Now she knew the captors wooed the women into thinking they were their saviors and the outside world would do them harm.

Still holding hands, she and Marcy ran through brambles that scratched their legs. They came out of a heavily wooded area, and up against a tall fence, blocking them. They inched along the fence until a hastily built patch appeared. Without exchanging a glance or a word,

Celia and Marcy kicked it in and crawled through it. They landed in a grove of trees fronted by a row of very large homes, all nearly identical.

At the back of one of the houses, a pit bull on a chain lead made a beeline toward them, snarling. Celia and Marcy backed up against the fence, hands covering their faces. The dog lunged off the ground. Celia saw nothing but sharp teeth in the dog's open mouth through her spread fingers. Marcy's face crumbled as she dug her fingernails into Celia's hand. Celia held her breath, her heart slamming against her chest. The dog jerked back in midair and hit the ground not three feet away. The fierce dog yelped as the chain around its neck rattled and it remained quietly on the ground.

They found a large playhouse that duplicated in miniature the McMansion beside it. With a finger, Marcy lifted her nose in the air at the show of wealth. The interior of the playhouse smelled of fresh pine, but a damp dog bed in the corner wafted a disagreeable odor.

"These people around here don't believe in decent bedding for doggies." Marcy scratched the back of her head. "I wouldn't mind living in that mansion though."

On the phone, Celia googled the name *Vladimir Stompovich* and read the bio aloud: "The CEO of V & S Industries, Vladimir Stompovich runs trucking, shipping, and import/export products. The article said that Vladimir's businesses stretch all over the globe—Moscow, Mumbai, Delhi, Mexico City, Veracruz, Phnom Penh, Nong Khai, Sacramento, Los Angeles, New York, San Diego, and Philadelphia."

Vladimir's shipping line brought merchandise-filled containers into the States. Celia knew the large ports in big cities, Philadelphia included, handled big containers. Several operations had been the subject of investigations but all had ended in exoneration. The few times his businesses had been raided, the containers were found to be filled with machinery from China or clothing from Thailand. One raid happened in Philadelphia where a local VIP announced that sex trafficking was a myth and the media incited people needlessly. *Was someone tipping off Vladimir Stompovich about raids?*

Celia called Allison again.

"Where are you now, Allie?"

"I have an idea where to go, but what can I say to Justin? Add to that, I'm worried about you and Marcy." There was a hesitation. "Why haven't you called the police?"

"The women aren't willing to go to authorities for good reasons. This cartel has a long reach."

"A cartel?" Allison screamed. "Are you mad?"

Celia held the phone away from her ear for a moment. "One of the cities in this illegal web is Philadelphia. I'm scared for you and Marcy's family. Go now." Celia had trouble getting the words out. "You must hide. They say they know your location."

The complete silence descended on Celia like a concrete wall collapsing on her. "Marcy and I will make our way to Philadelphia. We'll get through this, sweetie."

"We will? This can't be happening again, Mom. WTF?"

"They know everything about us. They will try to hurt you because we've escaped and know too much. They'll do everything to stop us."

"No way! I have a different name from you."

"I hope that works for now. They can always find it. We need your help. We have no money and no credit cards. Do you have one we can use? I'll pay you back."

"That's insane, too. I can give you my number and CV, but why would they accept that without a card? And, anyway, how will you remember the number?"

Celia looked at Marcy. "Okay, I'll remember the first half and you remember the back half."

"Go for it," said Marcy.

"And, Mom," said Allie, "the answer to my secret question is Dad's name—capital G for Gabriel."

"I'd rather forget that."

"This is not the time to get sarcastic."

"You're right." Celia still seethed about Gabe—how he'd torn down her confidence with verbal abuse, among other things. "How will I find you?"

"I'm taking you at your word. I have to go to my basement locker to get a bunch of clothes. I know a B & B in the Northern Liberties section. A friend owns it."

Celia pictured a huge sub-basement under the hospital. "Is there room in the basement where we could hide?"

"That dank, damp, cavern? It has all these alcoves where cast-off junk is stored."

Celia's brain revved up. They had to find a place. "Is there a separate entrance to get into the basement?"

"I only know where my locker is, and there's a fire exit on the side of the building. Oh, I guess there are delivery trucks that unload at the dock in the back. And there's another service entrance that you unlock from the inside."

"If they all lead to the sub-basement, maybe we could hide there. Please double-check it."

"This is going from one big insanity to another."

"We must hide until we plan a strategy and see who we can trust.

I'll try to buy a temporary cell phone to keep in touch. Got to dump this one or we'll be traced." Celia steeled herself to the idea of a possible hiding place. "When we get close, I'll call you to meet us at the side entrance that leads to the basement. And please be careful." Celia softened her tone. "I want you to keep your belongings even at the B & B. Prepare to move in with us once we get there."

Allie's voice dropped to a whimper. "Mom, I have a good life here. You're asking me to give it up? The answer is no."

"Listen," said Celia. "These guys are out for revenge. You've got to do this right away." Celia spoke with a grimace as though Allison could see her expression. A year ago in Florida, she'd done good detective work, but this impossible situation went far beyond her powers.

There was a long pause. "Please, stay in touch," Allison said, her words were weighted with fear.

"I love you with every fiber I have," said Celia. "I'll see you soon."

Marcy whispered, "Too much fucking danger. We're dead meat." She had tears in her eyes.

"Call Lionel." Celia's thoughts flashed through her head like a thunderstorm. She pressed her temples.

"His mother-in-law lives out in the country. I'd say we all go there but it's a tiny house, and he'd be really pissed about me uprooting him. He still mentions how I deserted him by running away with the guru when he was just a kid…"

"Join the club. We're damn screwups." Celia said. "We go out for a drink, and look where we are! Why can't we have a peaceful life? I just want to paint, not bother anyone, and live in sunny Florida. You just want a nice, rich boyfriend. Is that too much to ask?"

Marcy wiped her eyes with her sleeve. "Beats a rocking chair."

"Ha. If we live long enough a rocking chair doesn't sound so bad. I'll do everything age-appropriate and join Edith's nasty group of gossipers if we get out of this." Celia gave a sarcastic grin.

"Edith? Are you fucking nuts? I'd die first. She almost got us arrested. I wish they'd run her out of Boca Pelicano Palms and then we'd be fine."

"Listen, girl. We might never get back home again." Celia grabbed the phone from Marcy's hand and dialed 911. "Let's try."

"Hello, I'm here in Pittsburgh." Celia gave the dispatcher the street sign names she'd seen on the run. "My friend and I just escaped from a house where they keep sex slaves. It's a three-story residence, painted totally white. Please come quickly."

"How is this accurate information?" the nasal-sounding dispatcher asked.

"We were in there. I set a bunch of the women free. Some were under fourteen."

"We've been called to that house before and there was nothing out of order. It's the only white house on that street. Maybe these women were friends or family. We would need probable cause and then get a subpoena."

Marcy leaned over and said from an inch away. "What if it was your daughter?"

"Madam, there are laws that we follow. Can you come down to the station and file a complaint?"

"No. We're hiding from them." Celia threw the phone down and dug her heel into it as though punishing it for her frustration. "I'm scared there's a mole in the police department. And, they might have a trace on it."

Marcy dug her hand into her bra and pulled out a small bundle of twenties. "Remember, I told you that after that rash of robberies back home, I started keeping my money the old-fashioned way?"

"You weren't kidding," Celia smirked. "Now we have to figure out how to get to Philadelphia."

Chapter 8

Celia ducked her head out of the playhouse. Except for the chirping of birds, it was quiet. She focused on the darkened sky, then the house in front of them and the thick-trunked trees surrounding it. The leaves barely moved. It looked as though time had stopped.

Beneath a large portico stood a Rolls and a Range Rover. Sneaking closer, Celia saw a Honda Prius looking like a handmaiden curtsying to the expensive cars.

"They call them the Honda Pious because some residents in Florida feel superior driving them." Marcy sounded as though her snarky spunk had returned.

"Disposing of those batteries just creates another environmental hazard," Celia whispered, although no one seemed to be around. "Why are we talking like this, for God's sake? We're running for our lives."

Marcy breathed deeply. "I hope at least some of the women and kids make it to a safe place." Marcy pressed her nose against the window of the Rolls.

Celia walked around, trying all the handles on the cars. Only the Prius door popped open.

"The cheap one is a go. Figures," Marcy said. "That's the one they give to their kids or the maid."

"Keep it down." Celia sat in the driver's seat and rooted in the well. A key sat in a change pocket. Marcy got into the passenger seat and Celia let the car slide to the street on the sharp downward slope. She made a half-turn at the bottom.

"Let's hope the family is out of town for a month or longer."

"Yeah, we can only hope." Celia turned the wheel and the motor, her hands shaking for fear people would appear from the house. She put the hospital address into the GPS.

"Where are we headed?"

"There is a route off the highway. Follow signs heading east on Route 30 and then 202." Celia glanced at the dashboard.

"Mazel tov to us," said Marcy. "I just want a hot shower."

"Sounds good to me."

"Can we do some sightseeing?"

"Just let me drive."

"Let's go to Atlantic City. I feel like I could hit the jackpot. It might be our last roundup before we're done in. So, why not have fun?"

"Just try to stay quiet. There's no fun here." Celia slapped the steering wheel like an exclamation point.

"Spoilsport." Marcy crinkled her nose.

Minutes later, Celia spotted a gas station and a small diner and aimed for them. She slowed when she saw a woman staggering, hugging close to a row of stores. Her short, clingy dress was awry and smeared with dirt. She limped and kept looking over her shoulder.

The streets were dark; rows of stores, windows layered with dog-eared, yellowed signs, dotted their path.

"Doesn't that look like Nikki?" Celia asked.

Marcy shifted forward, eyes wide. "What, what?"

They followed her slowly. But when she saw them, she started to run. Celia waved a hand out the window. Marcy leaned out the window and called to her. "Hey, Nikki. We're the ones who got you all out of that house."

The woman slowed her pace, stared at Marcy, and stopped. She stumbled and bent over as though trying to catch her breath.

They drove up closer to her, and without a word, she opened the back door and threw herself across the seat. She passed out.

"Poor thing," Marcy said. "I'd love to kill the bastards trading women's lives for money. They should rot in hell."

"I agree."

"What the hell do we do with our new passenger?"

"I'll just keep going," Celia said. "I'm afraid the police might put her and us through hell. We have to move on and Nikki is out of gas. We're committing a bunch of offenses—car theft for one thing." Celia frowned. "She'll probably be afraid the police will arrest her for prostitution and/or drugs."

"We're used to criminal charges." Marcy harrumphed.

"I've run out of magic." Celia put the car in motion and took a sharp turn. Marcy rolled toward Celia then back against the door.

"Slow it down."

"Oh," a weak, high voice groaned from the back.

"It's okay, sweetheart," said Marcy.

"I tried to follow the women, but lost them. Head hurts." Nikki spoke as though a hand squeezed the words out. "They hooked us on drugs, then took more money from us. Don't have a dime. I'm going through the shakes."

In the rearview mirror, Celia saw her squeezing her abdomen. "I'll take you to the emergency room."

"No. They search hospitals. I think I'm going to be sick. Oh, my God." She dry-heaved.

Marcy opened the back window. Nikki leaned her head out. Celia eyed her in the rearview mirror and saw a trail of blood trickle from her forehead down her face.

"If they catch me, it'll be bad. I had the kid with me but they caught up to us. I grabbed the guard's gun and ran like hell. Left the poor kid behind."

"Oh, shit," Marcy said, biting her lip.

"It's my birthday. And this is my present. Here," she said to Marcy as she held out the gun, "for you. I don't want it. If they catch me with it, there'll be…"

"Hells bells no," said Marcy.

"Okay, give it to me," said Celia, imagining all the pain inflicted by those men. She tucked it into the deep pocket of the housedress Zutka had given her. "Tell us more of what the organization is like."

"Easy as shit. Russia, Ukraine, Italy, Croatia, Turkey, Albania, and many more get together to export women and children with forged visas and passports. They either kidnap the girls or tell them that they'd have good jobs in other countries, and they'd owe very little money. Funny. Once the girls get captured, their debts run up." Nikki did a thumbs-up and took a breath.

"Food, a dump to sleep in, shit-eating clothes, documents, travel, transportation, fucking guards and I mean fucking. Then the drugs those turds force us to take. All deducted from salaries they never get anyways. And they get moved from city to city to stay on the run from the good cops. The pimps keep their passports. Lots of women defend these creeps because they believe they are their lovers, their only protectors. What bullshit."

Celia understood how something so depraved could happen. She'd read of women being brainwashed to such extremes that they would defend those that abuse them. In this case, she saw how they fell in love with evildoers who claim to protect them from a hostile society as Nikki said.

Nikki seemed wound up as she continued. "These assholes entice vulnerable girls and women through romance, forcing them into prostitution from day one. Massage parlors, strip joints, hotels, motels, all in on the take. They keep them without a dime and their debts last a lifetime—which might not be that long."

"We'll use the damn gun if we have to," Marcy shouted. "Those poor kids."

Celia recalled a day in Florida, two years ago. Marcy had given her a picture of her two-year-old grandchild. Celia asked to do a portrait of him, and Marcy's face lit up. Stanton had bought her painting supplies. She had already begun painting startling portraits in which the subject was identifiable, but all other brushstrokes spoke to an inner spirituality or personality.

She had cut a section of canvas and stretched it on a frame. It sat on an easel for a month, like a finger beckoning to her each day. When she started painting the child's portrait, the process lured her into the canvas till she imagined living in real time with the child.

She squeezed paint—royal blue, sienna, yellow oxide, white, and celadon—on the palette. The sharp scent of turpentine and the heavy, citrusy scent of linseed oil relaxed her. Her hand started to paint before she had any thoughts in her head of where to start. She'd worked incessantly on the piece and it had turned out well. The baby's face emerged in warm sunlight, a happy glow of innocence, as though the very air swirling on the canvas protected him from harm. Would she ever have that satisfying feeling again?

She pondered the children who were violated and used. Whatever their future, those children would suffer for the rest of their lives.

A black SUV was following close behind them. She looked around the tiny, no-name town east of Harrisburg and sped up. It was nearly a straight shot east to Philadelphia. She had to keep going.

Nikki moaned, the sound ripping out of her like thunder rolling down a mountainside. She pressed her temples with shaking fingers. "How did they find us?"

Celia checked the rearview mirror again. The SUV was bearing down on them. Celia had nowhere to go except straight ahead. She hit the accelerator, but the SUV kept pace.

Nikki sat up, her face red and swollen. "I want to kill them. We must do twenty, thirty men each day or they take more food away."

She reminded Celia of a baby bird. The SUV was now forcing them off the road toward a small office park. At the very end, Celia saw a neon sign in the shape of a naked woman, curves and nipples blinking red. It hurt her eyes.

At the end of the parking lot, a man opened the passenger side door of the SUV.

"No," Nikki whispered in a hoarse voice. "It's Vladimir. He's the boss. This is where they take us to work."

"We're fucked," murmured Marcy.

Chapter 9

Celia blinked to clear her sticky eyes, and for a moment wondered if she and Marcy had rented a dark, smelly room. Her body ached as though her joints had separated. Explosions detonated in her head. It seemed weird to have been sleeping sitting up on a hard surface. She shook her head to clear it and suddenly remembered they had been stopped by Vladimir and his men who had broken the car windows and hauled them out. Then they were injected with something.

What about Marcy? Celia tried to stand but landed on her knees. Slowly, she rose, hitting her head on what seemed to be a shelf. The intense sewer smell choked her.

A naked bulb above her head shed a dim light, its conical beam barely reached the floor. She saw the shapes of women huddled together. A hard thump and bump told her she was in a in some kind of vehicle, and they were moving fast. She held on to the shelf to keep from falling.

"Marcy," she called.

A woman hissed, "Do you want those fuckin' animals in here? Shut up."

Celia heard a groan and bent down.

Marcy looked up at her, blinking her eyes. "Celia?"

"Are you alright?" She examined Marcy's face and saw scratches.

Marcy threw her arm across her face. "Think so. The lights are too bright," she mumbled.

"There's hardly any light. Just close your eyes for a while. I have no idea where we are."

"You don't want to know," a frail voice fluttered up to Celia. She looked down and there was Nikki. Celia hugged her and smelled stale sweat.

"We're heading to the Philadelphia ports," Nikki said. She waved her hand around the huddled women. "These are some of the girls who got caught running away from the house in Pittsburgh. And we have women here who came in shipping containers from all over the friggin' world."

"What are we traveling in?" Marcy asked, wrinkling her nose. "It smells like shit."

"It *is* shit." Nikki gritted her teeth. "We're in a shipping container loaded onto a truck." She laughed like a saw cutting logs. "First class, baby."

"Them's buckets of shit. We pray they empty them at the next stop," a voice in the rear spoke up.

Celia tried breathing through her mouth. Still, the after-smell stung her throat. "I'm sorry you got caught, Nikki. You're brave." Celia touched Nikki's shoulder. "Did all of them get caught?"

Nikki snorted. "Some got away, thanks to you both. News travels around here. At least they gave us shots of drugs. One thing for sure, I'm in this crap hole, travelin' deluxe right with you. No getting away from these fuckwits. We're in for life. If another mob catches us, they give us back to the one who owned us first."

"How do they know who that is?" Celia asked.

Nikki sneered. She wheeled around on her heel and raised her hair. Her bare neck had a barcode tattoo.

Paper plates littered the floor. Celia feared moving, not knowing what she might step on. Twenty-five women were wedged shoulder-to-shoulder, as if glued together. Several glared through half-closed eyes.

"So, we're in a container, right?"

"Right. Probably transport us to some, um, exotic place, you know, with palm trees and margaritas." Nikki gave a short grunt.

Celia touched something hard in her pocket. The gun! The men hadn't bothered to search her. She fingered it. After the trouble they faced in Florida, Stanton had insisted she take shooting lessons.

"Well, I'm not becoming anyone's madam. Fuck that," Marcy shouted.

A girl sniggered. "No, they fuck you real bad if you don't do what they say."

"Celia, we've got to get out of here." Marcy gripped Celia's hand. "How long have we been in this thing?"

"Just one day for us," Nikki said. "This container came from California. Now, we're all one big happy family."

"A girl died just before we reached our last stop," a voice said out of the dark.

Marcy inhaled deeply and retched.

Nikki pointed up. Three small holes were in the ceiling and two on the side just below. "Sit quiet, and don't move. Save your breath. Not much air gets in. Sleep till we stop. Girls are quiet cause they know."

Several women stared at Celia and Marcy.

"We have to report this to the police," Celia said. "Will any of you go to the police with us?"

"You crazy. They kill family back in Thailand." A tiny woman clutched her chest. "Police in America arrest for being whore and deport. Family die."

Marcy half sat up and leaned against the wall. "I can't do this. I want to die."

"Stay strong," Celia whispered. "Remember one of the cha-cha rules we used to say over and over? 'Create your own inner receptive space. It allows for healing…'"

Marcy looked wistful. "I made fun of those rules but now they might help. That oddball, neighbor woman gave them to me when I was a kid."

"Remember this one? 'Trust yourself. Be your own best friend,'" Celia said.

"Trusting myself is not good. I got us into a shitload of trouble."

With that, Celia had an idea. "Marcy, tell them what happened to you and why we got into trouble in Florida. Tell them about Melvin dying on top of you during, uh…making love."

Marcy's eyes got the slightest glimmer of light. "You bet." She waved the women closer.

Marcy stood, holding on to the shelf. "Celia and I are best friends. We met at a cha-cha lesson and it was love at first sight for us. It's a dance…"

"The cha-cha," Nikki said. "Some of us know it."

Marcy, standing unsteadily, wrapped her arms over her bosom and shimmied. "We were three friends, Celia, Deb, and me." She grabbed Celia's arm. "Well, I was really hot stuff. Men fell at my feet."

The women laughed. One of them asked, "How old?"

Marcy continued with her patter, ignoring the woman. "We live in a gated community in Florida. So, my boyfriend and I were making out in his office. He threw all the stuff off his desk and we made mad, passionate love." Marcy cradled herself tighter. "What a night."

Nikki laughed hard and pressed her stomach. A woman in the front said, "You funny. Two old people doing it." Loud guffaws filled the trailer. More women moved closer.

"Lo and behold, my Melvy drops dead on top of me in the middle of the best…well, you know. He was a big guy." Marcy held her hands out wide. "I couldn't move. Just managed to get my phone and call my two best friends. This woman here and another, Deb, came running to my rescue. They freed me, and it wasn't easy."

Some women giggled.

"What a sight," Celia picked up. "At first, I thought Marcy was under a mattress. Maybe he weighed close to three hundred pounds." Celia held her arms out in front of her stomach.

"Well, he was dead, really dead," Celia said. "What a shock. We tried to revive him, but it didn't work. Now the problem was, Marcy, um, she'd been in trouble before and the people where we lived insisted she be evicted if she got into trouble again."

Marcy scanned the women clustered in front of her, all eyes set on her. The response uplifted Celia.

Thank goodness they're enjoying the diversion.

"If I got evicted, I had no money to go to a new place."

Marcy seemed to sense the sudden pall and shifted her position. "So, we get the idea to move Melvy to his apartment as though he died there. That way I wouldn't be accused of, uh, indecent stuff, or whatever."

Celia touched Marcy's arm to signal she wanted to tell this part.

"So, we got a wheelchair, huffed and puffed, and pulled Melvy onto it and got him back to his own bed." Celia wiped her brow with a finger to emphasize the effort.

"Nothing like women helping women," Nikki said.

Marcy looked at her. "I loved Melvy. Wouldn't have hurt him for the world."

"He was a good guy, in his way," Celia said.

The group applauded and a few whistles cut through the muggy air.

"Just shows," said Nikki. "Got to keep a sense of humor to get through."

These women could be our daughters! They pause in the midst of catastrophe to laugh, be amused by stories, and share what little they have. I'm sure there is some backbiting at times, but in a crisis that is as bad as it gets, they've turned their suffering into acts of community that show the beauty of humanity.

Their laughter was like wind chimes singing in the wind, wiping out being knee-deep in debris. Celia wanted to keep these moments alive, keep the momentum of replicating the pleasures of real life. The truck slowed then stopped, and the sound of a train whistle pierced the walls. They'd have to wait for the train to pass.

Celia straightened her legs. She grasped the shelf above for balance, arched her back and tried to soften the kink in her neck. Someone asked for more stories.

"We'll tell you how we met. It was at a cha-cha lesson," Celia said.

Marcy grabbed Celia's hand. Celia began humming a cha-cha rhythm, "Let's Get Loud" imitating one of her heroines, Jennifer Lopez. Marcy sang the words, swinging her hips.

The women joined in, clapping their hands. Celia and Marcy

seamlessly did the steps—one foot forward, one in place, then one, two, three in place and repeating, but stepping back. Soon, all the women stood in a straight line, held hands, and followed in step.

At first Celia thought Marcy forgot the words. Then she realized she sang to Celia's humming but improvised the words of their Rules of Cha-Cha, the ones they'd tried to live by a couple of years ago. When Marcy was fourteen or so, a middle-aged, dark-skinned woman from Puerto Rico who briefly lived in her neighborhood gave her the rules. During their lessons, Marcy dug them up. Celia took them to heart.

Marcy sang in rhythm to cha-cha rhythm, "Ay, ay, ay, learn your steps, discipline liberates. La, la, la, don't be afraid of resistance, it opens new horizons. Cha-cha-cha, it is dangerous to fear risk, we may never know joy." Marcy stopped dancing, pressed her hands to her face and sobbed. "We might never know joy again. Oh, my God…"

Celia hugged Marcy. The rules had once sustained them in the darkest of times, but the times had gone deeper and darker now.

They heard pounding on the wall that separated the cab from the truck.

"They're telling us to stop the noise," Nikki said, holding her index finger to her lips.

Several women began coughing and gasping. Celia pressed her chest. Marcy panted.

The truck restarted, and Celia started devising a plan for the next stop. She leaned over to Marcy. "I still have the gun. I guess they don't search old women, thank goodness. I'm going to use it when they open the door," Celia said to the group, hugging herself. "It's fall—chilly."

"Yeah. We have nothing warm," Nikki said.

They stared at the small, battery-operated heater that sputtered pitiful shots of hot air.

"What did we miss when we were out cold?" Celia asked Nikki.

"They shoved in a couple more girls and dropped off others. I could hardly sleep, so I saw. Those dickhead truck drivers stop for food, things we don't know about."

Celia noticed that all the women had scraggly hair and dirty faces, except for Nikki who wore a creased but nice simple red dress and stiletto heels. Her pale skin, green eyes, and pouty mouth gave the impression of constant surprise.

"They were taking me to some other strip club, but changed their minds."

"I wonder where we are now." Marcy looked around as though seeking a window.

"We just keep going around in different directions." Nikki sighed. "Some dropped off and then new ones aboard."

"I still don't get what exactly happened at the bar," Marcy croaked.

"You don't know?" Nikki said. "After they knocked you out, you guys were driven in by the Boss's chauffeur in a snazzy limo. Too bad you weren't awake enough to enjoy it."

Celia's thoughts turned to planning. *How can we overpower the drivers? It's going to be a real challenge to find a car.* She leaned toward Marcy. "I read that a lot of containers end up at ports on the East Coast. The hospital where Allie works is near the ports."

"So? Suppose they dump this container on a ship that goes to Hong Kong? And what makes you think one little gun will mow them down?" Marcy asked. "They'll most likely have an army waiting."

Celia had no answer.

Chapter 10

However filthy and smelly the container was, it seemed to act as a fortress, a protection from the violent men out there. As long as they were moving the evil they faced didn't exist. There was an easy camaraderie among the women, as though they were in boot camp. As long as they were traveling, they remained far from the slavery in strip clubs and massage parlors. Far from degradation and dehumanizing beatings and rapes. They only had the drivers to occasionally contend with—a relief from hordes of men manhandling them.

Celia sat against a wall. *Stanton…his khakis and blue striped shirt…his crooked smile, endearing, gentle, and rubbing his cheek the way he does when I tease him.* These images kept her sane. On the flip side, images of Allie lying in the alley behind the hospital murdered by thugs sent her heart banging in her throat.

Lack of air forced her to black out for seconds at a time. When she came to, exhaustion overtook her, but she couldn't sleep. Marcy and the other women seemed to sleep for a few hours. The stench of buckets, unemptied for days, seemed to wrap her in sewage.

I should pray a little…doubt anyone in the great beyond might get my message. They don't even know my address.

Then she did something unexpected. Celia prayed for her death.

She drifted into her unpleasant memories. She thought about her marriage to Gabe. *I missed every red flag for years. I took his criticism of my artwork and constant criticism about how I mothered Allie. He was dead by the time I figured out he'd been playing me to keep his own secrets under wraps. I wish he'd lived long enough for me to tell him off big time.*

Stanton had encouraged her to paint again, to follow her passion. He believed in her talent. She imagined inhaling the heavy, oily, acidic, lemony scent of linseed oil. *Wish I could bathe in the stuff.* She most loved the swift movement of her bands as she put paint to canvas, as though her fingers worked in their own mysterious way. Her style relied on neon colors at the edge of her portraits to speak to the individual personality. As recognizable faces appeared under her fingers, she wanted to fall to her knees in supplication to the miracles she produced. She'd done several of Allie from memory; she had encased her in violet, hot pink, and hunter green. Stanton had posed for one and when she asked if she could do a second he had said, "This one will be your interpretation of me." He liked that she had used strong colors, blues, burgundies, and deep purples. He said the portrait "vibrates with intensity."

A sudden stop. Terror appeared on all faces as though one. Stops meant the end of whatever peace the containers afforded them. Now came the endless lines of men.

If they ever got out of here, they're going to need mentoring and therapy. I could use mentoring myself, somebody clever enough to get us all out of this.

Here it was; the places where they'd stay or a temporary stop before they were shuttled elsewhere. The days of metal walls protecting them was about to lift and spew them out into hell.

The smell of gasoline partially obscured the stench inside the container.

The truck started, and slowly bumped over what felt like big ridges in the road and stopped again.

Celia reached for the gun. She shared her plan with Nikki and asked her to make it clear to the other women.

"If we're at a port, I'm guessing you all will be divided up for transportation to different locations. At least, that's how they usually do it. Once we're outside, don't move until I tell you." She pulled the gun out of her pocket and heard a collective gasp.

"I'm going to use this and point at whoever is out there. As soon as I do, you all run. Best thing is to find a police station. I know, some of you are afraid of dirty cops and people who won't believe you or will deport you. But not all are dirty. If you talk to the authorities, maybe they'll catch the scum. You can ask for sanctuary based on fear of torture or murder."

Marcy piped in. "We have to put as many of these animals as we can in prison."

Rumbling. Door panels opening. Sunlight poured in. Celia blinked wildly. It hurt her eyes. *Okay, what did I learn at the shooting range? First, release the safety. Grip the handle firmly with your lower three fingers and keep the pressure constant. If you loosen the pressure on your grip, the pistol may shift in your hand, which will affect grip alignment and trigger placement. Use a two-handed hold whenever possible for better alignment.*

"Get your asses out," a rugged male voice yelled, echoing throughout the container. "One at a time. Don't try to run. Try it, and we'll beat the shit out of you bitches."

Celia froze. Only two drivers were out there.

Celia and Marcy squeezed to the back. She gripped the gun with her right hand, conscious of finger placement, just like her instructor had taught her, and held her hand behind her back. They were parked near a deserted gas station with a small bus and an SUV parked near empty gas tanks. The air was cool, refreshing, reviving her slightly.

The men were inside the container now, hustling the women out.

Celia and Marcy took their time as they moved to the front of the container. They saw the driver push Nikki to the ground and began to unzip his pants. He stood over her. But she refused to move.

"Touch her and I'll shoot your brains out." Celia raised the gun with a perfect two-handed grip.

The driver widened his eyes in surprise.

Nikki stood up, brushed herself off, and spit in his face.

"Fuck! You whore!" he roared. Celia raised the gun and fired. It missed, but the driver stopped, his body shaking with rage. Celia turned the gun toward his partner. "Don't move." She had trouble catching her breath, but she managed to say, "Get over there beside your friend."

"Jake," said the driver. "You gonna let her get away with this?"

"She has real bullets," said Jake.

Celia gripped the gun and steadied herself. "Come on. Try to take me down."

"Make a move toward her and you're a dead man," Marcy said, moving next to Celia.

Marcy motioned to Nikki to stand beside her. The other women collected behind them.

The driver raised his voice. "Ladies, you don't want to do this. We got your passports. You ain't goin' nowhere 'cause they'll find you and bring your fucking asses down. We're the only ones who can help. You know that ladies. We only want to help."

A petite woman with matted blond hair took hesitant steps toward him.

Celia motioned her to stop. "Sweetie," she said softly. "Don't believe him. They only want to make money from your body." She turned to Nikki. "Nikki, you need to get into that van with the women."

"Where are we, though?" said Nikki.

Celia raised the gun in the driver's direction. "Harrisburg," he said. "In bumfuck Pennsylvania. And you need us now more than ever." He moved toward the van and SUV.

"Stop," Celia yelled. She pulled the trigger. A shot bit into the ground, grazing his heavy boot.

"What do you think you're doing?" he shouted.

She fired into one of the truck's back tires. "Who owns the vehicles parked by the pumps? And don't tell me you don't know." She fired into the other tire, in terrified awe at the destructive power she held.

The men looked at each other. "We don't. We got our orders to use those to get you all out of here."

"Give me the keys and your wallets," Celia demanded.

"Bullshit. You're out of your mind. No keys to you bitches."

"I might be a bitch to you, but I'm a bitch with the gun." Celia moved closer and shot at the tip of the driver's boot, cracking the leather at his big toe. He screamed and hit the ground. Blood seeped from the rip. Celia tasted bile at the back of her throat. *I can't lose it now.*

"I plan to use this gun at your crotch, then your heart. Give me the keys." *I've already shot four of six bullets, so I better know what I'm talking about.*

Jake reached into his jacket pocket and threw two sets of keys and his wallet in front of Marcy who picked them up. The wounded driver was screaming now. "She's a crazy cunt. Why'd you give her the keys and your fucking wallet?"

"Don't matter," said Jake. "ID is fake, ladies. Have at it."

Celia picked up the wallet and checked the billfold. Inside were six crisp one-hundred-dollar bills. "So, you two do everything in cash. Of course. I need the other wallet." *Look, the man is hurt and I sound so cold.* "Get it and help your friend, Jake," she said.

The other driver stopped for a moment and threw it at her before crumpling into a whimpering ball.

"Hmm," said Celia, pulling out another six one-hundred-dollar bills. "Marcus Williams. Thank you, Marcus. You need to find a hospital." Marcy handed Nikki a set of keys and six of the bills. "Can you drive?"

Nikki nodded.

"Go to a police station. Use the GPS. You can do it," Marcy said gently to Nikki. She turned to Celia.

"Oh, and hand over your cell phones, Marcus and Jake."

Reluctantly, the men threw them on the ground. Celia dug her heel into both cell phones, crushing them. Marcy aimed her foot toward the phones but twisted and stomped on the driver's ankle. Celia heard a crack and shivered. He howled and kicked the air.

"Shit!" said Marcy, stunned at her own actions.

"Okay," said Nikki, hurrying the women into the van. "Let's do this."

Marcy and Celia followed them. Celia trained the gun on the driver and Jake. Carefully, she got into the SUV.

"Okay?" Nikki called to them, once everyone was settled in.

"As good as we can be," called Marcy. "Take care, please. Let's hit it, Celia."

Celia started the motor. "I just hope Nikki finds the police." She paused. "Honestly, I don't think the women will rat them out. The thugs have their passports, visas, birth certificates—real or faked. They have to know they'll be safe with the police if they're willing to talk."

"Right now, we have to save our own asses," Marcy said. "Here we go."

Celia signaled Marcy not to reveal their destination. They jumped into the SUV and shot out of there.

Celia had only driven ten miles before she stopped just outside Exton. She could hardly keep her eyes open, and when she shook her head, the image of blood oozing from the driver's boot appeared. They had to stop or she would lose it. Marcy had fallen asleep the moment they got into the car.

She drove below the speed limit, looking for a motel where they would find a bed and a shower. Hunger clawed her stomach. Marcy raised her head, eyes still shut. "My stomach is growling. Get us some food."

Chapter 11

Marcy was softly snoring, her head lolling against the car door. Celia didn't want to wake her, but she had to. "Marcy, honey, wake up. Wake up!"

Marcy's head popped up, and she narrowed her eyes as though looking through a fog. "Where are we?"

"Outside of Exton and nowhere PA," she said, driving the car down a small, deserted street. A dull streetlight cast a glow over the hood of the car.

"You fucking saved us," Marcy said, her voice hoarse. "We might have been sailing off to Bosnia if you hadn't kept the gun."

"And you're pretty good yourself," Celia said. "Nice crack to the driver's ankle."

Marcy grinned. "You were my inspiration."

Celia smiled, hoping her fear didn't show in the darkened car. "We've got to find a motel. I'm falling asleep and we need to be sharp when we reach the hospital. And you look even more tired than I feel."

"I wish we would have done the deed." Marcy sighed.

"You mean kill them?" Celia's jaw muscles clenched. "No."

"Why not? It's revenge even though I got us into this mess. Things were going great guns in Florida. We'd have been just fine. I destroyed everything with my big mouth. Why am I always doing that?"

"Listen, those guys were gunning for two grandmom types. And we were right there. They'd have drugged us even if you'd kept quiet— something hard for you to do."

"You warned me to keep my big trap shut. Stupid, telling a corrupt bartender he was pimping women to rich executives and gangsters. Even sex trafficking them." Marcy slumped in the seat. "But thanks for saving us."

"We're not out of it." Celia bit her tongue. *Don't remind Marcy of the danger to our families.*

"I wonder if they know where we are by now," Marcy said.

"They'll be looking for us by plane, bus, or train. Driving on the back roads is the best choice."

Three miles later, she saw a sign for motels and food at the next exit and veered off the highway.

"Those dumb fucks won't find us, I'm sure." Marcy looked out the back window.

Celia glanced over at Marcy from time to time. *Is she going to do something crazy?*

"I just hope we delayed them by a couple of hours. They have no transportation or cell phones until maybe the morning, and they've got to get to the hospital."

"I want to stomp Stompovich's ass or whatever his name is," Marcy said.

Celia took a deep breath. "We need to figure out a way to beat him at his game."

"Better we disappear or we're screwed," Marcy said, her voice tight. "Best outcome is we live and our families aren't harmed. It's survival time." She waved her hands.

"Get real. We will never be safe as long as they're free. They'll hunt us forever. That's why we need an airtight plan to get them slammed into prison."

Celia maneuvered onto a road that paralleled the highway. Silos and bales of hay lined fields. The smell of horse manure was pleasant compared to the stink of sweat, shit, and grease that clung to their clothing. Marcy's beautiful red curls were matted, and her housedress was streaked with black stains. Celia was hardly better.

Celia turned into the motel parking lot, the bright red blinking neon motel sign with the letter L missing. She looked into the rearview mirror, checking for bruises and dried blood on her forehead and cheeks. A glance gave her the impression she looked like a mutilated prize fighter. Using the hem of her housedress, she wiped her face. At least the blood was gone. The gun was back in her pocket, cold steel against flesh chilled her skin.

In the faded yellow lobby, a young man sat at a scratched linoleum countertop, his head resting on his arms. It was only 6 p.m., but Celia could imagine that the tedium of holding down the desk at this place would put anyone to sleep. "Hello!" she said. He awoke with a start and stared as though still asleep.

"Is it possible to rent a room in the back farthest away from the road? We've been traveling for hours and I'm a light sleeper."

"Sure," said the young man, scratching his face indifferently as Celia signed in.

"How much?"

"$129.99 plus tax."

"Is cash okay?"

"Whatever," he said, taking the money and giving her change for the second hundred- dollar bill. He handed her a key.

"Hey," Celia added. "You wouldn't happen to have toothbrushes and toothpaste?"

"In the vending machine," he said.

They parked at the last unit of a strip of rooms and opened a creaky door. Whitish-yellow walls, a small desk with a dull glass top, and twin beds with worn, flattened gray quilts looked suddenly like heaven.

A palace compared to the container.

Celia went into the bathroom, undressed, and stepped into the shower. There was mold in the corners, but the water was strong and hot. The towels were threadbare but happily smelled of bleach.

She scrubbed her underwear, washed her hair using half of the little complimentary bottle of shampoo left on the soap rack. She used a damp washcloth to take off most of the stains of their housedresses, marveling at how their homely design reminded her of her mother who wore a similar cotton dress with the yellow and blue daisy patterns. Her mother had worn it for years, it seemed, and Celia had loved that cheerful pattern when she was a child.

"You finished in there, Princess Celia?" called Marcy.

"Sure am," smiled Celia, opening the door. "I was washing our ball gowns."

"They're nothing, if not practical," laughed Marcy. "Now, excuse me, I need a shower."

Celia flopped into one of the twin beds and got under the bleach-scented sheets. "You once saved my life when I was at the bottom," she said, as Marcy, her hair in a towel, slipped into the adjoining bed. "I'll be your court jester forever."

"When we laugh, it lifts me out of here and flies me to our cha-cha studio in Florida," Marcy said. "This bed even feels like clouds. The first real bed since…"

Soon Marcy was snoring lightly. Celia dialed Allie's cell. It went straight to voicemail. "Allie," she said. "It's Mom from a safe phone. I'll call you back in five minutes."

She waited five minutes, her mind racing. *Can't stop thinking about those women and kids.*

Five minutes later, she dialed again. Allie picked up right away. "Mom?"

"Allie, we'll be in Philly tomorrow. We'll be at the hospital by noon. Can you wait for us?"

"Mom, this is a mess. Please stop."

"No, I'm serious. Where can we meet you at the hospital? We'll hide out in the sub-basement until we figure this out."

Allie sighed and said nothing.

"Honey, this is not a joke."

"Oh, it's not a joke. Fine, I'll meet you at the service door, just past the entrance at 8th and Colorado. I'll stay from 5 p.m. to 7. After that, I'm leaving. I stayed at a Philly B & B. I didn't tell my fiancé because I don't know what to say."

"Thank you. I love you with every fiber of my being."

"Sure."

Chapter 12

The sun poured in through the slats on the windows. Dust mites floated in the chaotic overlap of sunbeams.

"Morning! It's 7 a.m. Rise and shine!" Marcy croaked. "We slept for twelve solid hours. I'm starving. Aren't you?"

Celia shook herself awake. She had shaken the towel off during the night. She wrapped it around her, got up, and looked through the window. Not much to see except brown earth. Even the drooping weeds in the dirt lot seemed to have given up. "There's a diner across the road. I love diner food."

It sat behind a blacktop parking lot that dwarfed it. Celia imagined in its heyday that there would have been standing room only, young couples canoodling in the back booths, the retired fireman's club yakking it up at the counter, the morning shift folks, and the retired couples ordering the bargain breakfast special. There was something so very wonderful about a well-loved diner.

"Bring…me…coffee…" Marcy said in a robotic voice.

Celia turned and smiled. "And pancakes, eggs, bacon, hash browns."

"Sausages. Danish. We've got to get energy and keep these bodies healthy. Never know when they'll come in handy."

"True," said Celia, heading to the bathroom, shivering all the way. Still, she smiled. It felt good to wear clean clothes.

"Well, we look a bit more presentable, don't you think?" she said when they stepped into the morning sunshine.

"Speak for yourself," said Marcy. "I'm smoking hot."

"Allie will be waiting for us at the hospital between five and seven tonight. Save your hotness for the sub-basement."

"The idea of that doesn't make me feel sexy."

It was a chilly morning, and they had no coats. Only one other car, a Honda Civic with West Virginia license plates was parked at the far end of the lot. They were the only ones staying at the motel. *That's good news. They probably figured out that we're on our way to Philly, New York, or some other port city.*

She rummaged inside the SUV's trunk, found a raggedy sports bag, placed the gun inside, and settled the bag in the back seat of the car. She wasn't going down without a fight. She stopped, tapped her head, and wondered how she'd gotten to think like a thug. Well, this was her second go-around with police, and she had to protect herself and those close to her. *Am I a magnet for evil?*

I've hidden all these years behind the protection of my parents and husband. I let them control my life, and make me feel invisible. Now I welcome the challenge. I even might be attracted to the danger. Is that the new me? I hope it's not the motivation propelling me to do some good in the world. But, have I become addicted to danger?

The sky was clouding up as though a rainstorm was headed toward them. They ran across the road. An underlying chill in the breeze reminded her they needed new clothes. *All we have is on our backs.*

The '50s style diner took Celia back into her morning fantasy.

White and black-tiled floors gleamed. Rotating green vinyl stools, mounted to the floor, faced the red, Formica-topped counter like soldiers waiting for an order to attack a short stack or hash browns. Sparkling white subway tiles were on the walls. Five coffee pots emitted ribbons of steam and an earthy fragrance. Bacon sizzled on the flattop grill, and a jukebox in the corner stood silent. A dozen or so patrons were sitting at the long counter. Half the booths were full.

Celia saw Marcy relax as the hostess seated them in a cheery, red vinyl booth. Celia searched the sparse landscape outside the window. Scrub pines and loose stones. On the motel property she saw a car without wheels propped on wooden boxes. The rusting wheel rims and rusted holes in the doors announced it had been there for a long time. She leaned back, exhaling.

The waitress, who looked to be in her mid-thirties, wore a starched, white dress stretched over her ample body. Her name tag said Betty. "Whatcha got in mind this morning?" Her cheeks and neck jiggled when she spoke.

Celia's stomach rumbled as she ordered scrambled eggs and ham with white toast.

"And I'll have," Marcy said breathlessly, "Three eggs over easy, double order of well-done bacon, ham, hash browns, a bagel, and a whole pot of coffee."

The waitress raised her eyebrow. "Sorry. We don't have bagels."

Marcy started to explain that every diner had bagels.

"We have whole wheat, white, or rye toast."

"Rule," Celia said in her softest voice. "Judgments immobilize the mind. They limit freedom of choice."

"Sorry about that. This is not Florida, after all, where they grow as many bagels as oranges. Rye toast for me, Betty."

"I'll give you an extra slice, hon. Looks like you ain't eaten in two months or you got some big appetite. How do you stay so damn skinny?"

Marcy grinned and shimmied in her seat. "Good genes, the only good thing I got from my shit-eating father. And I had to eat a lot of that."

Celia reached over and held Marcy's shaking hand.

Betty patted Marcy's shoulder. "I had one of those. I ran away from home when I was sixteen."

"We're soul sisters, Betty."

"I'll bring you some extra stuff. You ladies are nice." Betty turned toward Celia. "And not bad-lookin' for your age." She laughed in a gentle way. "Not like those three gals who came in looking homeless. Young things, they were. So skinny. Not much money so I gave them some free food. Poor things. Clothes were ripped, mud on their faces, and scabs on their arms." She pointed to her upper arm.

Marcy leaned over toward Celia. "Do you think…?"

"Sounds like it." Celia tapped the metal spoon on the table. "Looks like they didn't get in touch with the police. At this distance they got away on their own."

"That's sad, but I get why they'd just want to get lost in the crowd."

"Betty, please pack our food. We have to leave." Celia said.

Betty shrugged and went into the kitchen.

"Can't we have one meal sitting nicely at a table? I feel bad about those girls, but I'll die of hunger."

"What if they were followed? I don't know about that car in the lot. Let's get moving."

Betty came through the kitchen door with three paper bags. "Got this ready for some construction workers, I don't know why but you sure look scared. Want me to call police?"

"No, no. Thanks. You've been so nice."

Marcy pulled her stash of money from her bra. She paid the bill and gave Betty a forty-dollar tip.

After checking out of the motel, Celia gave Marcy a lesson on how to use the gun.

"Always wanted to be a badass," said Marcy. "And here we are in our own version of a Chekhov play with a loaded gun, so I had better learn how to use it."

"Okay," said Celia. "Step one, make sure you know how to put the safety lock on and how to take it off. See this lever? Make sure it's flicked to the left until you need to use the gun. Step two, hold the gun with two hands…"

"I read lots of hard-boiled detective stories," Marcy said. "This takes more practice than one lesson, obviously. I'll try my best if we're desperate. But, I'm happy you learned to use the rod at the shooting range in Florida."

"The rod? What, now you're a gun moll?"

"I feel like one. Why do we find trouble wherever we go?"

"I thought the same thing myself!" Celia gave a throaty laugh. "I think we are like magnets to crazy, dangerous situations. As long as we walk away intact."

So, Marcy feels the buzz too! Another reason we're such good friends.

When Celia finished giving Marcy the firing instructions for the gun, they hurried into the car and drove mostly on backroads, crisscrossing from town to town. Stompovich would know by now that they were driving their SUV, but Celia guessed they wouldn't report it. That would call unwelcome attention to themselves. Most likely they had lookouts on major highways. She hoped to stay under the radar. They didn't have far to go to meet up with Allison.

Marcy was staring out the back window, looking unsettled. *I've got to stay calm. I can't let Marcy know how scared I feel.*

They passed Downingtown. *Are we making ourselves too visible? Do those guys know where we're headed? God, I hope Allie meets us at the right time.*

She spotted a strip mall where they bought a disposable phone, two SIM cards, and used the bathroom. Even though Marcy had gone through half their food, she wanted more.

"I'm hungry again," she said. "I've got to eat, even if it's your arm." Marcy rubbed her stomach. "I hurt."

It struck Celia that when Marcy's stomach reacted to stress, it demanded to be filled. Back in Florida, every time a problem arose, Marcy needed comfort food. She'd always plowed through Celia's refrigerator, looking for leftovers. She pulled into a Wawa Food Market. While Marcy went in, she organized the trunk.

"Look!" shouted Marcy, returning with a grocery bag. She held up a green, metallic package. "Funyuns! Better than the onion rings at Bernie's Deli in Boca! Goes with diner meals. Please drive while I eat."

"Okay, party girl. Time to go," said Celia, shutting the trunk. She was about to get in the driver's seat when big slabs of hands crashed down on her wrist and yanked her away. The man grabbed her hair. She gagged at the intense pain, but managed to turn her head to see it was the truck driver who had tried to rape Nikki. He grabbed her by the throat. Before he tightened his fist, she yelled, "Run Marcy!"

The other man walked quickly toward the door where Marcy sat. She smacked the door open with a thud into his body. He hit the ground, bumping his head. "You bitch!" he shouted, in a shaky voice. He had trouble getting up. Marcy reached into the sports bag, grabbed the gun, and jumped out of the car. Celia could hardly breathe but kept Marcy in view out of the corner of her eye. *Are we going to die?*

Marcy kicked the man on the ground in the groin, and as he writhed, she slammed his head on the ground, blood splattering the pavement. Celia was on her knees, the man throttling hard. Marcy pressed the gun against his cheek.

"Let her go, this instant," she shouted. He poked Marcy in the stomach with his elbow and she dropped the gun. He reached over to pick it up, but Celia kicked it in Marcy's direction. Marcy grabbed it, stepped back, aimed, and pressed the trigger, the recoil jerking her arm. She clipped the side of his knee.

"Yeow," he screamed, reeling backward.

Someone shouted, "Call 911!"

"Get that fucking motor going, Celia," Marcy said between gritted teeth, and jumped into the passenger seat.

Celia gunned the motor, and they took off, nearly running over the squirming man on the ground.

Marcy wiped sweat from her forehead with her sleeve. "Whoa. The gun's harder to use than I thought. Please, let's not make this a regular thing? You'd think they'd have caught up sooner. But, damn, they won't be after us any time soon. That guy's going to need knee surgery."

"They probably tracked the women first." Celia took a deep breath. "God, Marcy, you saved my life. But we may have Philly cops on our tails soon. We need to get rid of this car." Celia's voice was hoarse. She rubbed her throat. "I owe you big-time. I'll wait on you hand and foot in our new digs—wherever they are. You're a damn good fighter. Who knew?"

"I watch all the action shows and used to practice karate," Marcy said, pride in her voice. "I took lessons secretly as a kid, planning to beat the hell out of my abusive father." Marcy shook her head. "Fighting is my substitute when I don't have a hot sex partner." She flexed her muscles. "Well, maybe food is next. Then fighting."

They both understood some of the psychology underlying this madness, but for different reasons. Danger filled Marcy's need for intimacy when she didn't have a lover in her life.

What's my excuse? That I'm challenged for the greater good? But it's more than that.

She gave Marcy an ironic smile. "In the past it's been sex that got you into trouble. Now it's just plain risk-taking. And I go along with it. I must be crazy." Celia looked out the windshield, swerving to miss a car that suddenly stopped. "Philly driving," she muttered.

Chapter 13

When they entered the city, the number of skyscrapers seemed to have doubled since her last visit as though guards had stormed the city and hovering helicopters protected the pedestrians. They were four miles from the hospital, and Celia looked for a parking lot. A stolen car close to the hospital would tell their pursuers where they were hiding. They drove west on Walnut and left the car parked in an open lot in West Philadelphia, near the University of Pennsylvania and Drexel campuses.

Celia found a screwdriver in the trunk of the car and removed the license plates. Marcy snatched the screwdriver and rubbed off the VIN buried just below the windshield.

"There, it'll take a while to trace this car."

They walked a few blocks to the 30th Street Train Station to grab a cab. She glanced at Marcy and pointed to a dirt smear on her face. "Maybe a quick wash up for Allie."

Inside, she marveled at the grandness of the station's towering columns. At one end of the massive open waiting room, *Angel of Ascension,* a monumental and mysterious statue of a winged man, rose about four stories.

Marcy clucked her tongue. "They gave that winged behemoth a little wee-wee. Out of proportion."

Voices echoed through the enormous space as people bustled to their trains that waited outside on unseen tracks. Celia stopped, looked up, and saw the latticed ceiling five floors above. Windows rose from the second floor, allowing light to bathe the area. Something almost spiritual in the place struck her. A cathedral of light and shadow. Marcy tugged her arm to move along.

In the washroom, they splashed soap and water on their faces, hands, and arms, then used paper towels to dry off. Women came and went, glancing at them with disgust. Celia didn't care. The warm water felt good.

Making sure no one was tracking them, they went outside and hailed a taxi. Driving east, they crossed the Market Street bridge over the Schuylkill River. Celia envied the eight oarsmen rowing on the placid water below.

She'd read about the tourist spots of the city when planning a trip to visit her Allie. This was one. The eight men on the long boat made a small wake with their paddles as they skimmed the water. If only she could do that for the rest of her life!

She caught a glimpse of Boathouse Row. The large, old boathouses along the riverbanks were outlined in lights at night, showing their configuration like line drawings. They were homes to the rowing clubs, fraternities, and social clubs. The fading sun sent rays skidding off the calm surface of water.

A suffocating sadness enveloped her. The joy of dancing the cha-cha, taking art classes, going to museums, falling in love with Stanton, even sipping a cocktail at happy hour. When would they ever see that again?

Celia spied City Hall with a bigger-than-life statue of the city's founder, William Penn, on top. It looked so elegant and patriotic it brought tears to her eyes. If only sightseeing the city was on the top of her agenda. "Why the hell is everything making me cry? Even that statue is heart-stopping."

"Ahh, it's not so elegant." Marcy studied the statue. "If you look at it in a certain way, the rifle he's holding on his hip, at the level of his groin, looks like a big penis. He should trade his with the statue at the train station."

The cab driver snickered.

Celia laughed. "Girl, you are too much! Here we are, running for our lives, and you're making penis jokes."

"Well…if we don't laugh, we'd probably have heart attacks and die." Marcy shook her head.

We need the comic relief. Marcy is right. But it only goes so far.

They headed for the Delaware River. Center City was bounded by two rivers about six and a half miles apart, the Schuylkill on the west side and the Delaware on the east, which flowed into the Chesapeake Bay and the Atlantic Ocean. The major ports on the Delaware were not far from where Allison worked.

Twenty minutes later, the cab left them off at the hospital.

"Thank God, you made it." Relief filled Allie's anxious face when she saw them. Celia reached for her as did Marcy, and they collapsed into a hug. "Are you both all right?" Allie stepped back. "You look like you've been digging for coal."

Celia scanned the street then urged them inside.

"I'd rather have been digging for gold." Marcy brushed a lock of Allison's rich black hair from her forehead. "Still gorgeous. She has the same heart-shaped face, green eyes, and dimples as you do, Celia."

She turned back to Allison. "Despite the dark circles around your mother's eyes, you're hot-looking babes."

"Not bad yourself, Marcy," Celia said in a tired voice. She tried to sound upbeat and got a big grin from Marcy. "Enough of the mutual admiration society," Celia said. "Are we okay to stay in the sub-basement?"

"I checked it out, and it's pretty awful. I don't think it's habitable," Allison said.

"Oh, shit," Marcy said. "Let's find a hotel."

"We can't," said Celia. "They're looking for us."

Allison led them to a freight elevator. When they reached the sub-basement, she herded them through an open archway. They followed what seemed like blind corridors until they came to a six-foot entrance. They were surrounded by a big cloud of dust and a musty, damp odor. Celia sneezed, narrowed her eyes, and peered into the haze and the dull lighting. Marcy coughed.

Celia glanced at the useless items the hospital had abandoned: broken chairs, pieces of hospital bed frames, dented meal carts, dust pans, mops, and stacks of dingy mattresses. They maneuvered around piles of cinder blocks, two-by-fours, rusty struts, and dented, metal containers of cleaning fluid.

Allison reached up and pulled a string hanging from a bare bulb. Mice scattered. Celia jumped back and Marcy cupped her mouth.

"After what you've gone through, you let a few mice spook you?" Allison asked. She placed her hands on her hips. "Soon it'll be time for my questions. Your story had better be good for disrupting my life."

Celia grimaced and waved away the dust curling around her head. "Let's go." They came across another pile of junk: jagged wooden doors, dirty curtains, curtain tracks, stair railings, and metal chairs piled high against the walls, along with a dozen splintery wooden cabinets, each about six feet wide by eight feet tall.

Dim bulbs cast gummy, yellow shafts of light, highlighting whirling dust spores. In the next room, the pungent odor smelled like decaying animals.

Allison pulled a cord overhead. A weak beam of greenish light filtered down. She flicked on a lantern on the floor with a strong, white beam. "Used this in a blackout at my apartment."

The light flashed on a cracked, gray archway up ahead. They moved forward slowly, then quickened their step, passing into a darker, massive space.

"I walked through all the open spaces and this one seems to be the most isolated. Least amount of clutter and furthest from the elevator. I checked it out for an escape passage as well. There are a few narrow ones that take you to the delivery dock, or that side door we came in through."

"We can't live here. It's creepy," Marcy said, wrapping her arms over her abdomen.

"It's the last place they'd look." Celia shivered. "Get used to your home sweet home."

"Improvise. The dance is a palette to explore the unfamiliar." Marcy said dramatically. Celia and Marcy threw their heads back and placed their feet as though to start a cha-cha.

"What?" Allison said, looking confused.

"Just some dance rules we use to get by in life," Marcy said. "Not sure they work down here."

"It beats being dead," Celia said. "It looks like this place once served some purpose?" she asked.

"Early on a couple specialties were down here. It was the Radiology Department. They built a new one. Residents used to sleep down here, too," Allison explained.

"I bet there are lots of items we can use to set up housekeeping. It's a free-for-all furniture grab. We'll use the bed after we beat the dust out of it and use the cleaning stuff," Celia said. She popped her eyes open to make an upbeat face. "We might check out architectural magazines for good design ideas. We'll set a trend. Life in a hospital basement at no cost."

"We might as well live on the street," Marcy said.

She's not wrong. "It's insulated underground—cool in the summer, heated in the winter," Celia said. "And all the food we can steal. Those cubicles over there are our bedrooms." She pointed to several indentations just big enough to hold a single bed and a small table.

"Yuck. That's disgusting." Marcy's voice sliced through the heavy, damp air.

Allison rubbed her forehead. "There is a bathroom about thirty feet from here," she said. "Plumbing is working. We have lots of cleaning equipment down here. There's rust remover, too. The toilet and sink need a good cleaning."

Allison stared at Celia. Celia turned from the look because she knew what was coming.

"You must tell me what the hell is going on?" Allison's question was more like a demand.

Celia stepped back, as though about to defend her position.

Marcy widened her eyes. "It's unbelievable," she whispered.

"Try me," Allison said loudly.

"Let's set this place up first and then I'll tell all." Celia picked up Allison's lantern and walked through the junk areas just outside the main, cavernous room. She scoured through the piles. Climbing on ridges of broken bed frames, she waded through tables, old dishes, and silverware. She gingerly held two urinals. "We can use these for wine decanters."

"Yuck," Marcy said.

"Got to laugh or we'll cry." Celia tossed them back.

"What about clean showers, decent toilets, stuff like that?" Marcy asked.

"A bit harder. I stole hospital gowns so you look like patients and scrub suits so you can look like staff, depending what we need. I'll tell you where the empty rooms on the floor are. They all have clean bathrooms and showers. When finished, you'll dress normally, like visitors, and leave via the elevator. Hit the SB button and come down here. I can give you my badge for admission; hopefully you won't get stopped. It has my picture." Allison took a deep breath. "One at a time on the floor. No one knows what anyone is doing in huge hospitals. They're all in their own silos."

"Ingenious, Allison," Marcy said. "You thought of everything."

"When you two tell me that our lives are in danger, I go into desperation mode and move like a tiger. Learned that the hard way." Allison opened a badly dented tool box, revealing a variety of tools they could use.

Celia searched through the piles. She pulled metal night tables and swiped at the dust with the edge of her housedress. Allison tore old sheets for rags. While discussing the best way to clean, they pulled out pieces of furniture, dragged them into the alcoves and assigned cubbies. "Just like in grade school," said Celia.

They adjusted metal framed beds and hammered them where they had been bent. They filled buckets from the bathroom with water and poured in liquid soap. Old brooms would do for brushes. With broomsticks, they banged the dust out of the mattresses and sprayed them with antibacterial cleaner. Then they swept the concrete floors and washed them down.

"Medical residents have their own lounge, bathroom, and showers," Allison said. "If hospital rooms are filled, we can use their facilities late at night. It's when there are smaller crews and they're too fatigued to care. It's important we look like staff if we go on the floors. Don't forget to wear the scrub suits and badges that I give you."

"How will you get badges?" Celia asked, sitting down on the bed.

"You might say I borrowed blank staff employee cards, printed your names and departments. I can photoshop pictures. I have used computers that they tossed and work fine."

"Girl, you are a genius," Marcy said. "Like mother, like daughter."

Celia shined the light on Marcy. "Well, what's the verdict on our new digs now?"

"It'll work," Marcy said. "When do you think we can break out of here?"

"I don't know," Celia said. "We've got a lot of figuring out to do. We're not even sure how these gangs cooperate." She stopped, trying to put her thoughts in order. "Like, how do we get those pedophiles arrested? I'm sure they've covered their tracks." Celia followed the trajectory of Allison's puzzled expression as she stared at Marcy's distressed face highlighted by her thick red eyebrows. Although it wasn't masked by makeup, it looked good. "As soon as we have proof that those animals are sex trafficking we'll move on it."

"I did a bit of snooping online and saw very little about women going to the police," Allison said. "I still don't get why you won't contact law enforcement."

"We already tried. No one would believe this story. They'll demand a good deal of concrete evidence before they even stir. It'll be hard to persuade them that we were kidnapped. Most of the women they take are girls from five to maybe twenty-eight. Even if a police department believed us and went to investigate, the bad guys would likely be gone by the time they get there. They have moles in the police force, so they can get inside information and simply move the women." Celia folded her hands. "They've probably moved out of the house in Pittsburgh. And the women are scared to rat them out for fear of their families being murdered."

Marcy interjected, "Not one of the women we've met has been willing to cooperate with authorities because of the threats. Besides protecting their families back home they're told the police are the enemy and will arrest them for prostitution, then deport them."

Allison tapped her foot. "For God's sake. How did you get involved?"

Chapter 14

Celia gave Allison an abbreviated version, leaving out how Marcy sent the staff at Fritzie's II in an uproar. "We walked into the wrong place at the wrong time." Celia saw the look of horror on Allie's face and shuddered. "The name of the Mafia boss is…"

"I don't need to know. Just report the restaurant," Allison said.

"With us on the run, they'll be on their guard and stay clean as a whistle—on the outside," Marcy said.

"Remember," Celia said, "Mafia organizations of all nationalities cooperate in sex trafficking. Big time power. I read that it's an eighty- to ninety-billion-dollar-a-year business and counting. They might have a cop or two on their payroll in each city." She hesitated. "We need a plan to get them. Even with proof, they surely can make their bail, and none of us will live long. It has to be airtight because they can flee with passports in foreign countries."

Allison started to speak. Her voice choked. She cleared her throat. "My fiancé is a doctor at the hospital. Is he in danger?"

"They didn't mention him."

"Oh, goodie," Marcy said. "A doctor. A mother's dream. Does he have a doctor father?"

"Shush," Celia said.

Allison paced. "Well, let's see how long he'll stay around when I become imprisoned in this filthy basement." She stared at her mother. "And I'm pregnant. It's my second month."

Celia's jaw dropped.

"Great," Marcy squealed, then stood and hugged Allison who received the hug stiffly.

"This is thrilling, Allie," Celia said, caressing Allison's cheek. "I'm going to be a grandma."

Allison frowned and stepped back. "What's great about having a baby down here?" Her eyes dulled.

"We'll be out of here by that time," Marcy declared. "I hope."

Allison turned her back and unpacked clothing. "This hospital is at 3rd and Pine in case you go out," she said. "What am I saying? Do not go out." She reached into her pocket and removed a plastic card. "This card opens the elevator doors only employees use."

The damp, ashy-smelling, cavernous room felt fairly safe to Celia. If only she could lock herself in. But she had to face the daunting job of somehow digging out.

Allie seems to be handling this flood of dangerous news not as badly as I thought.

In Florida, Celia had gotten a fleeting glimpse of Allie having a wonderful relationship and future. Allie had moved there after leaving a husband who had consistently cheated on her. When the new relationship imploded, Allie felt driven to leave Florida. Philadelphia had welcomed her, had promised a great future. She'd developed a career in healthcare administration and had found a man she loved.

Philadelphia was an easy city to navigate. In recent years it had emerged from its sleepy reputation as a horse and buggy rest stop between New York City and Washington D.C. It now bustled with energy.

Celia knew Allison loved Philadelphia, even though it was a beset with big city problems: dirty streets, bus smoke, spit on the sidewalks, homelessness, a high homicide rate, and urine-stained alleyways. On the upside were great clothing shops, excellent restaurants, superb art, the Philadelphia Museum of Art, and the Barnes Foundation. Celia remembered Philly weekends when she still lived in New York; very good little theaters, the Philadelphia Orchestra with its present superlative conductor, Yannick Nézet-Séguin, and Comcast skyscrapers vying for the tallest on the skyline. *Too bad I won't be taking much advantage of all that.*

"Justin is one of the best doctors in the city and beyond. He's done great research and brought prestige to the Philadelphia medical community," Allison said, interrupting Celia's thoughts. "He's an interventional radiologist who has written books, and he's on the teaching faculty of Temple Medical School." Allison took a deep breath. "How can I tell him that my mother and her best friend are on the lam from a worldwide Mafia empire that forces women and children into prostitution? And how they got involved with the lowest scum on the criminality scale? How about his reaction when I tell him our lives are in danger, along with our baby?" Allison rubbed dirt from her fingers. "I'm going upstairs to clean up papers and help my assistant do payroll and our expense accounting. Then I'll come back to my penthouse apartment in the sub-basement." She made a disgusted face and started to walk away.

Marcy gave her a wan smile. "Do you think it's wise being seen?"

Celia echoed the question. "Don't go."

"I don't think these criminals will come to a hospital." Allison turned her tag around that showed her picture and the name. "I don't have your last name, Mom."

Celia breathed deeply. "Thank goodness."

"What happened to your boyfriend, Stanton?" Allison dipped her head as she eyed Celia.

"He's in Florida. Can't imagine he'd have anything to do with me now. I put him through misery this past year. I took my rotten moods out on him. We had fun when I felt good."

"Not to mention your mother told Stanton she was coming to visit you and hasn't contacted him since."

"Listen, I have to get my work done. I'll see you later." Allison turned toward the opening.

"Wait," Celia said. "I've got to pee, but our little bathroom needs more cleaning."

"Get that scrub suit on. Put this blank ID around your neck and keep your arms crossed around it. Follow a little behind me and I'll point out the public bathroom. Then come back down quickly."

Celia did as she was told and followed behind Allison by ten feet. When they emerged, no one was around. In the elevator they stood apart with Celia's arms crossed, hiding the ID card but leaving the string visible.

When they arrived at the second floor, Allison pointed Celia toward the bathroom. Someone stood in Allison's way. A sweet-faced, nerdy, mid-fortyish guy in a scrub suit with a lab coat over it. *Is this her Justin?*

Celia kept walking but could almost feel Allison's nervousness like sparks from a damaged electric cord. She heard the man's voice.

"Hi, sweetheart."

Celia knew it was the last person Allie wanted to see right now. She half-turned and saw Allie kiss his cheek. "Hi honey. I'm on my way to do payroll."

Celia stopped, pretending to tie her shoe. She kept her face averted.

"Hope it won't take too long. I'm getting off at six. Want to have dinner?" he asked in a pleasant, deep voice.

"Ah, I'm meeting my mother. I'll call you."

"She made it! When can I meet her?"

"Um, she's disorganized and a bit disoriented. I'll get her settled in, and I'll call you."

"Where'd she decide to stay?"

"She has her eye on a B & B. Love you." Allison pecked him on the cheek and hurried away.

I am blowing up Allie's hard-earned, stable world. Now what?

After leaving the bathroom, she made her way back to the sub-basement, trying to claw out a plan from her exhausted brain. Nothing. She jabbed the button several times as though it would make the elevator go faster. When the doors opened her heart pounded. From now on she'd have to pay attention to every person she passed, and every detail no matter how small.

"Maybe in a month or two those bastards will forget we existed." Marcy said. "We're small potatoes to them. Right?"

"We freed a bunch of their money-machines. It meant so much to those truck drivers to track us across the state of Pennsylvania, one with an injured foot, no less. And they nearly caught us," Celia said. "That means the organization will be hot on our trail." She rubbed her forehead as though it might propel ideas. "They know where our children live."

"We can contact politicians…"

"These women don't vote so they're low priority." Celia blew out a frustrated breath. "Picture this. Two aging women go to the police to say, without a shred of concrete proof, save for the location of a house in Pittsburgh that's probably abandoned by now, they were kidnapped by a sex trafficking ring," Celia said in a quivery voice. "Ringleaders move the stable of women from place to place if they suspect they've been outed. As for the women, we know they won't talk."

Allison came through the opening into their living space. "What's going on?"

Marcy perked up. "I vote for contacting the authorities. We call newspapers to get some publicity. By the way, I'm good at handling interviews, and I'm very photogenic, as we all know."

"Marcy! Are you crazy?" Celia's voice was constrained. "We come out in the open to people who think nothing of killing us like they'd swat a fly."

"I second that." Allison shook her head. "Where is your head?"

"That's what I'd like to know," Marcy said.

No one laughed.

"My son, Lionel, might never talk to me again. He still hasn't forgiven me for running off with the guru for all that time when he was a kid."

"Just think of ways to crack this horrible situation," Celia said.

"Ladies, there must be someone who could help us," Allison said.

"Allie," Celia began, "we are dealing with vicious, sociopathic killers."

"I owe it to Justin and our baby to end this soon," Allison said in a hushed voice. "I want this baby born in a proper hospital and to have a good life."

Celia stood stock still, picturing Justin delivering his child in this dungeon. *How awful.* "Allie, it will work out. I promise." *What am I promising? I have no idea.* "You'll have your baby in a proper delivery room, with Justin by your side." *If I nail these bastards soon.*

It occurred to her she hadn't paid much attention to Allie while they got the furniture dusted and arranged neatly and the place into a semblance of order. *Just as I did the whole time Allie was growing up. How sad that I've overlooked a true human connection with my daughter.*

"The good news about living here is that I can walk up to the maternity ward in minutes and see your baby," Marcy said out of the blue.

"You can hardly show your face." Allison said. "Plus, I hope to heaven this is all sorted out *before* the baby comes. We can trust Justin, but the news about the baby put him on a cloud. I don't want to ruin his happiness just yet."

I don't foresee that. Unless we desert the women and go on the run.

"My choices of men have been shitty, except for Justin. He's gentle and kind," Allison said, looking dreamy. "I can have that home in the burbs with a white picket fence. I used to laugh at the thought. Now I want it desperately. You turned my world around."

"I am so sorry for that." Celia sought a way to change the conversation. "You'll need healthy food while we're here." Celia placed a hand gently on Allison's belly.

"Hospital food may not taste great, but it is nourishing," Allison said. "I can sneak into the kitchen and gather the untouched leftover trays. There are always bunches of them."

I have to figure out a way to get Allie out when it's time or we'll all go feet first.

"Can we get Wi-Fi down here?" Celia asked.

"Yes, I know the passwords. You'll have two of the best laptops. Music has to be low-volume," Allison said, "so it doesn't reach someone who might be walking around the front space."

"No sex, no music." Marcy snapped her fingers. "Maybe a little pot?"

"Pot, no. The smell is too stong. Wine, yes," Allison replied.

"I need food and sleep," Marcy said. "That's all that's available to us. Poopers."

Allison opened her backpack and removed aluminum-wrapped sandwiches. "I managed to sneak these off a tray headed for a meeting. I'm hungry all the time now."

Sitting quietly on rickety empty wooden boxes, they munched ham sandwiches.

Chapter 15

"Guess who called me while I was upstairs?" Allison said, bunching the foil from her sandwich and dropping it into a battered trash can. "Stanton."

In the middle of bringing a water bottle to her lips, Celia froze. "What did you tell him?"

"He was really worried. I didn't know what to say. I said I hadn't heard from you or Marcy for several days. Apparently, you told him you'd call him once you got settled. He said that lately you've been moving in your own mysterious ways." Allison looked at Celia. "I agreed."

"Tell him we went on a fun tour through rural Pennsylvania," said Marcy. "It's all true except for the fun part."

"I told him I'd call him when I heard from you, Mom."

"Should I call him?" Celia felt a rush of warmth through her body at the thought of seeing him. Not only did she miss him, but she also had guilty pangs for her indifference over this last year. *He means a lot to me.*

"I don't know if we should tell anyone," Marcy said in a trembling voice.

"If you trust him, we should," Allison said. "He was so helpful with the fraud investigation last year."

"I trust him," Celia said emphatically. "What he did for all of us is nothing short of miraculous."

"I think it's a good idea. We need his help, someone who can come and go without being noticed," Allison said. "I don't want Justin involved."

Celia took a long swig of water. "Stanton did the most to help lock up the case back in Florida."

Allison winced.

"Sorry to bring up a sore subject," Celia said softly.

"I've gotten insights into myself since then. I walk carefully now." Allison's voice turned steely. "I've come to like myself."

"Let's vote," Celia said. "Should we confide in Stanton?"

Celia and Allison raised their hands. Marcy looked at them and half-raised hers.

"I'll call him, but we need more disposable cell phones. Did you get rid of your cell, Allie?"

"I did after your last call. I can say I misplaced my phone and that's why I have a burner temporarily. Stanton can be the outside person who can get us disposable phones and other stuff we might need."

Celia smirked. "That's if he even will come." Celia bit her lip. "Let's hope Stanton's forgiven me."

"Why else would he be looking for you?" Allison said.

"Maybe to kill her for acting so awful to him this last year?" Marcy said, her voice an octave higher.

Celia didn't say a word.

When she called Stanton and heard relief in his voice, the knots in her stomach untied. She told him only that a terrible situation existed. "I'll hop on a plane right away," he said. "And Celia, I'm so glad you are all right."

His words pierced Celia's heart. He didn't even press her for information.

Around midnight, Allison met Stanton at the side exit as he exited from an Uber. She led him toward their living quarters. Celia stood at the entrance, tapping her foot and humming a tuneless song. She studied his incredulous expression as he sidestepped the maze of hospital castoffs. Once through the debris, he stood face-to-face with Celia. His look turned anxious.

"Welcome to our new abode," Celia said.

He gave a soft whistle as he scanned the area, but when his gaze landed on Celia, he smiled broadly. Celia felt as if she had found the full warmth of the sun after a frosty morning.

He took her in his arms and gently kissed her on the lips. "What's going on? This is a joke, right?"

Celia froze. *He'll probably walk out when he hears the story.* "I missed you so much," she said. "I'm sorry that I cut myself off from you. Now, I see that it was a mistake."

Stanton took in the room. "What do these digs include? Room service with eggs Benedict and espresso?"

He puts on a good front, but will he recover from this shock?

"Can I stay over sometime for a pajama party?" Stanton asked, playfully. "Is this a cement version of that hotel in the arctic made totally out of ice? I have never stayed at a hotel like this. It's really original."

"Why would you want to?" Allison asked.

Marcy's face turned haughty. "We have the very best service and food. Three hospital food trays a day."

"This is not a joke," Allison said. "We're dealing with worldwide Mafia organizations." Her voice sounded grim.

"Not the best way to learn about the underbelly of the world, but we'd love to have your company," Marcy chirped. "It's so nice to have a man around the, uh, the dungeon." She rolled her eyes. "The ambiance sucks, and the food will be disgusting. You are entitled to your own room, er, cubby. You can be our game changer by bringing us some wine and pizza."

"And a tool kit with electric saws, chisels, and hammers," Allison added.

"We owe you an explanation," Celia said.

He stared wide-eyed as she related what happened. Then she waited for him to leave.

Stanton bent his knees as though about to run a race.

"Sorry, I should have stopped you from coming here. It was selfishness on my part."

"I didn't expect a room full of flowers, but this is more like a punch to the gut."

Celia expected this, but her heart sank. "Thanks anyway, Stanton."

Marcy leaned over toward Stanton. "Can you get us supplies from the outside before you go?"

Celia gave Marcy an evil eye. "Stop that."

"Who said I'm going to go?"

Allison said, "We'd never blame you."

"Just give me a list," he said. "I might not be as crazy as you two, but I'm in. My digs are excellent. Next to Celia's room."

Celia wanted to jump into his arms and kiss him. She resisted with every fiber in her being. *He can't be serious.* She reached into her pocket and pulled out a list she'd already made. "I won't be shy," she said. "We're in a bad way. We'll also need a radio or a small TV."

"You can get some money from the ATM. I'll give you my password," Allison said.

"No, if they have bank connections and suspect you in any way, they'll know you tapped in. I'll do it to my account to help pay my, er, um, rent. I'll bring a splitter so several computers can be used at the same time." He ran his hand through a tangle of white hair. "I can splice into electrical wires down here."

"He's not just a pretty face," Marcy said. "His forensic accounting work led him to electronic hacking."

He gave a wobbly grin. "A hacker only when necessary. As a forensic computer person, I worked on court cases mostly. I can do things around your new fabulous quarters. Too bad we don't have a garden."

Celia recalled his tales of gardening and sunshine. She thought his voice was a bit hesitant and he might bolt at any moment. If only she could run out the exit and inhale the air even if it was filled with stagnant sewer smells. Maybe a little marijuana wouldn't be a bad idea. "Are you sure you want to stay, Stanton?"

"We need lots of candles, wine, and a few hot meals, and this place will be paradise," Stanton said. He slid two rickety metal chairs over to Marcy and Celia.

"Like paradise in a horror movie," Marcy said.

Celia teetered at the edge of the seat. This past year, painting had been the only activity that lifted her spirits. It had obscured how much she loved Stanton. *Is he the silver lining in all of this?* Though he looked solid and proper on the outside, inside his soft, sweet charm set her skin tingling.

"Celia," Stanton said, hesitantly, "I get why you won't call the authorities. Don't you think you should reconsider?"

"Police want proof. Women won't talk. Even if we could get these Mafia thugs arrested, they'd be out on bail and we'd be really vulnerable. You'd be exposed as Allison's fiancé might be. They can wipe out witnesses and get away with it."

Allison let out a small yelp. "Don't forget my baby. I'm pregnant."

Stanton's face lit up. "Congratulations!" He paused. "But it does put another light on this predicament." He then turned back to Celia. "Any plans?"

"Right now, we're sitting ducks. No one hears of old broads being kidnapped by the sex slave trade." Celia heard a soft groan from Marcy. Celia gave her a warning look. "The only way to have a normal life is if we get irrefutable proof so they don't get out on bail and are in prison for life.

"The money made globally for sex trafficking is multi-billions—close to the drug trade. Not that long ago, sex slaves in this country were virtually ignored by authorities, and the public is all but unaware of it. Most people think it happens only in foreign countries and that belief has served as cover for these guys," Celia finished.

"People, there's work to be done," Stanton said, standing up. Then he wobbled slightly. Celia instantly put the chair under him. He sat. "I feel like I have the worst hangover. Last minute flight out of Florida and all this news. At least, the best news is Allie's baby."

Marcy came up to Stanton and took his hand. "As I said, I'm to blame for this awful mess, not Celia."

"Then we'll sacrifice you to the gang." Everyone laughed except Marcy.

"That's going too far." Marcy stepped away from Stanton and arched her back.

"Just joking. Let me ramble a bit. In my work I found that criminals have a high recidivism rate after being in prison. These guys have probably been caught once or twice. So, the authorities know that and keep their eyes on them. If we get them convicted and with a previous record, for sure a new sentence will be long," Stanton said. He grinned lopsided. "We need a plan."

"Let's just make this dump shine," Allie said. "I don't want Justin too upset."

"We'll do a bang-up job." He looked around.

"I'll settle for livable," Celia said.

Celia and Marcy stood in the darkened hospital kitchen with only the nearly full moon pouring in blue-tinged light. They wore scrubs, their hair was under surgical caps, and they wore surgical masks over their faces—just in case cameras were on. The cafeteria was closed and they didn't know how long Stanton might be on errands to buy needed supplies.

Huge stock pots and oversized frying pans hung on racks overhead. A portion of the meals were provided by food services, but much of it was cooked right here. The mammoth pantry with non-perishables was locked. The kitchen served three meals a day to hundreds of patients, numerous residents, interns, and staff. Stacks of white dishes lined the shelves. Celia found the walk-in refrigerator behind the fifteen-foot-long preparation table. She opened the door, and the lights came on. It was stocked with stacks of trays containing grayish meatloaf, lumps of potatoes, and wrinkled peas. The trays stood next to bags of ice.

"Grab some trays. We've got a gourmet meal for tonight," Celia said. "I'll go for bottles of water."

"No wonder they didn't lock the refrigerator," Marcy said. "No one would steal this nasty-looking stuff." Marcy filled a plastic bucket with ice. "Put leftovers to eat something from the Stone Age."

Celia took a few dishes, glasses, dish towels, and cutlery on top of the cart. Filching stuff gave the sensation of doing it for the greater good of saving lives. They placed as many trays as would fit. Everything got covered with a huge tablecloth and placed on the ice buckets.

They tiptoed out of the kitchen and headed to the back elevator. When they reached their hideout, Allison greeted them.

"Couldn't sleep." She held several flimsy blankets and spread them out on the sandy concrete floor. "Found more light switches," she added. Overhead, a ghoulish green lighting came from half a dozen bare bulbs.

Although Marcy put on a bright smile, the corners of her mouth quivered. She set the trays on the blanket and removed a handful of candles from her pocket.

"Where did they come from?" Celia asked.

"While you were grabbing up stuff, I went through some drawers. Kind of plain, stubby, but candles nonetheless. And matches." She lit a match, heated the bottom of several candles and pressed them to the concrete floor.

"Dinner by candlelight," Allison said through pursed lips.

"We need those candles to get some heat into this damp dump." Marcy shivered and leaned over the flames.

Celia felt a chill in the dank air as she sipped a bottle of water. Marcy grasped Celia's free hand.

"I'm missing your fabulous Italian meals," Marcy said. She turned to Allison. "Even her scrambled eggs sound pretty good now." Marcy's giggle didn't match the worried look in her eyes.

Then they sat cross-legged in a circle. Celia removed tinny forks and spoons from the cart and they began eating.

"This is delicious," Marcy said, making a face. Then she dropped her fork, stared at the plate and started sobbing.

"It's all right," Celia whispered. "We're in a big mess, but we'll beat this together." Celia inhaled the dusty air, trying to convince herself as well.

"We're gonna die like dogs in this pit." Marcy's body shook.

Marcy doubled over in a heap. Celia helped her up to her cubby where she settled herself on a lumpy mattress and covered herself with a sheet and thin blanket.

"Go to sleep, too," Celia said, returning to Allison. "Marcy and I will get this place looking half-decent tomorrow. Stanton got tooth-paste, toothbrushes, and all the other stuff. He'll bring good food to-morrow."

Allison grinned and pursed her lips. "You always wanted a house-husband."

The word husband brought Celia up short. "You're referring to your father who made a mockery of our marriage?"

Allison stood and backed away. "He was still my father, and he was good to me. I want to honor his memory and not degrade it like you." Allison's voice rose.

Celia remained silent. *This topic is our nemesis. Right back to square one.*

"And where are our new lives?" Allison gestured to the cold, masonry-walled space around them. "And bring my baby into this world? You can't blame me for being angry. I finally had everything going right, and you have destroyed it all." Now Allison was sobbing.

Celia held her hands. "I'll get us out of this come hell or high water."

"Even if we move out. There can be much worse waiting for us." Allison stomped off and threw herself on the bed in her compartment. The bed springs squeaked, but held.

Celia stood there for a long time. Then she stumbled into her cubby and flopped into bed, thinking of Stanton. She had a moment of guilt at getting the largest cubby. Everyone insisted. Why in the world had she not appreciated the man more? He had the kind of loyalty and caring you don't find very often.

Chapter 16

Awakening early in the morning, Celia thought again of Stanton, longing to be in his arms.

Do I deserve his love in the midst of all of this? Okay, okay, collect your wits about you. Get up and get busy. No sense clouding your brain with romantic notions. Wouldn't be the first time I deceived myself by allowing love to cover up a desperate situation. No more self-delusion.

She went to the little bathroom at the back. Splashing her face with water, Celia tasted metal. Rust, she thought.

When she walked back to the main area, there was Stanton, piling rough blankets on the floor. "Later I'll nail them up to give everyone a little privacy in their bedrooms, you'll excuse the description." He smiled. "Oh, and by the way, good morning," he said in a soft voice. "They're still sleeping."

She almost jumped for joy when she spied the mini refrigerator, microwave, and double hot plate. "Never thought I'd be so excited to see those appliances."

He held a blanket up to see if the width was right for the entrance to the cubby. "Got a refrigerator from a junk pile along with other stuff. Even these curtain hangers. Got all kinds of dumped equipment out there."

"Magnifique," she replied. "What comfort you bring, Santa."

She made her way to her cubby and dressed in her scrub suit. When she walked into the common area, Stanton had his back to her and seemed oblivious. Bending over, he fetched eggs out of the little refrigerator. She watched the way his body moved, the way the material of his shirt stretched over his wide back, straining against the outline of muscle and the curve of small love handles that she knew so well. The pan sizzled with hot butter as he cracked the eggs into it.

She saw a coffee pot on the floor. "How the hell did you get so much in here?"

"I piled it up in cardboard boxes, bought a small hand truck, and acted like I was delivering stuff for the hospital." He brushed his jeans. "No one stopped me." He jammed his fists into his pockets. "Even bought the kitchen items. You've got loads of outlets to plug into."

With his clean, soft hands he didn't look like the usual delivery man. His jeans had an ironed crease and his shock of gray hair was noticeably well-trimmed. Whatever worked.

"I also got a supply of toiletries—you know, soap, paper products, and aspirin, and all the stuff you'll need."

She didn't want to wake the others so they sat down at an empty cable wheel Stanton found behind some cabinets. They could use it as a table. Celia felt a tinge of comfort and dug into the fluffy eggs, the best dish she'd ever eaten.

"Real salt and pepper," she said. "Wow. You are a wizard, but an insane one. Why do this?" She put her fork down. "I wasn't so great to you for a while."

Celia felt his eyes searing through her. "I'm sorry I pushed you this past year. Deb and Allie moved away and Marcy became your rock. You were in shock and grieving and needed time. Of course, I felt left out and miserable. I acted like a baby. Now all that is compressed into a thin line I can step over. I love you. Don't you know that?"

"I love you, too, Stanton. But I'm a bad griever. I'm sorry."

"I came this close to walking away," he said, illustrating an inch of space between thumb and index finger. "I know I'm not patient. Didn't know if we'd get our relationship back on track. Once we found each other, I didn't want to lose you again." He looked around. "I don't care where we live. You are my home."

Celia sat back on the wobbly chair and almost tipped over. She caught herself. Her breath quickened, overwhelmed. "I was wary of you when we met in Florida after so many years had passed since we were lovers in college. When you moved to California and ghosted me I didn't trust you after that."

"Haven't I made up for it? I've got scars on my knees from begging your forgiveness."

Celia grinned. "As it should be."

A noise behind Celia made her jump up. Allison stood outside her cubby in flannel pajamas, rubbing her eyes. "Hi, Stanton. Do I smell eggs?"

Stanton made more eggs. "I'm the executive chef at this resort."

"Going to the bathroom." Allison's bedroom slippers tapped lightly as she walked away.

"I feel useful, but, Celia, um, Celia…?"

"What is it? Speak up. You're rambling."

"Can I sleep with you tonight? No fooling around. Just hugging." He flipped the eggs. "I miss your touch and the vanilla scent of you. And you do have the biggest cubby."

"Do you like the scent of sweat? No real showers for a while." Celia's heartbeat accelerated.

He turned to her and gave her the look of longing that she hadn't seen in a long time. "Your sweat is intoxicating." He tapped a spoon against the edge of the pan.

For a long time, they stared at each other until Stanton turned off the burner and walked toward her, arms open. She had no trouble folding into his warm body. He stepped back and cupped her chin. "Is that a yes?"

No, no, no. "Yes," she said. The thought of sleeping next to him made her giddy. *Where did my resolve go? I promised myself to use all my energy to fight this mess. I guess I have some reserve for Stanton.*

Chapter 17

That evening Stanton returned with more supplies. "The gate at the ramp was locked," he said, "but the side door was still open."

"I taped the lock so it would remain open," Allison said. "In large hospitals like ours, a single door can be overlooked. Whatever you have in that box smells like heaven."

"I ordered steak frites from Parc restaurant," he said. "You ladies deserve the best." He pulled a bottle of Grey Goose from the bottom of the box along with a small bag of ice.

"The vodka bests the steaks," Marcy cried, helping Stanton put the box of food on the cable spool. Celia liked the idea of using it as a table. As a child, she'd had one in her backyard and used it for pretend teatime. Hearing birds chirp and watching sunsets had quieted her forever-squabbling parents—at least for those few minutes.

Celia set places with flatware she'd snitched from the hospital kitchen. Stanton pulled plastic juice glasses out of his pockets, dropped ice into each glass and poured a generous amount of vodka over the cubes. Celia poured orange juice for Allison. Stanton slipped the steaks from their boxes, reheated them along with the frites, and set a porterhouse on Allison's plate. "You first, my dear. You're eating for two."

"By the way," Allison said, "I told Justin everything. He doesn't know what to make of it. I told him that I'm scared and he advised me that I can ask for maternity leave for my suddenly precarious pregnancy. I'm thinking about it only because I don't want to be here all day. He understands why you're afraid for me, and said I should live with him. But I know too much now, and I don't want to put him in danger, too. Because I have a different last name from yours, Mom, I think I can pull it off."

"Oh, Allison," Marcy said before surrendering herself to the decadent, perfectly rare steak, "he sure sounds like a keeper."

After dinner Stanton brought a pan of water from the bathroom. They washed the dishes and dried them with towels.

Allison folded her hands together. "Good news. I can take one of you to shower later tonight. I found an empty room. Only one a night. Wear the hospital gowns I gave you. Don't think they'll notice what looks like a patient being led by an employee."

"I'll save my shower for tomorrow night," Marcy said, yawning.

Stanton stood and smiled at Celia. "See you later," he whispered.

The simple beauty of warm water nearly sent Celia into a swoon. *What a luxurious gift. Something I always took for granted. I wonder where Nikki and the women are tonight? I wonder if they have the luxury of warmth, hot water, and good food? I hope.* Guilt closed her throat.

When she finished showering, she found Allie in the hallway talking to a security guard. Her knees went weak. But Allie was lifting her tag and smiling.

The guard frowned. "Pretty late to be walking a patient around."

Allie glanced at her. A warning to play along. "She wandered off and I'm bringing her back to the eighth floor."

"Oh, the looney ward," the guard smirked.

Celia put her head down and pretended to shuffle.

Allison frowned. "We don't call it that, sir." He dipped his head and gestured for them to pass.

They entered the elevator. When they reached the sub-basement, Celia stepped off, but Allison stayed on. "Just popping in to see Justin. Be back soon."

Celia fell into a dreamless sleep but fear, crawled into her bones. She heard a creaking noise and sat straight up. Stanton stood over her. "What? It's 5 a.m." She had been dreaming about being trapped in a fire, and her heart was still hammering against her ribcage.

He eased into the narrow bed beside her and rubbed her back. She sighed into the warmth of his body. Stanton gently kissed the back of her neck.

"You smell of springtime," he whispered. "Move over a tad."

"Not much wiggle room." A trickle of light drifted over the top of the blanket Stanton had nailed up. A cloud of comfort washed over her as he kissed her cheek, her upper arms. Soon he ran his finger over her shoulder. She wished she could crawl inside of him, merge with the flow of blood through his veins, see the structure of his bones, the pumping of his heart. Discovering in him all those unknown thoughts, buried secrets, would bring her to a safe place.

He pressed against her. "These hospital gowns are handy things, aren't they?" he whispered as he untied the strings and gently lowered them over her shoulders. He drew in his breath. "My beautiful Celia," he said, kissing her shoulders, hands, her lips.

She kissed him back, seeking what had eluded her for some time—a connection so deep that even a long separation did not erase the feel of his body against hers. Something stopped her. "Maybe this is not the right time. I'm afraid. My body is not ready."

"You've gotten a little bonier. Still, looking at your body is like worshiping before the altar at a temple."

She turned to him, nestling into his warmth. "Do I have to give a sermon? I'm bad at that." When he cradled her in his arms, the hollow in her chest ballooned with joy.

She traced a scab beside his lip.

"I had a duel with a swordsman about who gets you."

Celia stifled a laugh. Even muffled, the laugh opened floodgates of warm waves through her body.

"I cut myself while shaving," he whispered. "When Allie told me what was going on. I freaked out."

She kissed him and felt the urgency in his lips.

She imagined they were on a warm, secluded, moonlit beach, the sand giving a gentle scrub to her back.

"I love you," he said. "You make me feel like a teenager with raging hormones."

"How can we feel this at our age? I thought desire went poof."

"It's a myth," he pressed against her. "I am your loyal seducer. Haven't you heard? Sixty is the new forty. I only wish my back knew that. You do know that orgasms are healthy for you."

"Funny," she said. "We breathe rapidly when making love but also when we're afraid. What do you make of that?"

He put his finger to her lips. "Maybe such ecstasy makes us afraid we'll die in a blaze of glory. Living without ecstasy makes us afraid we'll die never having tasted such splendor."

He looked her straight in the eye. "Do you still feel as though you don't want to make love? Think about this. We don't want to run from a previous life altogether. Otherwise, we surrender and fall into their trap. We'll be fearful without a break. Fear saps our strength and our mind."

"I have trouble holding on to that." She leaned over and kissed him hard on the lips.

"I don't have protection," he said, grinning.

She laughed. "Having a baby at my age would get me into the New England Journal of Medicine."

"Ahh, but me man." He quietly smacked his chest. "Me can make babies."

"Sure, Superman. You can be up all night when it cries, and you can have fun changing poopy diapers."

"Don't you just walk a baby to the nearest fire hydrant? I can pick up the poop with a plastic bag."

"Right. Just don't tell Allie how you intend to babysit." She bit her lip. *Don't say it, Celia. Don't ruin this moment by saying we might not be there to enjoy babysitting.*

"Man, I'd love to babysit you." He leaned over and ran his tongue over her bottom lip. The feel of his breath mingling with hers sent waves of electricity through her.

He rolled off the bed and onto his knees. Leaning over, he ran kisses from her toes to her inner thigh. Her hands sifted through his hair.

Heat suffused her as pleasurable currents coursed below her belly. He pressed his mouth between her legs and remained there until she slipped to the edge, and then she urged him upward. Her hips swayed as though moving to distant strains of music.

He entered her and soon they moved in a synchronized rhythm, slowly at first then quicker as he pressed inside. Together, they tumbled into a delicious void. When her body shifted into a sweet stupor, she drifted off to sleep.

Stanton awoke shortly and shook Celia. "I'm thinking," he said, inhaling shakily. "We have to get the police involved."

I knew the delightful infusion of a past world wouldn't last long. "The case has to be airtight so that no one gets out on bail and comes after us. I'm sure they can get to us even if we're in the witness protection program. They've got gangs all over the world. Lots of people in their pockets."

"This will go down in history as the most bizarre romance," he said.

She grew quiet for a moment. "You've seen what they're capable of doing. They sell a child for sex and kill the sick women if they can no longer produce."

He tightened his arms around her. "My bad for ruining our deal. Let's make the most of our time together. I'm forever beside you. You know that, don't you?"

She did know that. It amazed her that a man born and raised by emotionally distant parents had so much empathy. It hadn't come easy to him. She recalled how she'd chided him for thoughtless acts. *He is a man who has changed. I hope I can trust that.* She rested her head on his chest, grateful they'd met again in Florida—widow and widower.

"If we beat our crazy upbringings, we can beat this," he whispered. "My iceberg parents, partying it up every night, then my unsatisfying marriage, and you with a husband who ignored you for years and did you dirt."

Stanton sat up and folded his arms around his knees and half-smiled. "I thought I'd inherited the emotions of a wooden board." Stanton brushed her hair back with his finger. "Meeting you again, I fell in love for real. For the first time in my life, I'm not afraid to show my passion. I walked through my marriage in a fog most of the time, no fault of my wife."

He ran his hand over her hip. "I'm alive with you," he said, his eyes turning inward, as though reading his own thoughts aloud.

She kissed his cheek. "Know that I can't give you one hundred percent of myself, despite what you deserve. I've got to protect Allie and the baby."

"I get it, but let's improve our pillow talk," he said, holding her close. "Just hug me."

After ten minutes of complete silence he said, "I'd better get dressed and make us breakfast."

Later I'll tell you, no more lovemaking until we get some measure of justice for the women. Our moments of stolen, intoxicating intimacy are not fair to Allie and Justin who are innocent. There's Marcy who yearns for love. How can I be so self-indulgent?

Celia threw on a bathrobe and noticed that the industrial-sized containers of disinfectant that had been outside their hideaway had been stacked against the wall. Stanton must have prepared for a good clean-up. She washed her face and brushed her teeth. When she smelled bacon, she realized just how hungry she was.

As Stanton stood over the frying pan, she hugged him from behind. "Please be careful when you leave here, honey. Anyone could have passed by when you went for those cleaning products. It wasn't far from the elevator."

"No worries. I didn't see a soul."

After breakfast, Stanton left to meet a client in Center City Philadelphia. An idea struck Celia.

Chapter 18

After breakfast, Marcy and Allison got to work scrubbing. It was Wednesday and Celia knew the stores were open late in Center City. Stanton had bought her and Marcy jeans, T-shirts, and red and white Philadelphia Phillies baseball caps. Now, she got dressed and pulled the baseball cap low over her forehead, tucking her hair into it.

Before heading to the first floor, she hung the fake tag Allison made her from her neck. Allison had taken photos to attach to the ID cards she'd swiped. They looked perfectly authentic and gave her a boost of confidence.

She walked past the nurses' stations to reach the front door. The hospital was busy as usual and no one paid the least bit of attention to her. Stanton had given her cash and her first purchase was a shopping cart at Target on Chestnut. In a CVS, she bought dried fruit, beef jerky, granola bars, nuts, prenatal vitamins, and milk. Next, she went into the Ross Department Store and bought sweaters and light jackets for herself and Marcy.

On her way back to the hospital, she noticed a man striding across the street wearing a black suit and black tieless shirt. Three burly men in tracksuits followed behind him, casting penetrating looks in all directions. Their biceps stretched the material. Celia squinted at the man in the suit as her heart revved up.

Could it be Vladimir? This close to the hospital?

She turned toward a shop window, pretending to scan the dresses on the mannequins, but instead watched the men's reflection in the window. *It is Vladimir.* At the next corner she made a quick turn and picked up her pace, pulling the cart behind her.

They're looking for us and if we're not careful, they'll find us.

When she reached the hospital, she went to the side of the building and climbed the five steps to the access door. The tape Allie had applied did the trick. Celia took a deep breath, maneuvered the cart through the door, and slipped inside.

The boxlike entryway led to a dark hallway. Once inside, she bent over to catch her breath. Her heart raced.

Without a word, Celia went into her cubby. Stanton, Marcy, and Allison busily scrubbed the walls and floor. She needed to collect herself. Still shaking, she thought of her late husband Gabe, how he had told her she had no talent or smarts, how he had mentally beat her down to a pulp. She bought into his brainwashing, like the vulnerable women who were beaten down by their pimps. She stayed out of fear of the world and with the silly notion that there was something wrong with her and that she could change to please him. Wrong! Then she found best friends in Florida—and, *thank karma,* Stanton. With their support, she had thrived and learned how to face what life threw at her. Until now.

She missed painting, missed the soothing effect it had on her. Her comfort had been in knowing Allie had found a contented new life. *Until I messed that up.*

Marcy stepped in front of her, holding a rag and broom.

"Out there. Been scrubbing the bathroom. Didn't hear you come in. Where you been?"

Celia pointed to the cart. "Listen," she said, grabbing Marcy's arm. "While I was running errands, I saw the guy who drugged us at the bar. It's Vladimir. The scum of the earth is close by and probably looking for us."

Marcy's eyes widened. "What the hell… Did he see you?"

"No, but he's strutting around outside like he owns this territory. Maybe he has a bead on us. I'm scared out of my mind."

Chapter 19

Wearing her identity card, Celia went upstairs. She noticed a woman in housekeeping gear wheeling a cart of linens, surgical masks, and scrubs into a closet. *That's exactly what I need.* Celia waited and pretended to read the fliers on a bulletin board. The woman began stacking the shelves. When she finished, Celia waited until she closed the door behind her and walked down the hall, turning the corner.

Stepping into the closet, Celia filled the cart with linens, pillows, and towels. *I'll need to bring this cart back immediately. I'm sure they keep inventory, but I've got to take the risk.*

A hamper in the corner was piled high with dirty linens and caught her eye. "V & S LTD/LINENS" was printed in large letters on the front. She gripped the edge of the cart. V & S Industries was the name of Vladimir's shipping company. They were all connected.

Stop it Celia. You're seeing conspiracy stories everywhere. But I did see him.

She pushed the cart down the hall, holding her head high, smiling to a passerby now and then. Tasting bile in the back of her throat, she thought about the children, boys and girls alike.

If I could only find out when and where the shipping containers arrive.

Down the hall, Celia saw a man in a sleek, charcoal black tailored suit, leaving an office in front of her. *I have to stop thinking every man in a European cut suit is the creep who kidnapped us.* But he sure looks like Vladimir.

He waved to an attractive, dark-haired woman and sidled up to her. Cradling her elbow, he leaned over, whispering in her ear. The woman smiled. *Is it just my imagination? Or is that woman blushing?* He turned and she saw his face. Her heart nearly burst. It was Vladimir.

She grasped the cart's handles as tight as she could. Blood pounded in her ears. *I can't think straight.*

Back in their quarters, she unloaded the cart with trembling hands. Allison was loading food into the small refrigerator: sandwiches, potato salad, fresh fruit, and salads.

"Hi, Mom. Just got some catered leftovers from a meeting. I waited for someone to bring out the cart. I told her I needed anything they hadn't used for another conference."

"She didn't think it was odd?"

"Hell, no. This hospital has six hundred and fifty beds and there are four buildings. No one knows one from the other." She scrutinized Celia's face. "You look like you saw a ghost."

"I saw the guy who drugged our drinks and shipped us off to Pittsburgh. He acted like he belonged here." Celia paused. "Maybe I'm cracking up, but…"

"Mom, you're coming undone. What the hell would he be doing here? We take care of sick people. Why would a criminal be here?" Allison sighed.

"My question exactly." *Can Allie's fiancé help in some way? Would he know this Vladimir? Why hasn't Justin come down to meet us?*

Celia set the table. Even though they'd cleaned, scrubbed, and sprayed the place, it still smelled like musty socks. *I hope there are no floods when it rains.*

"Leftover hospital food is our feast," Marcy said, eyeing the spread and stepping out of her cubby. Celia had tried to make the hospital food look appetizing. Marcy wore a yellow peasant blouse and red capris Celia had bought her from the sale rack at Target, knowing her style.

Marcy did a quick cha-cha step and bowed.

"Not exactly a feast. The bologna is like eating plastic," Allison said.

Celia's mouth felt stuffed with cotton. She didn't know what to think.

Chapter 20

Celia's confusion about whether she had seen Vladimir or not plagued her. She would return the cart and check it out for sure. She dressed in plain clothes and put the Phillies cap back on.

As she pushed the empty cart along the fifth floor, she veered into the administration wing, the doors marked with names of the administrators on gold plaques.

Through one of the open doors, she glimpsed the man and the young woman she had seen earlier. He leaned toward her as she looked at him with total adoration. With head down Celia hurried past the office and saw a nameplate on the door: "VLADIMIR STOMPOVICH."

Go back now. Don't look right or left. Straight ahead. No doubt about it.

She left the cart at the housekeeping door. *Just what am I doing?*

She returned to find Marcy scrubbing a wall with a long-handled brush. She set it down and walked over to Celia. "Are you sick?" Marcy frowned and put her hand on Celia's forehead.

"I'm sickened."

"What's going on?" Allison asked, stepping over the threshold.

"Bad news," Celia said. "I'm right. It's Vladimir Stompovich. He's here, right here at Rudrow. I saw him up close, cozying up to a beautiful young woman. His name is on the door."

Allison pressed her hand to her cheek. "Where exactly did you see him? We have business sections on different floors."

"I stopped on the floor where I got the cart. I know I wasn't supposed to go there but…"

"Your hand hit the wrong elevator button," Allie said, fury in her voice.

"He acted like he belonged here, like he owned the place. So damn confident. I hate to say it, but he *is* handsome. He and the woman looked like a celebrity couple." Celia put her arm over her eyes, trying to dispel the image.

"Was the woman tall, slender—dark, long hair?" Allison asked.

"Yes."

"If that's the right one, her name is Svetlana. She's from Russia, but speaks English very well."

The name sent a shock through Celia. *Svetlana.* Zutka's daughter?

"Vladimir Stompovich, I don't know him personally, but he's chairman of the hospital board and a big donor. I've done some work with Svetlana in the year I've been here. Justin would know," Allison said, her voice a shaky monotone. She called Justin on her cell and walked away.

When she hung up and came back, her face had gone white. "He's a businessman in international shipping. The two are an item." Allison rubbed her forehead. "They can't be criminals, can they?"

Celia stiffened. "What do you know about her?"

"She checks my budget. She's assistant to the comptroller. But this guy, they gave Vladimir an office because of his generosity." Allison took a deep breath. "He donates a large amount of money to the hospital."

Celia knew the double-dealing of many boards. *If you scratch my back, I'll scratch yours.* Obviously, Vladimir had the linens business, which was part of his larger operation. For sure his linen business brought in much more than his donations. The shipping containers must be part of the insidious-sounding LTD.

"Does your board of directors walk the line between honesty and duplicity?" Celia asked.

"Well, from what Justin said it's not all on the up-and-up. Board members get perks; trips to resorts, credit cards, contracts between board members and the hospital. Vladimir supplies linen services, another is a lawyer for the hospital and so on for every member. In return the board gives approval to execs for everything they ask for." She took a deep breath. "Vladimir Stompovich donates big—probably more than a million a year."

"That's chump change for a guy like Vladimir," Celia said.

Allie nodded. "Other than that, I don't know."

Something struck Celia. She hoped she still had the picture Zutka had given them of her kidnapped daughter. Why wouldn't Svetlana contact her mother if she had a good job in the US? *Svetlana didn't appear to be a victim.*

She dug through her bag for Zutka's picture. After a while, she found it. Definitely Svetlana, only a bit younger looking.

"Ladies!" she heard Stanton call. "I brought dinner."

Relief flooded Celia. "Where have you been? I've been worried."

"You knew where I was. What's going on?"

Celia shared the story, words tripping over each other. Sweat broke over her forehead.

Stanton set the bags down. "What the hell?"

Celia, Stanton, and Marcy sat around the table, lost in thought. They waited for Allison who had gone to see Justin. Questions needed answers about Svetlana and Vladimir. Justin had given little information. He did have work stress. Because of his MBA received before going to medical school, he took on a part-time job as purchasing agent. The administration pleaded for him to take the job. Promises to quickly find a replacement hadn't materialized.

Celia trembled at the thought; *the man who wants to kill us has an office upstairs. But then, hiding in plain sight had worked so far.*

"I'm here for as long as it takes," Stanton said. "I'm here to help."

Marcy said, "I feel so bad for Zutka. Why would Svetlana make her own mother sick with worry?" She tapped Stanton on the shoulder. "What did you find out?"

"We can tell the police to go to the docks and stake out when the next containers come in," said Stanton. "He could send some containers with TVs and some with women. My understanding is that Customs and Border Patrol can open anything, anytime with incoming shipments. Also, they x-ray many containers but not all. Don't know the formula for why they pick some. There could be a bribe to keep them from x-raying Stompovich's containers. To get a subpoena as you already know, we'll need serious probable cause."

"We need to get information when the containers come in." Celia said. "What can we say? 'Hey a container full of women is coming in,' unless we knew it for sure and what time it would arrive." Celia paused. "Can they reroute a ship if they know police are waiting?"

He half smiled. "I wouldn't put anything past them. I'm sure they have it down to a science. In my experience in dealing with crime, almost anyone can be bribed if it's enough money."

Marcy seemed to awaken from a concentrated daze. "Looks like Zutka's daughter is part of this crime ring."

Stanton refilled their glasses. Celia pulled the picture Zutka had given her from a folder on the table. With a trembling hand, she said, "It's her for sure, the one I saw talking to Vladimir."

"She was taken at age sixteen three years ago. Her poor mother is worried sick," Marcy said. "Zutka helped us escape, hoping we'd find Svetlana. And here Svetlana is, strutting about with her killer boyfriend."

"Maybe it was the only way she knew to save herself," Stanton said.

Allison burst through the door. "I got it." She waved papers in the air.

"Thank goodness you're here," Celia said, raising her voice. "What do you have?"

"Justin gave me a list of the board of directors. But he still wants me to move into his place. I convinced him he'd be a target, too, if I did."

"Let's see if it adds up." Celia and Stanton looked at the list. After each name, Justin noted what connection they had with Rudrow: hospital accountant, hospital lawyer, building contractor for additions, hospital insurance agent, catered deliveries, and ambulance company. "All these members are making money from this place."

"The board usually agrees with the administration because they have a huge investment with Rudrow," Stanton said. "It's business as usual."

"If he's importing sex slaves, he's bound to be involved in other criminal activities. He'll need to be laundering cash not reported to the IRS," Celia said.

Stanton tipped her chair forward. "Huge amounts of untaxed money are hard to hide. He probably uses the linen business and others just for that reason."

"We have to be sure," Allison said.

"That guy is so good-looking he's almost a cliché. At the bar, he looked like an elegant gangster," Marcy said. "But a hot, elegant gangster."

Allison shook her head. "This is ridiculous. Just a short while ago, I lived in a fairy tale. All was right with my job. My Prince Charming was taking me away to paradise. What the hell happened?" Allison looked directly at her mother.

Chapter 21

"We need to get down to the docks to find out which containers hold the women and when they arrive," Celia said as Marcy, Allison, and Stanton leaned toward her soft but commanding voice. "Then we get those bastards dead to rights." Celia looked at each one. "Anyone have anything to add?"

"With Sherlock Celia and me on the case, we'll find a way," Marcy's voice boomed. She was wearing her blue scrub suit. "Fashion trend for, ahem, mature women." She giggled. "Maybe I'll find a doc in this joint who'll whisk me away to his McMansion. I don't mind a cookie cutter mansion. Hell, no."

"Be more concerned to see justice done and to get out of here," Allison said, irritation in her voice.

"Allie is right on. Been doing homework and it gave me an idea," Celia said.

"See? She's got that brain zooming," Marcy said.

"Let's hear it," Stanton said.

"There are at least five thousand doctors in the US who have fake credentials. We know any kind of documentation or credentials can be bought for the right price. Law, medicine, tech degrees, PhDs—you name it they make it. Just have to find the print shops."

"The hospital uses a legit printing company. You need one that is underground." Allison said.

Celia eyed Stanton with a raised eyebrow.

"What do you intend to do?" Stanton asked. "A little iffy if you ask me."

"I'm working it out. I'll need documents that say I'm from the Centers for Disease Control and Prevention."

"The CDC? Why?" Allison asked.

Stanton smiled. "I think I get it. The fake docs are your ticket to hanging out on the docks."

"Good thinking, Stanton. I saw where the CDC reported a hepatitis outbreak among stevedores. They're trying to head off a pandemic around the ports. Workers need vaccines—and lectures on hep C and how to prevent it. I'll be the CDC person who starts the ball rolling. And, if I run into real cases, I can refer them to the hospital."

"Maybe I can get a job," Stanton said. "You can be the Philadelphia director of the CDC. I can be your assistant?"

"Damn straight." Celia poked him gently in the ribs.

"I'm in," Marcy said.

"But I'll need a driver's license and an official looking badge to match my credentials. One set for Marcy, one for me."

Stanton paced. "I'll pay for it, and check my old hunting grounds. In my world of computer forensics I've met some interesting criminals along the way. They've had connections like underground places that do just that kind of phony printing. Anything you want. MD degrees, law degrees. Driver's licenses are a dime a dozen. I hope it doesn't land me in jail." He half-smiled. "Might take a bit of time."

"That's it," Marcy said. "Stanton's our master criminal. Just what we need."

"Whatever you're getting into, you have to be on guard," Allison said. "Don't get too cocky. Vladimir knows what you look like."

Celia stood.

"Brilliant," Marcy said, grinning.

Allison seemed to sag, as though a hundred-pound weight had hit her. "My thickening body is tired all the time. I'm heading to bed." She massaged the back of her neck, and walked to her cubby. "When you find the underground sources, do we all have to deal with those shysters?"

"We work together, we're a family," said Marcy

"Hey," Celia said, "remember we're asking Stanton to get involved in criminal activity."

"Good, then we'll turn him into the police when this is over." Marcy slapped her thigh.

"You know I am a bit of a coward," said Stanton.

"Get over it if you want to hang with us," Celia said, smirking. "I kind of like being in charge," she said to no one in particular.

"Once we get out of this, don't be bossy. I'm a fifty-fifty kind of guy. You do the creativity and I do the dirty work."

Celia smiled. "When did you get so clever?"

Allison slipped a note under the utility closet door, telling the housekeeper what time to be there, and if she showed up there was some money involved for her. Celia insisted she go herself so as not to upset the housekeeper. As she rolled her cart slowly to keep the wheels from squeaking, she saw how few people roamed the hallways at 9:30 p.m. and that quiet prevailed.

When Celia located the closet, she found the door locked and no one answered her light tap. She stepped into the bathroom next door to wait. Celia trembled, wishing she could dunk her head under the cold-water faucet. She opened the door a crack and waited for ten minutes. When she started to think she'd been stood up, the housekeeper passed by. Celia stepped out and the housekeeper jumped back. Celia motioned for her to go ahead.

The woman opened the door, looking up and down the corridor. Celia stuffed a hundred- dollar bill in her hand.

"What you want? Why give me money?"

"I need room heaters and four heavy blankets. I know you have them here in the hospital storerooms." *It's already getting cold down there.*

The woman backed against the wall, shaking her head.

Celia gave the woman another hundred-dollar bill. A sharp grimace on the housekeeper's face pinched her lips. Celia put a hand on her shoulder to try to calm her.

The woman shook her head vigorously and motioned for Celia to leave. "No entiendo lo que quieres decir." She tried to give the money back.

"I think you do understand what I'm saying," Celia used her strongest voice, the one that had overtones of a growl. "I beg you. It's for a good reason. I promise." Celia felt awful. She realized that desperation had compromised her moral compass. "I hope you will trust that you're doing a good thing. Please take the money. I swear I'll never do anything to hurt you."

Celia saw that housekeeper was trembling. "I am so sorry."

"I no take money," the housekeeper said, handing it back. "But wait here. I get. Have old stuff."

"Thank you!" whispered Celia.

As Celia stepped into the elevator, a man in overalls hurried in just as the doors began to close. She stood in front of her filled, covered cart despite the fact that nothing showed.

"Hello," he said in a gravelly voice, regarding the panel of buttons with a surprised look. "You pushed the sub-basement? Nothing but storage. I gotta get cleaning stuff. Where you headed?"

Celia felt herself grow lightheaded. "I must have gotten turned around. I'm looking for the second floor."

"It's tricky because from this old building you've got to cross a bridge on the second floor to get to the new buildings. I'll take you back up and show you how to do it." He grinned.

"Thank you, but I'll be fine."

"Nope. A gentleman helps a lady."

She now had to take the long route and hope for the best.

"Gonna clean out level two once and for all and dump all storage bins in residents' lounges."

She sucked in her breath.

"What do you do?" he asked, staring at her cart.

"Er…I'm in…housekeeping. That's why I have this cart."

"A supervisor, huh?"

They arrived at the sub-basement.

The janitor turned to her. "Just make sure the doors don't close. I won't be long." He hit a button that held the doors ajar.

The man turned on several lights Celia didn't know existed. She stared into the empty space and the darkness just beyond. Suddenly, like an apparition rising out of the swirling dust motes, Stanton appeared. His face brightened when he saw her standing in the lighted elevator. He walked straight toward her. A short partition separated Stanton from the janitor. She had a view of the janitor's back and Stanton hurrying toward her. *Oh, God. Stanton stop.*

She stiffened her spine until it ached, as though using her body to push him back and began waving frantically as he scanned the shelves along the walls while he walked to her. *Does he think I'm waving like a nut because I'm happy to see him?*

In a minute, the two men would come face-to-face. She heard a loud rumbling and saw that some large cans had fallen to the concrete floor beside the janitor. The noise made Stanton stop, and she waved wildly again for him to go back. At the same time, the janitor emerged with arms laden, and Stanton backed up into the shadows.

The janitor got back into the elevator, and Celia punched the button, but her sweaty fingers slipped off. The man did it for her.

"You all right, lady? You look awful pale."

"I'm fine," she said, her voice cracking. "I can find my way now by myself as soon as you get off, I remembered I need something on the sixth floor," she said, her heart thumping against her rib cage.

Arms filled with metal cans, the man looked happy to grant her wish and stepped off on the second floor. Celia quickly pushed the button to the sub-basement.

Stanton rushed toward her. "What the hell was going on?"

Celia explained and Stanton apologized. "I almost ruined the whole thing. I was looking for more cleaning crap."

"I told you about the dangers. The light was on. You take foolish chances."

"But I'm taking a chance on you," he said, smiling sweetly.

"That's pretty dumb, don't you think?"

When Celia and Stanton entered, Marcy was just finishing hanging white hospital sheets on the freshly cleaned walls.

"My, it does look better, more like a snazzy apartment." Celia said.

"I just rebuilt this damn dungeon and you smirk. It's cozier now." Marcy's voice had a touch of annoyance. "And Stanton climbed the stepladder to help."

"Sorry. We just had a harrowing incident." Stanton gave her a quick rundown.

Celia took long, slow breaths. Her eyes swept the area. It did look better. The floor had been swept and washed as close to clean as it would ever be. Tattered blankets had been laid out on the floor to give some color.

"You've both done a great job," Celia said.

"I can see career changes for us," said Stanton. "We'll start a cleaning and security company."

"Look," Marcy said. "Allie found another refrigerator discarded near the dock. It's a little banged up but it'll do as our wine cellar. We can have a feast and Stanton brings the wine. I'm getting to like this. I'd like it more if I had a hunk to share it with. Do you think I could pretend I'm a doctor in these scrubs and meet up with a doc on Tinder?"

"Tinder is for much younger people." Celia said, feeling her heartbeat settle to nearly normal.

"Like we don't have enough trouble." Allison mumbled stepping out of her cubicle, rubbing her eyes. "You guys are making so much noise it woke me up."

They had upgraded their table to a slab of wood on top of two sawhorses. Celia set it while Stanton took sandwiches out of the fridge. He then sat down at his computer. "By the looks of the emails, no one at my community has noticed I'm gone."

"Maybe your grumpy ex-girlfriend, Edith, misses you." *It still rubs me raw that Edith created serious trouble for me and friends and Stanton remained a friend of hers.*

Stanton huffed. "She was never my girlfriend, just an acquaintance."

"Harrumph." Celia gave him her playful evil eye.

Marcy leaned over the table, inhaling the briny scents of corned beef and pastrami.

"From the Famous Deli, at 4th and Bainbridge," said Stanton, looking grateful for the change of subject. "Just for you, Marcy"

"I might decide to stay in Philadelphia," Celia said. "I can't wait to be a grandmother."

"Can the baby call me Aunt Marcy? My grandchild calls me Cee-Cee."

Stanton shifted, looking uncomfortable. "Hey, talking about kids, I've been thinking."

"Isn't that dangerous?" Marcy asked.

Celia half-grinned.

"Let me finish," Stanton added, standing up. "I'm thinking about volunteering to entertain as a mime on the pediatric cancer floor. I did it for years at Boca Raton Hospital and the kids loved it. I might pick up some information about the comings and goings at the hospital. And these kids need a good laugh."

"I don't think it's a good idea. You're exposing yourself," Celia said.

"Risky," said Allison. "But at this point all bets are off, anyway."

"I'll check in with the hospital volunteer office. I can get a reference from the team in Boca Raton."

"Well, isn't that a genius plan," Marcy said. "But they'll have your name on file."

"I'll take the risk. I'm not officially connected with any of you," he smiled at Celia who felt her heartbeat tick up a notch. "Well, maybe one performance."

"Vladimir and Svetlana are just down the hall from Pediatrics," Allison said. "Are you sure, Stanton?"

"Yes. The offices being that close might be an advantage." He gave Celia a penetrating glance.

Allison seems oblivious to his underlying suggestion. She'd hit the ceiling.

Chapter 22

Early the next morning, Stanton went out. Allison was on her way upstairs to see Justin. He had scheduled an ultrasound before the hospital got busy.

"You know, Mom," Allison said, a frown crossing her face, "Justin doesn't understand how you and your friend, who live in a retirement community, can attract life-threatening trouble. I don't get it myself."

"Neither do I, to tell you the truth…"

"I'm going up."

"Please be careful," Celia said. *Please, please, please.*

Celia and Allison spent two days at their computers gathering information, researching all they could about the hospital layout, the administration, its players. Marcy hung over their shoulders. Desperate for volunteers, the hospital had verified Stanton's credentials, and he was scheduled to perform this afternoon for an hour just after the children had lunch and before the afternoon lull.

Celia thought about how to use Stanton's performance to an advantage. Once she was on the pediatric floor, she could cross over to the business offices and case out the spot where she had seen Vladimir and Svetlana. She pictured the look of deepest despair on Zutka's face.

Svetlana, now about twenty, and Vladimir, maybe about fifty, made the oddest couple. She knew that abused women sometimes fell for their captors. In Svetlana's case, coming from apparent poverty, she could also imagine the life that Vladimir offered her. *She agrees with his life of criminality even if it is dangerous and against her better interests.* For all she knew, he may have told Svetlana that her mother was dead.

Celia quickly retrieved the picture of Svetlana. The likeness was so close. Just one more time to verify it.

It was time to go upstairs. She tied her hair back in a bun, the kind Marcy insisted looked like a donut plunked on her skull, put on scrubs and the fake ID on its lanyard around her neck. When she reached the oncology wing on the pediatric floor, she noticed a group of kids in the hallway accompanied by nurses. Standing on tiptoe, Celia peered deeper over the group and saw Stanton in a tuxedo-like costume, his face painted white with exaggerated lashes. He was wearing a red beret and blowing up balloons. *You look adorable. I can see how much the kids are enjoying your performance.*

Some of the kids were in wheelchairs and some stood, wearing hospital gowns. They smiled and cheered. Many had lost their hair, and their eyes drooped, but those big smiles meant everything. There were two stretchers with children on their bellies, heads propped with Styrofoam chin-holders, giggling. Others watched from their hospital beds, looking out of the glass walls of their rooms. She suspected Stanton wouldn't learn anything new regarding Stompovich, but she could see that he genuinely enjoyed bringing a bit of happiness to the kids.

A woman who looked like the photo of Svetlana stared directly at her. Stomach churning, she slipped into a room where a child barely held his head up from the pillow as he tried to watch Stanton through the glass wall.

"What's your name, sweetie?" Celia asked.

He had trouble keeping his eyes open. "Rasheed."

"Do you want me to help you see the show?"

His eyes fluttered open, and he smiled. "Yup."

She held his soft, limp, hand. He leaned his bald head against her shoulder.

"Are you my doctor?"

"No, sweetie. But you have some of the best doctors in the world." Celia gripped the remote and raised his bed so that he could see better through the glass.

"Oh, he's making a dog from that balloon." Rasheed huffed out each word. "Do you think he would make one for me?"

"I'll make sure he will."

"Yeah, for my birthday. I'm gonna be twelve in two days. Maybe I'm too old for balloons." He waited. "But I like him."

"I'll make sure he'll be here just after the clock strikes midnight on your birthday. Okay?"

Rasheed nodded his head.

She waited until Rasheed had fallen asleep. Outside his room, she looked past the crowd and saw Svetlana clapping her hands with glee.

No question it's her, all right. Damn, if she isn't coming right toward me.

She stopped and touched Celia's arm. "You like the mime? I saw you smiling. I always love the circus. My mamma always took me as kid." A nurse was beckoning Svetlana. She smiled and rejoined them.

She's wistful about her mother who is worried to death and risking her life to find her daughter. Could she have contacted Zutka? What if she doesn't want to be in touch with her mother? Maybe Svetlana thought it better that her mother believed she was dead. I'm putting Zutka's life in danger with these maniacs. Stanton emptied many offices on the floor with some doors left open. Makes it easier. Can't go in now as Svetlana seems concentrated on me.

Celia tried to plan how she would sneak into Svetlana's office. Now she watched Stanton make a pot of coffee, open a box of apple cake, and cut a slice. He had been asked to do another performance which he agreed to.

He'd changed out of the costume, but his face held traces of white pancake makeup around his temples and ears. The coffee warmed her and the sweetness of the apple cake reminded her that simple pleasures could create moments of happiness even in the worst of situations. Celia had painted the slab of wood that made their table a beautiful sea blue with figures drawn on it. With the table set off against the billowy white sheets nailed to the walls, she could almost imagine that she and Stanton were sitting in a taverna on a Greek island.

"Those kids are so damned cute." His eyes teared up. "It's incredible how brave they are." He cleared his throat. "Don't know how oncologists do it."

"There's one child, Rasheed, who can't leave his room because he's too weak. I want you to meet him. In two days, he'll be twelve."

The idea of bringing a bit of joy to Rasheed upped her mood, filled her with all the beauty life still held. One day, she hoped, Rasheed would be well. One day, they would again lead regular lives—worrying about bills, a leaky roof and taxes, all of which looked rather small now.

"I'll be happy to visit him when I do my next routine."

"How did you learn those tricks?" Marcy asked, pouring a glass of orange juice. "Did you go to mime school in California?"

"Don't need a degree to do simple tricks, but I took classes in the art of mime at college. I loved Marcel Marceau and the poetry of movement, how we can tell stories, evoke shapes and moods without using a single word. One summer, during college, I worked for an amusement park as a mime and I learned the art of turning long balloons into dogs, rabbits, and monkeys. You could see the delight on children's faces, but also their parents and grandparents too. I loved doing it when I first moved to Boca."

"We need to be careful. Svetlana loves the circus. I'm hoping she turns up. While you're holding her spellbound, I'll try to sneak into her office. Maybe I can find something."

"What the hell does a beautiful young woman see in a shlock-meister pedophile like Vladimir?" Marcy asked.

"I think it's a situation where the victim falls for her captor. Vladimir comes on like he is the only trustworthy person in the world, and the rest of the world is out to get her." Celia paused and gazed at Stanton. "Stanton, be careful. I don't know how often he's on the floor."

After a morning away, Stanton arrived with bad news. "Sorry, but I've been unable to find a good underground printer for the Centers for Disease Control documents. I have a lead but it'll take some time." He pressed his lips together. "I know you're all disappointed."

Celia felt like a fist smacked her head back. "I know you're trying, but please try harder, Stanton."

"Whoa. I'm doing the best I can."

"I know that."

"I've got a performance now, and have to go upstairs. If you want to try to do what you set out to do on the floor, it has to be now. Hospital said this is last one for a few weeks. I'm rotating with two other volunteers."

Later, Celia felt her throat tighten as she crept past the back of the crowd of delighted children and staff. Stanton was wrapping balloons into the shape of little dachshunds and had promised to pull a real rabbit out of a top hat. Svetlana was in the crowd, giggling.

Okay, here I go.

She walked nonchalantly toward Svetlana's office. The door was open a crack. Inside on Svetlana's desk sat a brass plaque next to a picture of Vladimir. The plaque said that Svetlana was "ASSISTANT TO THE COMPTROLLER." *Fast climb of the corporate ladder when you're so young and know the right people. How is the hospital administration approving of this?*

At a prominent angle near the edge of the desk sat a picture of Svetlana and Vladimir, his arm around her waist. Her beautiful face glowed, and long, black, wavy hair shone with blue highlights. Her large, wide-set eyes were pools of the deepest black that stared back at Celia.

She slid a desk drawer open and went through some papers. Nothing in there made sense with the job title: political posters, car wash ads, menus, and pens. *Looks like this job is just for show. You'd think she'd be considerate enough to make it easy to find the good stuff whatever it might be.*

It seemed pretty obvious her benefactor kept her in this job. How deep did Svetlana's involvement in the kidnappings go? Had she gone along to save herself from rape and torture? Had she fallen for her captor, or the money? *If she's the real point-person, then she's using her good looks as a smoke screen.*

More paper. Nothing but ads for cosmetics and clothing. She pulled the drawer out as far as it would go, reached into the back, and pulled out a wad of balled-up paper. It was a handwritten note… *A container ship coming in.* That was all. No destination, no arrival time, nothing.

She imagined what Zutka would say if she knew. *She'd be so happy to know Svetlana is okay that she probably would accept almost anything. And how would I tell her? Your daughter is involved with Vladimir's organization that kidnapped her? And she's been brainwashed to help them?*

She thrust her hand back in and felt a partition that she easily opened. It startled Celia, looking at a framed picture of Svetlana and Zutka from maybe a decade ago. Zutka appeared rosy-cheeked and prettily dressed. On the back cardboard she peered at what looked like a password: Svet_Vlad@2020Phil. *Probably not operational.*

Celia put everything back in place. It squeezed her heart to know that mother and daughter had been ripped apart.

Svetlana had kept it hidden. Zutka mentioned the death threat if Svetlana escaped or didn't cooperate. It was the Mafia's anthem, no matter the nationality, to intimidate. And kill they will. She found a pen on the desk and wrote down the password on the palm of her hand.

A flurry of voices in the hallway. Had Stanton ended his performance? At the door she peeked out. A group of nurses passed by. The majority of spectators remained focused on Stanton. She slipped out, rethinking her strategy.

There is something I can do. It's time.

Walking down the hall in her scrubs, she passed Svetlana chatting with a group of children. *So innocent-looking.* Does she have a heart? She slipped into Rasheed's room. As soon as he saw her, he gave a half-smile and tried to flip his hand as though sending a ball through a hoop. His arm dropped and he closed his eyes. She kissed him on the forehead.

"Can you stay?" he asked with eyes shut.

"Sure." Celia sat at the edge of the bed. She silently prayed for the child's life. "Do your parents visit?"

"My foster mom and dad come most nights after work," he said, his voice ragged. "They're taking care of my big sister. She comes. too." He sighed. "My real mom couldn't take care of us when my dad died. I really miss them." He suddenly looked so very tired. "My foster parents are nice and they're good to us."

His mouth moved. No sound came out. She clasped his face in her hands, worried he'd stopped breathing, but he opened his eyes and looked at her with love. "Can you keep visiting me?" he whispered.

"Of course. Do you like music?"

"Yeah. I try to play the guitar. Well, maybe just a little. And I like to draw."

She imagined teaching Rasheed to paint. When Rasheed got well, she'd be living in Philadelphia with Allie and Stanton and her grandchild. She could visit Rasheed and give him drawing and painting lessons.

"Do you like Mr. Mime?" Rasheed whispered.

She nodded. Very much.

"Maybe you and Mr. Mime will get married?"

Celia laughed. "We're too old."

"I have something to tell you." Rasheed's voice rasped. "This guy came…to see me… another guy with him. He said he wanted to know if I knew Mr. Mime. I said, 'No.'"

Celia sat up straight. "What did they look like?"

"One guy was big. Real big like a monster."

"What about the other guy?"

"Dark hair. Dark dude clothes. That's all I remember." Rasheed closed his eyes.

"Rasheed, don't talk to anyone about the mime or me, okay? Call the nurse right away if they come back."

"They were nice to me. The guy in the suit gave me comic books."

She didn't want to burden Rasheed with the truth. "I'll bring you comics and anything you need for drawing."

"Okay."

Her body turned ice cold at the notion they suspected Stanton.

The next morning, Allison was outside her cubicle sipping herbal tea. Stanton had left to run errands. She explained to Allison what Rasheed had told her.

"This is too close for comfort. Are you sure you can't call the police?"

"What would I say? Svetlana could say she or her cohorts just visited a very sick kid because they felt sorry for him. Asking about the mime is no big deal. I know the drill. Then we'd be outed."

Allison shook her head. "Do you think he knows Stanton is connected to you?"

"Maybe a nurse in the crowd told Vladimir that an older white woman in scrubs visited. No question he's hunting us and getting a lot closer. What bothers me is what happened to Nikki and the others. Nikki put her life in jeopardy to help us get away. I owe these women."

"Well. I just heard something awful," Allison said. "They're investigating huge deficits the hospital has been incurring. In the last three years they've purchased much more equipment and controlled substances than ever before. Sometimes doubles of the same item. An increase of about ten million over the last three years. Demand hasn't risen enough to explain it, and they haven't even located half of the orders."

"Does Justin know any of this?"

"Yes. His administrative assistant says it's Justin's responsibility to explain the deficit since he was part-time purchaser. Justin has all the receipts and records.

"When Justin found out, he demanded they bring in a forensic accountant or he'd go to the press. He said his accounting for orders was accurate.

"They are in the midst of an extensive inventory check. As I said, much of the expensive equipment and controlled substances that were ordered could not be found in the hospital." Allison cocked her head.

"So, what's happening? It's definitely an inside job," Celia said softly, sensing Justin was in the middle of something terrible.

Allison looked at Celia with a cynical smile. "If anyone can figure out what's going on, it's you."

"Honey," said Celia, "there's a scam or theft idea for almost anything that involves money whether it's big government or a non-profit charity." Celia rubbed her chin. "It points to someone in the comptroller's department as the inside person. They couldn't be so remiss. Isn't Svetlana involved there?"

"Yes, I thought in name only. I'm wrong. Justin filled me in on the big picture. Svetlana does have the position. Truth is, no one understands how much she knows about finances."

"It's not only Svetlana. To pull off such a big scam there must be more people involved. Who in the upper echelon has dealings with Vladimir?"

"The chief financial officer of the hospital, Ramon Valez, has a chummy relationship with Vladimir. There's Barry Chester, the comptroller who is Ramon's lackey. But the CFO couldn't be so crooked as to allow theft of equipment and drugs. All at the top make a fortune in salary and benefits."

"Vladimir has to be involved. How long has he been here at the hospital?"

Allison stared at Celia. "Three years? He was friendly with Ramon even before."

"The board has a fiduciary responsibility to oversee financial activity. They don't seem to be doing that." Celia frowned. *This mess is getting deeper and darker.*

"They need a mole in the accounting department and cooperation from the CFO. I wouldn't be surprised if Vladimir has customers in foreign countries who'd be happy to pay sixty cents on the dollar for medical equipment and drugs. While the crooks pay nothing for goods and maybe little cost for the shipping. Vladimir owns an import/export company."

Allison shivered. "How did you figure that out?"

"Just a little more experience in the underworld. It's not a given though."

"If you're right, and I believe you are, they have it all so tight. Justin might get caught in the middle."

"Maybe that's just what they want."

"We'd be battling Goliath without even a slingshot." Allison clasped her hands. "Mom, we might never leave here. And Justin doesn't deserve this." Tears rolled down her cheeks.

Chapter 23

A flash of harsh light hit Celia's eyes. She jumped up and saw a man who stood in the semi-shadows, holding a large industrial flashlight.

Celia backed up against the wall. "Who the hell are you?" she gasped.

"Oh, sorry. I didn't mean to scare you," a pleasant male voice called out. "I just didn't know exactly how to find you. I guess I lucked out."

Celia moved forward, still feeling the imprint of rough stone on the skin of her back.

He held his hands up in a peaceful gesture and walked toward her. "Don't be afraid. I'm Justin Adonhuff, Allie's fiancé. I come in peace." He laughed a bit nervously. "I just want to talk to you." He focused the flashlight away from Celia and illuminated his own face.

Celia's stomach still fluttered from the shock. He was medium height and build, and wore wireless glasses over a thin nose. Sandy blond hair hung over his forehead, and his shoulders slumped slightly beneath a rumpled white lab coat. In contrast to his general, distracted appearance, he had penetrating, determined blue eyes that took in the surroundings very quickly.

"I don't know how to get us out of this jam, if that's what you want to know." Celia turned on the overhead lights.

"Calling it a jam falls a little short of the reality." He put down his lantern and stuck his hands in the pockets of the lab coat, stretching the openings. "To be honest, I have a stake in this hospital, having been here since finishing my residency. My department is responsible for a generous revenue stream. I'm the chief of radiology. Not bragging. Just background." He coughed and waved away a sheet of dust particles. "I also donate big time. It's, ahem, suggested that hospital paid professionals owe something back. That's why I took the part-time job as a purchaser. They pushed it on me so they wouldn't have to pay a full-time person. My MBA gave me credentials—not my personality."

"Allie says you know about the hospital's deficit."

"I have a vested interest in finding out what's going on because of my position." He folded his twitchy hands behind his back. "Allison briefed me about it, er, you all are in an awful spot."

Celia offered Justin a seat. "Welcome to our apartment, as we now call it."

She sank into a low seat and invited Justin to sit across from her. She hoped he'd reveal more, but he stared at her.

"Do you know him personally, this Vladimir?" she asked.

"Of course. I keep a finger on the pulse around here. More so now. My contract to keep my job has to be approved by the board every few years. We have a nice, but distant relationship." His chair wobbled. He shifted his body to keep it steady. "Vladimir says he's in mostly import/export."

"Importing and exporting sex slaves."

Justin didn't look surprised. "Allie told me. Not the tiniest rumor about that around here. He's very generous to the hospital through his charitable foundation. A million a year makes him a hero. I have trouble believing it."

Maybe generous, but possibly taking more than he's giving. "If the hospital keeps most of the beds occupied most of the time and is receiving generous donations, then why this huge deficit?" Celia wondered how much to trust Justin. "Why orders of expensive equipment and meds that can't be found?"

"Maybe it's an accounting mistake? Or even mismanagement. That's why I got them to bring on a forensic accountant."

In the past, Allie hadn't made the best choices in men. Celia juggled thoughts in her mind about how much to tell. "Marcy and I went to a local bar near Rittenhouse Square called Fritzie's II." Celia swallowed hard. "The bartender and Vladimir conspired to drug us. We awoke in Pittsburgh where sex slaves, young women and children, were living in this shoddy mansion." She knew her story sounded implausible. She knew she'd doubt it herself if she heard it from a stranger. "I know it's odd that older women would be caught in that web, but they needed us to help keep the young females in line. These women didn't choose to be prostitutes, and they were kidnapped or duped into believing that these men offered a better life for them."

Justin looked part horrified and part disbelieving.

"These people are velvet harpoons. Charm you one minute and shove a knife in your back the next."

Justin looked doubtful.

"As madams they demanded we turn in those who rebelled; pretending to be compassionate so they'd trust us. We were to make sure they took birth control pills—but only because pregnancy puts a woman out of commission to earn money." Celia watched as his crumbled face transitioned into fear.

He shook his head. "I've heard a few things on TV. I believed it happened in third world countries, not here in the USA. Even when Allie tried to explain, I kind of dismissed it as unreal."

"That's what most people think." It tired Celia to keep going through the entire drill, but this time it involved Allie. She continued talking of their escape and avoiding getting caught. "Worst of all, we were to give women false hope of being freed in time, as soon as they paid their financial debt. It doesn't happen. They're never given opportunity to pay off a phony debt." Celia eyed him directly. "These thugs are brutal, global pimps."

"But a global conspiracy? Maybe just one small gang of bad guys doing this." He shook his head. "Vladimir is a philanthropic guy."

"Stop believing in appearances." His naivete annoyed her, but she bit her tongue. She told him how drugs were forced on the women whose addiction keeps them enslaved. And how they must pay for the drugs as well as everything else to keep them broke. "Besides, he makes more in linens than his yearly donations, let alone what he makes illegally."

Justin frowned. "Wow. It's scary. You see someone who looks ordinary, and they're living a double life. Allie said you don't have enough proof to go to the police."

Not sure she convinced him, she pushed harder. "We don't. If we expose ourselves, Vladimir will kill us, our families, and anyone who helps us." Celia watched Justin's pained face. "Do you suspect he's the driving force in your situation with the hospital's, um, mismanagement?" She bit her lip.

"Jeez, man. This is over my head." He looked at her askew. "I'm hoping the forensic accountant comes through."

"Do you know where Vladimir lives?"

"He keeps a condo in Center City, but so do a lot of people. Also, he has a shipping company."

Celia realized she was grinding her teeth. *Relax, breathe.* "It might just be he's laundering huge amounts of cash at offshore banks."

Justin stood and wiped his forehead with a sleeve. "I don't want to minimize your predicament. I'll keep an open mind. I'll help where I can. My Allison and our baby are at stake here, too. They are my life."

Celia shook his fine, smooth hand. "You can help. You're there in the trenches. If you hear anything, let us know. Anything about containers in the ports?"

"Containers." Justin said. "Shipping is one of Vladimir's businesses."

"Right. Captives are smuggled from foreign ports in containers. They have a system where those containers rarely get inspected or they hide the women behind products like TVs."

"I know his containers mostly come in at Pier 60. Name of the company is V & S."

"Big help."

He turned on his heel and looked back over his shoulder. "I'm happy to be your upstairs contact. Feels like a spy novel." He shrugged, shoulders rubbing his earlobes, and left.

Celia went back to her computer, the light from the screen dizzying her. Fifteen minutes later, Marcy returned, hair damp and shaggy. Her face was red with a scrubbed look.

"Justin came by to introduce himself," Celia said in an offhand manner. "He was skeptical at first, but I think he's going to help us."

"Can we trust him?"

"We need an outside person in the right position to get information. I'm sure Stanton's mime act is under suspicion now," Celia said. "They're clever bastards. They must have made some connection."

"I talked to Justin," said Allison who joined them. "He told me he met you and hopes he can be of help." She sighed. "I'm taking a nap. Tired, tired, tired."

"We'll talk later," Celia said.

Maybe Justin should talk to Stanton. Both are highly skilled. Maybe they can come up with ideas. Come on Justin, be on our side. You seem like a sweetheart, and I want to trust you.

Chapter 24

A couple of days later, Celia arranged for Stanton and Justin to meet.

"So, young man," asked Stanton. "Do you have any information?"

Justin grinned as though he'd eaten the best chocolate ever. "Didn't make much of it at the time. I thought it was a nice gesture. But there is one receipt in my database where Rudrow donated some state-of-the-art equipment to a Russian hospital."

"Is it enough to account for the big uptick in the increase in buying?"

"Not by a long shot. Just a hint of what might be going on."

"Maybe it's a way to cover his tracks," Stanton said. "Or perhaps someone else is stealing."

"There's more. This I got from the assistant comptroller who works directly with Barry. It's a copy of the financial situation and inventory lists from Rudrow." Justin waved a stapled set of papers.

Stanton's eyes widened. "Give it here."

"I had trouble making sense of it, and I thought I had a business mind."

Stanton rubbed the back of his head. "Wow, here's something weird. The last time they did an in-depth audit of inventory was three years ago, just before Vladimir started donations to the hospital. Such big discrepancies would come to the attention of the comptroller way before."

Celia tapped her toe on Stanton's sneaker. "Three years ago is when Vladimir contracted for the linen business and got on the board."

"Shit," Allison said.

"Double shit," Marcy echoed.

"When I heard about the indebtedness recently," Justin said, "I thought they were just having trouble collecting payments due. People pay thousands to burn in the sun at expensive beach resorts, get skin cancer, and smoke their heads off. Then they fluff off hospital bills as irrelevant or crooked."

"Let's stay on track," Stanton said, gently.

"The assistant comptroller claimed any discrepancy came from a few electronic glitches."

"That would be Svetlana."

Justin nodded. "She's young, but whip-smart. I personally wouldn't have hired her but Stompovich is her mentor. And what he says, goes."

"This is a huge place to run with so many beds," Celia said, staring at the numbers. "But it's still a business. You'd think budgets and inventory would be of primary importance to a hospital. They let this go for three years?"

"How are errors in accounting handled?" Stanton asked.

"We're non-profit, and run inefficiently like the government," Justin said. "Not many are watching the store. I got turned down for a lot of X-ray equipment. I thought it was because of the budget."

"A massive deficiency like this can bankrupt this hospital," Stanton said, an edge of impatience creeping into his voice. "Ten million?"

"With fewer diagnostic units, patients don't get top-notch

care," Justin said. "I'm forced to share an ultrasound machine with other departments. Patients have to wait hours."

Celia read the spreadsheet and said, "There are many units ordered and delivered, but not to the hospital address. It's addressed to a port here in Philadelphia."

"I'm sure Vladimir didn't want anyone to see this," Stanton said. "Maybe he's going to fudge it since there's an investigation underway."

"Thank you, Justin, for getting this information," Celia said.

"It's great to see it under the light of day," Stanton said. "Corruption? Collusion? Crooks in control? It reads like a mystery novel."

"And the board has its own agenda for letting all this go," Allison said.

Marcy mumbled, "There's a conspiracy. When does it end?"

Justin looked taken aback. "The hospital approves my contract every three years. I try to keep my nose clean." He hesitated. "I'm afraid to take this to the top bosses. They might be involved. Nosing around has probably already gotten me on the shit list."

Celia caught Allison staring at her as though reading her thoughts. "Ramon would be ideal for Vladimir as an inside person. Barry, too."

"Barry's in a position to be in on it," Allison said. "Why else hasn't the comptroller reported it?"

"Ramon makes close to a million a year plus benefits." Justin brushed his pants as if he brushed away all the information created by the news. "I was warned not to make waves—in a not-so-subtle way. Barry has hinted before about my contract negotiations."

"This is all over the top," Stanton said, disbelief in his voice. "I did lots of forensic computer work on every type of crime, but never theft of equipment and drugs from an institution of this magnitude."

"You think maybe it is a computer glitch?" Justin said, a note of hope in his voice.

"A computer malfunction for three years and no one mentions it?" Stanton said. "No way."

"They're updating systems," Justin continued.

"Maybe to make sure it squares with the missing inventory before the forensic accountant gets to it," Stanton said.

"This is getting more complicated and dangerous," Allison said, hardly above a whisper.

"Justin, maybe back off for a while," Celia said, her fears skyrocketing. "We don't want them to know you have any association with us."

"This is my first foray into fraud," Justin said. "It's distressing… and if I'm in danger, so is Allison. I'm in this till we get it resolved."

"Don't go head-to-head with Ramon." Celia said. "Pretend you don't know anything."

"Yeah, and watch out for Svetlana. Lay low," Stanton added.

"I'll try." Justin shook Stanton's hand. When he shook Celia's hand, his had no heft, no pressure, as though she were made of delicate eggshells. She wondered if people who shook hands like that had some dark secret that they feared revealing. Or was he just afraid of what was happening?

"By the way," Justin said in a low voice. "I'm definitely going to keep my mouth shut. If Ramon is involved, well, the pressure they're putting on me…" He gave Celia a tight smile.

"I can help," Marcy said. "I can cozy up to this Ramon, get him to trust me, and maybe he'll spill the beans. I have an aura of sexual prowess that ignites men. They confess all."

"Marcy, not the time to put your charms to work." Allison said.

"Those people are hard-boiled and inured to your charms. If anything, it will get you killed."

"Oh, don't count me out. As you know, my allure is so overpowering that my Melvy dropped dead during, um, an intimate moment. My powers can kill." She grinned.

"What?" said Justin.

"Marcy!" said Allison, her face stern.

"My vibes are intoxicating. He'll drop right into my arms, I'll turn him on, and he'll turn himself in. I'm better than a priest." Marcy put her hands on her hips and shook them.

"Maybe cut the humor for now," said Celia. "Just ignore her, Justin."

"Excuse me? I'm not joking." She walked provocatively to her cubby, throwing her hair over her shoulder.

"I think you have a story for me Allie," said Justin. "Let's head up to my office."

"You have no idea what you got yourself into, sweetheart," said Allie.

"Oh, I think I do."

Celia knew any half-decent comptroller could have picked up the cooked books in all that time. Those who thought Mafia organizations went out of business were so wrong. These days they dodged publicity and worked under the radar.

Stealing had become incredibly sophisticated. Now they took over corporations, emptied the coffers, created phony bankruptcy scams, virtual scams, Medicare and Medicaid rip-offs, investment fraud, insurance fraud, food stamp fraud, and the endless list went on.

Chapter 25

Wearing one of Allison's business suits, Celia located the comptroller's office and walked in with an authority she absolutely didn't feel. Barry Chester had a small office that smelled of stale coffee and mildewed carpets, while an empty room deodorizer sat on a desk.

"Hi, I'm from Financial Compliance," she said. "I'm here to ask you a few questions." The badge she wore was new and listed her as a senior compliance officer. Stanton did a good job of finding a quality underground print shop. She grasped the paper with the data. It creased under her fingers and she set it next to Barry.

"Let's get started." She pulled a legal pad out of her messenger bag. "What's the situation with paid-for equipment delivered and not accounted for in inventory?"

Barry's eyes widened. He peered at her badge. His hands floated over the scattered papers on his desk. In the dim light, his computer threw a ghostly light onto his hands. His tightened lips had a blue glaze. It looked as if he'd had a heart attack.

"Oh, um, well, it's, ah, don't know. Something about equipment?"

"You are aware of it then?"

"Not really…um…some things were recently brought to my attention."

"It's looking like we paid millions for equipment that is

unaccounted for. Why is that?" She shook official-looking papers in front of his face, long enough for him to get an overall impression, then snatched them back.

He sat up straight. "Is this from the forensic accounting firm? Ah, I'm not really…er…kept in the loop."

"That's quite surprising," she said, putting on her sternest expression. "Who is in charge of the loop? Isn't that you?"

"Who sent you?" Barry tapped his pencil. "Who the hell are you? Police?"

She tapped her badge. "I work in Compliance, and Ramon sent me," Celia replied, keeping her tone abrupt. She didn't want to get chatty and misstep.

Barry seemed to melt into a vat of hot steam as his body went into slow motion. "I told you I wasn't in the loop." He stared at the ceiling. "Am I getting set up as the scapegoat?"

"Are you? What do you know?"

He threw his pencil down. "We did spot checks, but never an audit as encompassing as this one. Top level told us not to bother; it was being handled by this outside firm. I know the city is up-in-arms over hospitals in low-income areas because they make up the difference of money lost for uninsured patients."

Wow. He's trying to wriggle out of it. Who will they blame?

"These losses," she said slowly, "are off the charts."

"I'm going to get lists of every single piece of equipment and track it down," he mumbled. "I just need time. I'm sure it's a computer glitch." He blinked rapidly and gave her a gummy grin, his teeth yellowed by cigarette smoke. "Someone else took charge of inventory. One of the docs did part-time work purchasing stuff. That was all done without me. I went along or I'd lose my job."

Celia's stomach flipped. "You don't know the person's name?"

"Look, I just try to keep to my job. When higher-ups get involved, I do what they say. I suggest you do the same. Keeps a paycheck coming in."

"Thank you for your help." His light blue shirt had wet stains under his arms. The scent of fear-driven perspiration oozed from his pores.

"Hey," Barry shouted, "What's your name?"

She walked out of the office and down the hall.

At seven in the evening, Celia was in her cubby scanning the figures on the spreadsheet one more time. She inhaled the scent of potatoes and gravy. Through the parted curtain, Stanton appeared like an oasis. She saw the table laden with aluminum containers. Next, she heard movement and the excited voices of Marcy and Allie, anticipating a feast: mashed potatoes, peas, cranberry sauce, and a fat, browned turkey.

"What's the occasion?" Celia asked. "My mouth is watering."

"Well, it's almost Thanksgiving," Stanton said. "We're all working overtime and I thought I'd bring you something special."

For an instant, Celia had an odd feeling that the large space was a real home, as if it were the most natural place in the world for a sumptuous meal. She realized Stanton's presence might have something to do with that feeling of comfort and safety.

Oh, what the hell. Relax.

Allie and Marcy's faces glowed in the light of several lit candles.

Stanton smiled broadly, something he'd been doing more of lately. "For you, my dears." Stanton bowed. "Actually, I did all this to entice Celia to tell us what happened in Barry's office." Stanton loaded the plates with food and set them on the table. He smiled. "Ah, bless the supermarkets."

"I'd tell you all without a feast." Celia sipped the cabernet sauvignon.

"I'm salivating. It sure looks good." Marcy rubbed her hands together and took a seat.

They looked at Celia as they cut into the food. "I'm glad Allie tutored me in how to approach Barry. I just wanted to scare the bejesus out of him and get him to talk. He knows something, but is terrified to say. He told me not to meddle if I wanted to keep my job."

I have to tell them despite upsetting Allie? "The one thing that slipped out is that Justin might be on their scapegoat list."

Marcy draped her arm over Allison's shoulder. "We've got to protect Allie. Maybe we just go into the witness protection program… But then, I wouldn't ever see my son or grandbaby." Marcy held her napkin to her eyes. "God, what are we going to do?"

"I think if we get Vladimir, we get a big bunch of them." Celia paused. "Those hospital head honchos might know about Vladimir's sex trafficking. We must gather as much information as we can about how these criminals transport women—in detail.

"Allison, keep us informed about the ins and outs around the hospital. I'm working on a step-by-step plan to learn when containers come in. I'm sure Svetlana knows something about it."

"She's out of the office a lot, for hours at a time," Allison said.

"Bet I know where you can find her," Marcy cackled.

"Listen, we have a mountain of work in front of us." Celia's face turned red. "You, Marcy, are making too many jokes at such a tough time." Her voice turned up a notch. "Let's get real. Vladimir will escape punishment. He's stolen hundreds of thousands of women and children's lives. We live in a hellhole that we're getting to like, including me. Shows my insanity. One minute I'm la-de-da. And the next moment, claustrophobia sets in." She banged her fist on the table. "No more kidding around."

"You can't take it out on us," Stanton said softly. "No blaming."

Celia felt caught in a net. "You're right. I'm sorry. It's the frustration…"

Marcy rose and walked away.

Celia left Stanton sipping the last of the wine and walked into Marcy's cubicle. Marcy's eyes were red-rimmed and filled with tears.

"I'm just a mess," Celia said. "You are my friend and sister—for life. I don't know what I'd do without you."

"I know you care. I'm breaking down."

"I was only thinking about myself. I'll be more thoughtful. I promise. Get some sleep."

When Celia went to talk to Allison, she was fast asleep.

Celia returned to Stanton. "I think Marcy's okay with me now. Allison, well, she's asleep."

"Good. Now how about us?"

"We have to put us off."

A rat darted across the room. Celia gasped. Stanton grabbed a shovel and trapped it in a corner. Celia closed her eyes. She heard several rapid thumps with a shovel. When she opened her eyes, Stanton held the rat by the tail. He dropped it in the trash can.

"There's an incinerator on the way to the freight elevator," Celia said.

"I noticed some plastic bags. I'll wrap it up for special delivery."

"To Vladimir?"

"Who else? I'll buy some rat poison when I shop tomorrow."

Celia suddenly began to sway.

Stanton caught her before she hit the ground.

"You are my best friend," she whispered.

"You bet your sweet ass." He escorted her to her cubby, settled her in bed, kissed her gently on the forehead, and tiptoed out.

Chapter 26

"Rasheed is in bad shape," Stanton said. "I hate giving you the news."

He sat in front of Celia, hands clasped, in a doctor's long lab coat with a tag clipped to his breast pocket.

Celia heard a mournful note in Stanton's voice. Trying to stop him from visiting Rasheed was impossible. They sat in silence, Celia in her own world.

"It's going to be tough to see that sweet child now," Celia said at last.

"I know. He calls me Mr. Mime." He took her in his arms and hugged her tight. "I just hope Stompovich leaves him alone."

Celia tightened her arms around his neck. "Allie said Barry reported to the board and higher ups that a strange woman from Financial Compliance came into his office, asking questions. The staff will be checking IDs super closely, watching like hawks." Celia knew she looked careworn. "How will I visit Rasheed?"

"They can't watch the area every minute of every day," Stanton said. "I'll go with you."

Upstairs, Stanton sat on the edge of Rasheed's bed and Celia stood just behind him. Stanton awakened the child and gave him the chocolate chip cookies. Rasheed took two bites and stopped. His eyes fluttered.

"Rasheed, tomorrow I'm going to bring you a basketball to go with your new haircut," Celia said, moving closer and pressing her hand against his hot cheek. She lay drawing materials on the night table, and wondered if he'd ever use them.

Rasheed smiled weakly, gulping air between each word. "Those guys…"

"Were the same guys here again?" Celia kept her voice low so as not to upset Rasheed.

"Yeah, they…asked about a lady… Hair twisty in back." Rasheed squeezed Stanton's hand. "Name…is Mr. Stomp…um…something."

"Did they hurt you?" Stanton said, his tone soft.

"No, they…the other man's mean…wanted to slap me. Black suit stopped him." Rasheed fought to catch his breath. Celia put her hand on his chest and calmed him. After a couple of minutes, he seemed more alert.

Celia's heart banged against her chest. "You don't have to talk about those people."

Rasheed shook his head. "They asked for your name and where you live. I told them you were my friend, but…I don't know."

"Just relax, Rasheed. Now get some sleep." Celia motioned Stanton to the doorway as Rasheed closed his eyes.

Stanton kissed Rasheed on the cheek.

As they left, Celia said, "They have no pity."

"Celia? Are you okay? I heard you call out," Stanton lifted the side of the hanging blanket over the opening of her cubby. "It's 5 a.m."

Celia wiped her damp cheeks with her sleeve. "Where did you sleep?"

Stanton wore only his scrub pants. "In the cubby next to yours, the luxurious one with a semblance of a bed." He cocked his head and stepped in. "Are you crying?"

"I woke up, thinking about Rasheed. It's so hard to watch that child die. He's a reminder of what we've all lost. Rasheed is losing life. And we're dying in here, bit by bit." A sob broke from the depths rising to engulf her.

Stanton squatted in front of her and pushed her hair away from her face. "Maybe we can do something for Rasheed."

She felt his eyes piercing layers of her skin, exposing her heart.

"Whatever happens to Rasheed, let's arrange a scholarship in his name, that is, when we can get out of here," he whispered in a voice that sounded almost like a moan.

"Well, you've got the money. I'll arrange it."

"Deal." Stanton cupped her cheek.

"I hate this time of day," she said. "When the world is still asleep but about to awaken to possibility. I want to roll back to a time when I was in my own bed thinking about going to my studio to paint." She half-smiled. "And I was torturing you."

"S and M isn't all that bad." Stanton cuddled up next to her. Celia pressed tightly to him and soon drifted off into a light sleep, fraught with dreams of her, Marcy, and Nikki running down dead-end alleyways.

An hour later, Celia awoke in Stanton's arms. He slept. Each time he exhaled, his breath skimmed her forehead. She tightened her arms around his waist as he sighed and opened his eyes.

"There you are, my love," he whispered.

She felt resistance settling in, even as she knew that he was the only man who could reach the tattered, loneliest place deep within her. *I can't afford to give up another sliver of my will and become too vulnerable.*

"It's heaven to be in your arms, especially first thing in the morning."

"Don't kid yourself, Stanton," she teased. "It's lust, not love."

He laughed. "Love and lust, a mighty powerful pair. I feel we touch each other's souls as well as the physical connection."

She sighed. "With what's happening, you scare me."

"Whatever you want to call it, I like it."

"I don't know what's worse." She stared at him. "Saying you love me or you getting involved in this insanity."

I won't let myself fall in love with you again. My life is not my own.

"I'd better get to work."

"And leave me with all the housework?" He pouted.

Celia got out of bed, smiling in spite of her conflicted mood. She chided herself for a crushing yearning to be back in his arms.

Stanton slipped into his scrubs. Veins and tendons rippled across his arm muscles as he tugged and tied the strings. She pinched the love handles. He jumped back.

"That tickles."

She dressed and followed him out to the living area where he was unwrapping a granola bar.

"I don't want you to visit Rasheed. I'll go alone," Stanton said, putting on a shirt he lifted from a chair. "They'll be looking for you. They probably suspect you're nearby." He tugged at a button. "I'll tell Rasheed you send your love."

"And I do love him."

By 10 a.m. the following morning, Celia had calculated rows of numbers that, once again, corroborated their original estimate of the Rudrow Hospital's unaccounted for losses.

She gazed at the single cinder-block wall not covered with sheets. She imagined a garden of red, blue, and yellow flowers. She would paint them on the wall to cheer everyone up. She thought about Stanton. *Maybe the thrill of his presence has created an excitement that feels like love. Or maybe it's just the fact of confinement. It's so powerful as if I'm in the midst of an explosive emotional meltdown.*

Stanton had lived an exciting life in a way. He'd worked on the cutting edge of technology, and had participated in the rise of the internet. A childhood like his would have broken someone less strong. She and Stanton had been widow and widower when they bumped into each other in Florida. It wasn't an accident. She'd googled his name and found out where he lived. It fit into where she wanted to be—in the retirement village next to his. He had to miss that sunny world now, deep in this dungeon.

Does he see me as the missing link for bringing him back to a life when he's hit the brink? Does risk replace his tormented youth? Is my situation providing excitement as an antidote to an older man's humdrum life?

When he should run, he drew closer. Before, when she'd seen less of him, he'd pursued her, but not with the kind of passion he was showing now. Nor had she ever yearned for him this much. The real test of their relationship needed to happen in the real world, if they ever got there.

Stanton said he had errands to run. "But before I leave, I have a big surprise for you," he said, handing Celia a large manila envelope. Inside were the contraband cards and documents needed to prove she and Marcy were doctors from CDC: fake names, certificates, letters on CDC headings, and even post-doctoral fellowships, exactly what they needed to get themselves on the piers. She knew Vladimir operated out of several ports. The high number of hepatitis cases they planned "investigating" would be sufficient to give them entrée. "I said my guy was working on them. It took longer than he thought. Complicated stuff."

Celia and Marcy whooped. Allison slunk out.

She watched his back as he sauntered out. Unlike a lot of men she knew, he didn't appear to need adulation or unconditional love. He took her criticism to heart and tried to make changes wherever he could. He didn't have an arrogant bone in his body, nor did he judge people. But he could be annoying at times with his prattle about connecting souls or expecting more attention. When they'd renewed their friendship after many years, she'd demanded he be sensitive and empathetic. He took it to heart. When he overdid it, she told him to be kinder to himself.

I don't know if I'll ever be able to promise him all of me. But a bit less might be enough for both of us.

Celia opened her computer and saw an email from Allie. The message said that Justin had been called to a meeting with Ramon and Vladimir. They want to know why Justin opened up a hornet's nest about the financial losses. He told them it happened accidentally while he was trying to discover why he wasn't getting the equipment he ordered for his department.

Apparently, the Commonwealth of Pennsylvania is looking into a possible investigation of their own, depending on the results of the forensic accountant. They had the right since they received public funds from the state.

She went on to say that Ramon had made a big fuss and accused Justin of inciting the forensic audit when the whole affair was only a computer glitch. They also wanted to know if he knew the woman who had barged into Barry's office. Justin had told them he had no idea, but came back badly shaken. He and Allie agreed not to make any more waves.

Asking questions like that makes Ramon look as guilty as Vladimir. We'll have to be more cautious.

She made a cup of tea and watched steam rising and curling out of the cup. Finger-pointing had begun. Why did Ramon call Vladimir to the meeting with Justin and not Barry Chester? The financial implosion would hurt Justin and Allie the most.

Marcy cleared her throat, causing Celia to snap out of her daze. "You scared me."

"Sorry. Didn't want to disturb you and your lover, but I see he left. You keeping that tea to yourself? I'm tempted to roll tea leaves into a joint and smoke it. Heaven knows we can use it now."

Celia poured her a cup and told her to read Allison's email.

She gasped. "We've brought Justin into the hole with us. You don't think he'll give us up, do you?"

"Not if he loves Allie and the baby, he won't." Her head spun. "I hope."

"A lot of rumors will be floating around the hospital nursing stations in the next few days," Marcy said. "Somehow, this stuff always leaks out."

"Things are closing in, and we have no wiggle room. We have to stay away from walking hospital floors. The next step is to make contact at the wharf. We need to go there, but be prepared to run like hell if Vladimir shows up."

"His thugs will probably be around. I'm gonna love being a doctor. How do we go about this?"

"We're investigating hep C and for the CDC. Hep C is actually spreading among stevedores so if they look it up, we're golden. Once they accept us, I'm hoping to get information about the containers coming in."

Marcy sipped her tea. "On second thought, what use will the MD degrees do for us if we're dead?"

"You don't have to come along, Marcy. It's crazy and dangerous as hell. But the only way to convince the authorities is by catching them in the act."

"No, no, no. You are not doing this without me, get it? I'm in, and no two ways about it. We'll case the place first?"

"I'll ask Allie to get us stethoscopes and other medical implements from Justin. We'll do it tomorrow."

Fury throbbed in Celia's head. Those bastards had big-time hospital connections, and now they knew she and Marcy were somewhere in the area. Only a matter of time before they figured out where they hid.

Marcy went into her cubby and in a short time emerged, wearing a black T-shirt cinched at the back and artfully tucked into black leggings.

"What do you think? Am I doing a good job channeling Catwoman?"

Celia laughed. "Go change. We're not robbing a bank. We have to look like doctors. Put on scrubs and a lab coat."

"Well, I'm wearing this underneath. Timing is everything and I might impress one of the men at the docks. I like those stevedores with those six-pack abs."

"Girl, some of those guys are drinking a six-pack a day and their abs have turned to slabs. Don't get too excited."

Chapter 27

Despite Stanton's desperate warning to not visit Rasheed, Celia, in scrubs with a stethoscope around her neck, walked toward the child's room. When she reached his door, she saw that there were people in the room with him. Vladimir and Svetlana stood close to Rasheed's bed and Ramon, standing away from them, tapped his foot. Rasheed appeared to be breathing hard as Vladimir and Svetlana spoke loudly, as though he couldn't hear. Celia stepped away and stood beside the door where she could hear voices.

"Are you sure you haven't seen this woman?" Vladimir held a large picture up for Rasheed.

Damn, I posted that picture on Facebook ages ago. They were hot on her trail.

Rasheed's half-open eyes blinked. "Uh-uh. Nope," he said and closed his eyes again.

Vladimir and Svetlana glanced at each other. Svetlana, bending within inches from Rasheed's face, dominated the bed space. Vladimir stood stern-faced beside her.

"I know you saw her, kiddo. We're just trying to help. Do you know where she goes when she leaves?" Vladimir asked sweetly.

Celia backed down the hall and waited until she was sure they had left. Inside Rasheed's room, she clasped his hand. His fingers curled around hers as his eyes remained closed.

Hang in there, sweetheart. I'm sorry to cause you any stress or pain. You deserve only love and light.

"I heard that they're about to publicize the preliminary results of the audit," Allison said as she walked in. "Not the final."

Celia looked up from the computer. Allie looked disconcerted and spoke first. "Maybe that's why the evil triumvirate were in Rasheed's room, torturing a sweet child with questions. They might think Justin and I are somehow behind the audit."

"He's got double trouble," Marcy said, "and I add to their woes. They must be scared we'll finally report them to the police. If only…" Celia's eyes glazed over.

"Justin told me that they keep asking him where he got the information about the equipment," Allison said. "He kept his cool, but he's as worried as we are."

Vladimir's phantom presence had taken over all the space in the hospital in Celia's mind.

"From what Justin says," Allison continued, "Ramon is breathing fire, swearing to find out how this got out. Vladimir isn't hiding under a rock either. He's incensed."

"Barry might be the weak link," Celia said. "If he turns in evidence to the state for a lighter sentence, then we're only one step away from Vladimir."

"Hold up," Allison said, "Ramon claims that a philanthropist like Vladimir can't be involved. Barry claims the audit is fake. Ramon is saying he has it on good authority that a competing hospital is behind this; he says they want to destroy Rudrow and gobble it up at a bargain price."

Celia sucked in a deep breath. "Again, proof will be tough to find if Ramon and Barry cover for Vladimir."

Later that day, still dressed in her lab coat, her credentials in the briefcase, Celia gave a tight-lipped smile. She sat next to Stanton in the passenger seat of his car. Marcy sat in the back. Stanton had insisted on accompanying them, but agreed to Celia's request that he not go in, only if he had possession of the gun. Celia had forgotten about it until Marcy took it out of their sports bag. Stanton had then taken it and even bought bullets.

"What the hell?" she had said.

"Having a gun is serious business," he said. "And I've been licensed as a weapons expert forever. I've had to use one in the past and I'd do it again if I need to."

Stanton spun the wheel as they turned off Decker Avenue and headed up Shaker Boulevard toward Pier 60, which the locals called Shaker Pier. Celia had called several piers, pretending to be Vladimir's assistant, trying to find out where his next order of containers docked. The supervisor at the last pier on her list told her he knew three containers were due but asked her to produce the bill of lading number before giving more information. That's when she knew she'd have to go down to the pier and take a chance.

Celia had studied how the CDC operates in an outbreak. She now had a list on very authentic-looking CDC stationery of patients who had contracted the disease at Shaker Pier and others. She'd made an outline on what her "team" planned to do about prevention. Based on her research, she now knew as much as any professional. She and Marcy would educate and refer those they deemed at risk to the hospital for treatment or vaccination.

Maritime Shaker Pier on Shaker Boulevard turned out to be the busiest in Philadelphia. They had numerous in-house stevedore crews, and fast turnaround for the vessels that docked there. There was constant loading and unloading of huge ships carrying every kind of product in metal containers—the very same kind that would contain sex slaves. The containers were hauled off the ships by state-of-the-art top loaders and reach stackers.

At Shaker Pier, from a distance and through a gate, they saw the ships piled high with containers lined up along the dock. Each level had a several inches between them and the next level above. There were three sets of railroad tracks nearby for freight cars that picked up some of the containers, others were loaded on flatbed trucks in an endless reception line. Most drivers didn't need to get out of their cabs. The massive cranes loaded the cargo right on the truck's bed.

"Stanton, will our plan work?" Celia asked.

He gave a half-smile, but his eyes were worried.

Marcy shook her head for emphasis. "We gotta do this."

"You look at this pier, and it's the picture of legit, hard-working, industrious people," Stanton said. "Most of them don't know and probably don't care what cargo the containers carry as long as they can verify them according to the documentation."

Celia surveyed the weathered, wooden beams of the dock, the ten-story cranes, and the large hangars in a row lining the back of the dock.

Stanton's nostrils flared. "Remember, these criminals have no compunctions. If you stand in their way, there's no telling what they'll do but it won't be pretty."

"You have to leave as soon as you drop us off."

"Can't do that. As a matter of fact," he said as he reached into his pocket and withdrew what looked like a small, red buzzer, "push this button if you get into trouble. It's wired to reach me."

Celia took it and gave him a half-smile. "The gods are looking out for us."

He nodded.

Celia gazed toward the river, sailboats and motorboats skimmed the tranquil waters as though the devils in the world didn't exist. She wished she felt as calm. The sun lit clouds from behind, the blue sky peeking out. Ships lined the docks for blocks and blocks, business as usual, but even this daily, bustling scene had dark corners and in some of them tortured human beings might be loaded and unloaded at this very moment.

Stanton pulled in front of the gate and leaned out to speak to the guard. "Sir, I'm driving doctors from the CDC to investigate an outbreak of hepatitis C among the stevedores."

The guard who looked younger than his sun-weathered face raised a bushy eyebrow. "What outbreak? Ain't heard nothin'."

Celia started to explain when he cut her off.

"I know that shit."

Stanton took the papers from Celia and handed the documents to the guard. Marcy handed hers over.

"Only thing I thought they got was syphilis," the man snickered. "What the hell is the CDC?"

"It's the Centers for Disease Control and Prevention, US government," Stanton told him.

The guard brought out a thick hardbound book, licked his fingers, and flipped through pages. Celia saw he thumbed through what she'd discovered from the union website and what Stanton produced, using other secret means for getting information. She had the names of men on sick leave. It had taken an entire day to access the information. With Stanton's help, she'd honed her computer skills quite a bit these past few weeks.

"I know most of the names of guys here who are on sick leave. So, that's what they got?" He lost his brash attitude. "Jeez, man."

He opened the gate. "Do some good," he shouted in a gravelly voice. "These guys eat fish they get from these filthy waters. And you don't want to know where they go after work."

Celia asked Stanton to park in the lot. "I don't think I'll be that long on this first visit."

She and Marcy walked over a gravel lot, toward a building with a sign that said "OFFICE."

"I know we practiced night and day for the last couple of days, but it's easy to slip up," Marcy said in a squeaky voice.

Celia urged Marcy forward. She worried that her own face revealed how afraid she was. She took a deep breath. In her pocket, she felt the warning device Stanton had given her along with a tiny bugging device.

At the pier, huge cranes were emptying cargo containers from a six-story ship. Celia's heart skipped a beat. Just inside the office, she saw a sign above a door that said "SUPERVISOR."

"Yeah," a male voice shouted. Celia opened the door all the way. A bald, thin man was bent over a pile of papers. "I don't want to be bothered now."

"Ahem," Celia cleared her throat. "Excuse me. I need to talk to you. It's urgent." She and Marcy stepped over the threshold.

"Yeah." He looked up. "And who might you be?"

"I'm Dr. Ignatia. I'm here about the hepatitis outbreak. This is my assistant, Dr. Cross."

He stood up, his lips pressed together in a frown. "What the hell you talkin' 'bout, lady?"

"We're from the Centers for Disease Control, federal government."

He sat and glared at her beneath narrowed eyes. "Look, if we got somethin' going around, we can handle it." His crinkly eyes and thin, sun-wrinkled face with a pointed chin looked aggrieved. "Yeah, I know we got a couple of cases. Under control now."

"More than a couple. We're here on a federal mandate." She leaned forward. "Someone can be asymptomatic and contaminate a sex partner, their children, or friends." She handed him her papers. "People can get hepatitis C from blood, sharing needles or shaving razors, sex, and fish," she explained in her most businesslike voice. "Many infected people mingle with the public. And sickened stevedores can contaminate others. This could produce a massive epidemic. We want to try to nip it in the bud."

He paled as Celia went on: "The shipping industry has about ten percent or more of its workers addicted to alcohol and/or illicit drugs. They might share dirty needles. I'd guess about half of the workers have tattoos and body piercings. What do you think happens if equipment isn't sterilized properly?"

"Look, lady…"

"Are you married? Kids?"

He nodded.

"If it spreads to a pregnant wife the baby might get it. It can spread when a woman nurses her baby." Celia took a deep breath. "If this pier gets a reputation for refusing to help stop the disease, civil suits follow. Products get rerouted to other piers. Workers don't show up."

"All we do is unload containers." He looked up at Celia. "Let me see your credentials. These letters don't mean shit."

Celia reached into her briefcase and dropped a large manila folder on his desk. "Look to your heart's content. I'll be back in the morning with educational material that will make everyone aware of this disease. The key is to alert workers that symptoms might take a long time to appear."

"Whatcha gonna do for us?"

"People should be treated if they have the disease or receive injections if they made contact with an infected person. We refer them to local hospitals for that. You have excellent hospitals all over the city. I'm hoping that with education we'll nip it in the bud. We'll start a campaign to raise awareness for your employees, explain the symptoms, and direct them where to get help. Where can we set up?"

"Listen, keep it down as much as possible. I don't want any blowback from my superiors. I got my job to protect. I just been hearing pieces here and there. Guys go to the doc. I'm thinking like gonorrhea or something. They don't tell me the real shit." He slapped his hand on the desktop, yelped and raised his finger to his mouth. "Shit. Got a splinter."

"Let me see that." Celia opened the doctor's bag. She prayed there would be everything she needed. *Thank you, Justin.* "Hold his hand up, Doctor Cross," she said to Marcy.

Marcy took his hand and raised her head up at him. "We'll take good care of you," she said, her voice husky. "Does it hurt much, sweetie?"

Celia squeezed her eyes tight. She had no compunctions about Marcy using her feminine wiles to their advantage. Marcy had excellent timing for when to divert someone.

"Nah," he said, staring at Marcy's breasts. She gave him a sugary smile as Celia picked out the splinter with a tweezer and applied alcohol with a wad of cotton. Her hand shaking, she reached into her pocket, palming the listening device. Leaning over she threw the cotton in the wastebasket. The man continued staring at Marcy's boobs. Her shoulders jostled just the slightest bit. As Celia moved upright, she placed the listening device on the underside of his desk and it stuck.

"How's that?" Marcy asked, holding his rough palm as Celia removed a bandage and pressed the edges flat. *Couldn't have worked better.*

When Marcy stepped away, he seemed to snap out of his goofy staring. "Okay. Do it."

"We'll be heading out for now," Marcy said with the most subtle wiggle of her hips. "See you in the morning." They walked out to the parking lot, spotting Stanton's car. They both hurried, just short of a run. As they got close, she saw him smiling in relief.

"Marcy, your boobs did a merciful task," Celia said.

"Not the first time I did my part for mankind. I know when to hold 'em—and when to fold 'em."

Chapter 28

Allison, Stanton, Justin, and Marcy huddled around Celia as she turned up the sound on the mini-receiver. With intent faces, they waited but heard only the shuffling of paper.

"Yo, jerko. What time is the next shipment?" a harsh male voice shouted. It sounded like the wharf supervisor.

"The clothes shipment from Indonesia is due at 6 a.m."

"Okay, jackass, I'm out of here. Neary is on night duty."

"Tell Neary to fuck himself. He's a wiseass jerk."

"He's your boss at night. Shut the fuck up."

A door slammed, opened, and slammed again.

"Damn," Celia said. "I was hoping for more."

"We don't know if they're using code words, like maybe clothes means women," Stanton said.

"I'm going to get there at 6 a.m., when the shipment arrives," Celia said.

"Oh, shit," Marcy said. "So early?"

"I'm thinking you've both lost it," Stanton said, his voice sharp.

"You are endangering our baby's grandmother and godmother," Justin said with a sardonic tinge to his voice.

"I'm gonna be the best damned godmother ever. Whoopee," Marcy said with a grin.

"A gorgeous one at that," smiled Stanton.

Celia knew Stanton had social skills. He made sure to compliment Marcy.

"Oh, Stanton. You are such a good guy. If you weren't Celia's beau, I'd bring you a brisket like all the other single women at Boca Pelicano Palms."

Stanton and Celia looked at each other and laughed. When Allison looked confused, Celia said, "In Florida, the minute a man becomes single he is barraged by older, single women coming out of the woodwork. They besiege him with cooked meals. There's a saying that if an older guy can drive a car at night, dance, and get it up, he's gold. Two out of three gives him a silver star."

"Give you an idea," Marcy said. "In the sixtyish age range, there are about ninety-five men to every hundred women. Eightyish, it drops to only sixty-one men for every one hundred. They start becoming a precious resource."

"Justin doesn't worry about casseroles." Allison said. "I'm not much of a cook."

"You wouldn't go far in Florida, girl. Older, single women pursue older men with unending casseroles," Marcy said. "The second an old fart becomes single, the way to his heart is through his stomach."

"A healthy, nurturing woman who can cook is ideal. A guy gets a caretaker with homemade meals," Celia said. "Throw in a bit of sex and he's a goner. That's how to snag an old geezer."

"And I wooed Celia by reading every book I could. She never made me a casserole."

"Okay, everyone," Celia said. "We've got to get down to business and get work done."

"Got some bad news and more bad news," Justin said. "The forensic auditor was fired before his findings became public. They hired a new auditor today. Guess who recommended him? Vladimir, of course."

"We might be onto something with the docks," Marcy said. "Justin, we're hoping you can get pamphlets on hepatitis C for Dr. Celia who needs them for the morning lecture."

"Wow. Now that's an assignment that won't get me into trouble, for a change. This hospital has pamphlets on everything," Justin said.

"You really are the partner I always wanted my daughter to have," Celia said, looking lovingly at Allison.

Allison gave Celia a hug. "And you got lucky with Stanton."

"I only had to come begging on bended knee several times," said Stanton.

"Men have to work to deserve us." Celia said. "And be empathetic."

"What we all need is sleep," said Marcy. "Celia and I need to be up before five. Justin, if you could get those brochures now, I'll be forever grateful. Nighty-night all. Keep your nose to the grindstone—er, computer."

"Aye, aye, captain," said Stanton. "Are you sure I can't come with you lovely women, er, I mean doctors?"

"No," said Celia.

"Well, be very careful."

At 6 a.m., Celia and Marcy stepped out of their cab and stood at the wharf in their lab coats, black stethoscopes slung around their necks.

They trudged across a stone path toward the office and noticed the name "Jack" was now scribbled on a Post-it and tacked on the half-open door—a hurried honor to Marcy, in all probability. Jack waved them in all the while keeping his eyes on Marcy below chin level.

"Yuz look like good docs." Jack had a sleepy look with bloodshot eyes. "So, why the hell you guys in so early?" he asked, looking at them sideways. "I hear there's an outbreak at a pier a mile from here. Why don'tcha help them?" He pointed out the window. "I'll take yuz. Come back in the afternoon."

Celia felt a headache starting at her temples. *Why the hell is he backtracking? Did someone get to him?* She tried to be nonchalant. "You're first on our list. We're understaffed and can only do so much."

A loud foghorn blasted its mournful call across the dock. Jack ran out, shouting at the men, "Get yer asses in gear. I need truck guys to be out of here by nine."

Celia and Marcy followed. Some drivers were lined up, smoking in the cabs of their flat beds. A few drivers, toward the end of the line, had stepped out and were howling at some joke.

Celia reached into her doctor's bag and pulled out a handful of brochures. "Did you arrange for the workers to gather for a few words?"

"Jesus, woman. I got too much stuff. Do whatcha gotta do, but don't blast it all over the whole place."

Celia's jaw dropped. "How are we going to advertise a meeting? We need to hand out these brochures and tell them where the meeting will be."

"Can we have a place to hold the meeting?" Marcy asked in her sugary sweet voice.

Jack stared at her. "You gotta get outta my hair. Next door. It's empty." He hurried away.

"We'll put a note on the door," Marcy said.

Once inside, Marcy pulled Celia's computer out of her bag. They opened chairs that lined one wall. Marcy read her speech from the computer. Celia first put a brochure on each chair and next tacked fliers on the wall about a series of lectures to educate everyone on the spread of hepatitis C. The fliers asked people to inform each other about the program. The first meeting would be held at 10 a.m. that day.

They hurried out of the office, settled on a spot where the ship was docking and started handing out notices. Many men refused to take them and made snide remarks about letting in religious zealots and kooks. One guy glanced at it and stared at them.

"What the fuck is this? What outbreak?"

"Just come to the meeting and we'll inform you. Bring your fellow workers."

He stuffed the paper in his pocket and walked off.

Celia saw three cranes removing twenty-foot containers from the ship and placing them on the beds of eighteen-wheeler trucks. She handed Marcy the pamphlets. "Keep giving them out. I'm going to check out the containers."

Celia watched the men guiding the cranes, making sure the containers landed properly. When they all appeared to be engrossed, she slipped away and wandered over to the rows of parked trucks.

"Whatcha want, sister?" a truck driver called, leaning his head out the window.

"Uh, just curious about how the system works. What's inside?"

"I freelance. We just take 'em to whoever ordered them. Them other trucks with names on them are owned by companies." He looked around. "Get outta the way or some drivers might hit you. They do their runs without much sleep."

"Yo, doc," Jack yelled at her, gripping a clipboard. "Move it. My insurance company will put my head on a platter, which would make my wife happy. Anything happens to yuz guys, my ass is on the line. Get."

Celia hustled over to Marcy. *Is Jack chasing us away to keep us from seeing anything suspicious? Does he know about the women? Is he in on it? Are we even at the right pier?*

"Didn't see any air holes, but I can't get to the top," Celia said to Marcy. "If we call the police without being positive, we'll wind up screwed. I don't know what compelled me to come here without being sure."

"You took a shot. We're getting the lay of the land, and a better handle on what's coming down."

"Right." Celia shielded her eyes from the now blazing sun.

Marcy smiled. "I had swarms of guys coming over. Didn't mind it a bit." Marcy handed the remaining pamphlets to Celia. "Are you sure you know what to say at the lecture?"

"I've been practicing for days. They have a real problem here that they've kept under cover. It's a necessary mission we're on, though inadvertent. And remember all we talked about. The symptoms are: tiredness, upset stomach, yellow skin and eyes, dark-colored urine, weight loss. Untreated, there can be serious damage to the liver."

"These guys are reported to be big drinkers, you'd think the idea of hep C would scare the bejesus out of them," Marcy said.

"We might not find out much today. We might get more with the hidden bug under Jack's desk. After the lecture, we'll head back and tune in. If that's not working, we need some other plan."

"We shouldn't be so out in the open. We might meet up with Vladimir."

"Right." Celia took Marcy by the arm and headed toward the room. She needed to practice.

Chapter 29

Back in their quarters, Celia sat at the table in front of a laptop, thinking she and Marcy had done a good setup at the pier that morning, but little more than that. A few at the lecture of twenty-five hulking men had already experienced symptoms like persistent fever and lack of appetite. On a break she tuned her earphones in to the micro-recorder. She only heard Jack's occasional shouting orders and in between, only static.

The lecture had gone off without a hitch, but she had no luck figuring out what shipping container held what. Legit or not, the containers all looked the same, even those with company names emblazoned on them. Not one in sight with Vladimir's name.

It was now 2 p.m. and she knew Allison was in Justin's office, researching how the hospital's new audits were being conducted.

I hope Justin can get hold of a copy of the fired forensic auditor's draft report on Rudrow finances.

Marcy rested in her cubby reading a Vogue magazine Stanton had brought her a few days ago. He'd not shown up yet today, needing to buy more clothes. She tried to tell herself that he had a tad of a life outside, too. Maybe he found someone who wanted to play tennis with him. She'd played tennis with him many times. *On second thought, I don't want him to play tennis with anyone else.*

He'd mentioned a park in Fitler Square that had two courts. For just a moment she thought she might sneak out—no, no. Too dangerous. Celia missed tennis, dancing the cha-cha with her friends, and painting, for which she had no energy. She especially missed doing the cha-cha, feeling the rhythm coursing throughout her body while everyday problems floated into the ether.

Just as she closed her computer, Stanton walked in. "How's my girl?" he asked, setting a box of bread and lunch meats on the table.

"Stanton, I was thinking about you."

"Oh, really." He jiggled his eyebrows.

"I know you need some fun. Thought you might find a partner for tennis."

"No. I don't want to mingle with anyone."

"God, we are so locked in. I'd love to paint, but…it just seems sometimes that we'll either get caught, or be on the run for the rest of our lives. Those gangs are relentless. I know I can't stop the trafficking, but I'd like to make a dent."

He took her into his arms and stroked her hair. "I'm here for you. We'll get out and have a nice life together."

"Ever the optimist." Yet, the idea so appealed, tears blurred her vision. "You can always fix my computer."

He stepped back, placing his hand over his heart. "And you can always seduce me."

Celia sighed.

"How is Marcy holding up?" he asked.

"She loves being a doctor, and she loves men making goo-goo eyes at her. Believe me, you gave her the best present. She's reading *Vogue*."

Stanton reached back into a box. "Got these for you." He pulled out tubes of oil paints, brushes, turpentine, and linseed oil.

She stood so quickly her chair turned over. "You sweetheart. I was longing for these." She pointed to the concrete wall she had envisioned as a mural. Energy streaks ran through her.

After lunch, she set up her paints, squeezing dabs of sky blue, white, black, maroon, and pink paint on a nearby board to use as a palette. With her largest brush she made swoops of pink paint for the background of four feet by three feet. On top of that, in thick slabs with a smaller brush she swept on maroon mixed with blue. Constant, quick brushstrokes suddenly produced a child's head. Then swirls of circles of black turned into curly hair, eyes, nose, but the lips manifested in a sweetness of lines that appeared to be in motion— talking to her. Although Rasheed's hair had fallen out she envisioned it all grown back. After forty-five minutes, she stopped. Dropping the palette, she sat on the floor, legs folded under her. She felt a huge feeling of release of tension as though she sat on a bed of roses.

"That's Rasheed," Stanton said, awe lighting up his face.

All was quiet at Rudrow as it awaited the outcome of the mystery audit. Two days had passed since the announcement of a new forensic accountant. Short time for such a complex task. Worse news, Barry was to oversee it. The results of this audit appeared predictable. How would Ramon and Vladimir legitimize the theft? The atmosphere from the top tier seemed eerily quiet. Celia clamped her teeth so hard they felt wired together.

In her cubby, Celia began drawing Stanton's face on the sketch pad. She caught the tilt of his head, the slightly larger right eye, and his direct gaze. As she drew the softness of his mouth, she emphasized the corner with the tiny scar. The more anxious she became the faster she drew.

At three o'clock, Celia put away her drawing pad and googled websites on hospital theft and how supplies could be taken out without the robbery being exposed. As the rumor went, in some public hospitals, audits allowed for a certain amount of missing inventory to be overlooked before alarms were sounded. It wasn't uncommon for narcotics to be stolen from hospitals and sold to smaller, independent pharmacies and corrupt physicians, or on the open market. The word "sample" on any of the pills got shaved off with a razor blade and resold. A few overseers turned a blind eye to the theft because they got a cut.

Her fingers flew as Justin burst into the space. Even under the dim, yellowish lighting, his face looked collapsed and camera-flash white.

"I received a letter from Ramon, and the board of directors. They've also confiscated my computer. It had all the receipts that I put out for purchases."

"How did that work?"

"I'd order a full load of equipment then receive receipts for lesser amounts on equipment. They told me the missing units were canceled for budget reasons. And that they received discounts on lesser pieces, thus the smaller amounts on receipts. I was left with receipts for a lot less than I originally ordered. Obviously, the canceled items were still ordered and sent elsewhere. So, I am being held responsible for stealing the difference from the original order and the one much less. Sure looks like I did the nasty deed since my name is on both orders."

She took the envelope from his trembling hand and felt her cheeks burn. Due to the new audit, the hospital was investigating missing ordered items and Justin was to meet the administration to tell what he knew. Justin's signature is on both large and small receipts.

Barry's put his two cents in putting the "okay" stamp that pointed straight to Justin. He even had the audacity to suggest that Justin might be in cahoots with unnamed others. Also, he presented an account for a sham corporation in an offshore bank. Something told Celia that this was the easy part, with the real destruction yet to come.

Justin's eyes glistened, and he swiped at them with his hand. "This is my worst nightmare. I could go to jail."

Celia walked to the edge of the living area. She looked around to see if anyone had followed him. Nothing. She walked back, reminding Justin that large orders of equipment and drugs were going right into Vladimir's fleet of trucks and shipping containers. He surely laundered money with a sham corporation to hide millions of dollars of illicit cash. "It's time for Stanton to use his forensic electronic background to find the CEO of that sham corporation," she said.

Justin ran his hands over his hair. "Why can't we just tell the police? Call the newspapers."

"They set the stage to make it point to you, Justin. Vladimir has a ton of legitimacy about him. He's a philanthropist, on hospital boards, appears to be a legitimate businessman, and who knows what else. I'll fight very hard to find proof. You appear to be their scapegoat and they can make it look like you rented the containers via Vladimir Stompovich."

"What do I do?"

"Can you get your computer back so we can root through the receipts? Stanton can help with those things. Maybe work with criminal lawyers in Pennsylvania. Be careful about coming down here.

They'll put a tail on you for sure. Act naive. Say you never met me and that I took Allie away on a trip." She felt her body tremble and tried to compose herself. "Right now, I think we're okay, because they would have been down by now. Keep me posted."

"I'm not in the loop anymore, and I can't promise I'll get my computer back," Justin said in a rattled voice. "But there were rumblings even before you came."

"Like what?" Celia asked.

"When I thought the hospital might be in danger of closing a year after Vladimir joined, I asked Sam, the assistant comptroller, what was going on. He's the one who gave me the data spreadsheet."

"And?"

"He said he thought someone had done creative bookkeeping and that Barry kept it secret. He planned on changing jobs and he's happy to get out of here. He swore me to secrecy. Said he'd be canned if I told—lose his pension. He has three kids in college so I kept my mouth shut. I put it out of my mind. Now they want to hang me." Celia took a deep breath, trying to focus. Justin's revelation rattled her. "We've got to move fast. Maybe you can help me get into Vladimir's office, then Ramon's."

"I heard Ramon is taking a month's sabbatical."

"The gruesome threesome, trying to dodge."

"Uh…what if…if I can't get out of it?"

"I promise you will." Celia had no idea if she spoke the truth.

Chapter 30

Celia snuck up to the pediatric floor. Rasheed and his illness had invaded her dreams and she no longer cared about the risk. Through the glass she saw a male nurse leaning over Rasheed's bed. Distress filled Rasheed's eyes. From time to time, he writhed in his bed. An older couple was there too—a woman in a gray wool coat leaned against the shoulder of a man in a black denim jacket over which peeked a gray ponytail. Tears spilled down the woman's cheeks as she leaned forward to kiss Rasheed.

Minutes later, the man said something to the woman and, holding her close, escorted her from the room. When they walked past her, she smelled the faintest hint of lavender.

She slipped inside Rasheed's room. A series of shrill beeps and sounds rose as a nurse adjusted the tubes. He nodded at her. "That's about all we can do right now," the nurse said, and he was gone.

Celia's legs turned to rubber when she saw Rasheed's immobile face and fluttering eyes. She pressed his hand. "Sweetheart, I'm here," she whispered.

Rasheed blinked and gave her the barest smile.

"Don't go. Please honey. I love you. Your family loves you."

"Mommy," he whispered. "I love you."

Rasheed's skin had an ashen pallor. He closed his eyes and his chest wasn't moving. The heart monitor had a flat line.

"Honey, you are deeply loved. Mr. Mime and I will always love you. We will always be with you." Celia thought she might keel over. She rang the buzzer for the nurse and when he arrived, she asked him to stay by Rasheed's side.

"Who are you?" asked the nurse. "I don't recognize you."

Celia swallowed. "Someone who loves Rasheed."

"Sorry, but you'll have to leave if you're not a family member."

"I am a family member—in my heart."

"I'll still have to ask you to leave." He looked at all the meters hooked up to Rasheed and shook his head. "Poor kid."

When she reached their quarters, she put her head down on the table, and sobbed. That would be the last time she'd see Rasheed again. The hopelessness of life, the futility strangled her. What was the point?

Her chest ached, her sadness edging toward rage. Tears streamed down her cheeks. All the cruelty in the world. Where would it stop? She needed air. *Screw the danger.*

She walked out quickly, staying close to the lane of stores across the way. The fresh, cool air tasted like pears as she took in deep breaths. She ducked down a narrow, quiet residential street. After walking for half an hour beneath ginkgo trees shaking the last of their golden leaves, she made her way back to the hospital. Some workers were on the loading platform. She saw a nurse waiting on the side. Did she need air? Was the stress of work choking her?

At their hideaway, she found Stanton chatting with Marcy. She told them about the implications Vladimir had launched at Justin. She didn't mention Rasheed. *Not yet.*

Stanton's face hardened. "He held back telling us about his earlier run-in with the comptroller office."

"I'm beginning to understand the doctor mentality. It's hard work, but their intense focus from high school through medical school and residencies keeps them insulated from the real world," Celia said in a tired voice. "They often never learn street smarts."

Marcy piped in, "I agree with your diagnosis, Dr. Celia. I can't believe he'd stab us in the back."

Celia felt light-headed and plopped into a chair.

"No one leaves this place for any reason," Stanton said sternly. "Especially now."

"Stanton brought cans of tuna," Marcy said. "I'll make a tuna noodle casserole. Got to practice for when we get back to Florida." Her eyes blinked rapidly.

It's all about when we get back. A tuna noodle casserole, reminders of home, of the early years when that dish was popular. Oh, it was a creamy mess and I loved it.

"So, Mr. Computer," Marcy continued. "What's your plan for tomorrow and the next day?"

"We have to keep listening in on the bug, see if we learn anything. I'm still trying to get the true owner of the offshore bank. I told you how complicated that is so when we have more time I'll go into details. Made some headway." He opened a can of tuna.

Celia welcomed the reprieve about Rasheed. "Stanton, you're not just a pretty face. You are opening that can of tuna like a pro."

"Lady, I was reared on survival tactics. Learned how to use can openers early."

"I'm still learning about you," Celia said, faking an upbeat voice. "You had parents out partying all night and sleeping all day. It's abuse. How did you survive?"

"It's survive or go under. I like to swim."

Celia's cell phone rang. Her back stiffened.

"Who has the number?" Marcy asked.

"Allie's the only one."

Celia took in a deep breath. "What's up, Allie?"

"Been hiding out in Justin's office, trying to hack into hospital computers. I saw a group of men combing the floors. They walk in and out of rooms. Not a soul is stopping them. That bastard has too much clout."

Celia gripped the phone, her heart banging against her chest. "Get back here before they see you."

Marcy looked aghast. "We need to switch gears."

"Put another batch of disposable phones on the shopping list," Celia said, grabbing a pen. "Then hightail it out of here. Don't come back till we see how safe it is around here."

There was a long hesitation. "I will not leave you all alone."

"We'll keep in touch. Your going in and out exposes us now." Stanton's eyes reflected Celia's dread.

He pulled her to the side. "I understood why you kept me out of your life before. We both needed time. Now it's all hands on deck. I stay."

The emotion in Stanton's voice startled Celia. "Check into a hotel."

"No There must be something we can do right now!" His voice dipped deeper. "I could do something if I had some information."

"I've been thinking about a keystroke logger. You remember I used one during out fiasco in Florida. There's some we can get but not everything."

He scratched his cheek. "Right. It will only give you what she types. We also need what comes in and out like emails. But we don't have her password."

"Geez. I found one in her office. Not sure if it's the one she uses."

Stanton slapped himself on his forehead. "Why didn't I ask if you had anything resembling that? That's incredible."

"Who knows if it will work."

"It will be a bonanza if it does. I pay for a premium spyware that will allow us to record what's typed, emails both sent and received, chats, screenshots, and other things. Her computer won't detect the spyware. Do you know what kind of computer it is?"

"A PC. Hell, we don't need a keystroke logger? I am so behind the times."

"Don't jump the gun. We need to get into her office…"

"I can handle that. Hope it works."

Celia felt awful about treating Stanton like her lackey. *I've become a woman so possessed who destroys love when it comes too close. Seeking justice rises above everything else to the point of smothering my emotions. Marcy could go to her family and hide. Instead, she's here with me, trying to help the immediate world far from her son and grandchild.*

Do I kill love because I don't think I deserve it? Am I still guilty about how poorly I raised Allie? Why didn't I wake up to Gabe's shenanigans before he died? And why think about it so often? Guilt?

She recalled sweet memories she'd had with Allie when she was a child. The parks, playground, zoo, and she loved the ballet. Then Gabe had taken over and pushed her away from me. *All I can do now is get my daughter out of the danger I've created. And then there's Rasheed.*

"Why so quiet all of a sudden?" asked Stanton.

Celia took Stanton's hands in hers. "I'm trying to get some insights into myself. Not doing that well."

"Just relax now. We can all find glitzes in ourselves."

"There's something else. It's Rasheed," she said, inhaling deeply. That was all she could get out. Stanton's bowed his head and put his hand over his eyes. She didn't want to talk anymore, didn't want to think. Now, she only craved sleep.

Chapter 31

Allison slept, the sound of deep breathing emanating from her cubby. Celia was with Marcy, haggling about what to do if their hiding place was outed. Which hotel would be safest?

Soon, Allison joined them, kicking up dust as she dragged her feet. No matter how much cleaning they did, the place was sooty again in a few hours.

Celia grinned and patted Allie's stomach that now showed a lovely roundness. Three months and counting.

"You haven't gotten much pampering." Celia's throat felt scorched.

"Justin wants me to stay hidden." Allie crossed her hands in her lap.

"We are discussing going to a hotel if we get ratted out," Marcy said. "We'd take Justin. He can deliver your baby."

"It's been a long time since he delivered a baby, but we've got six months to go, and I'm not planning to have a baby in a hotel room. Anything going on with bugging the pier?"

"Totally silent for days. They might have found it." Celia marveled at how much more passive Allie had become despite the imminent danger. *Is it hormones or resignation?*

Celia rose and went to the bathroom sink to wash dishes. It took her to a focused, dulled state which gave her comfort for the moment. Her dulled vision caught Rasheed's wall portrait and she brightened. She had only known him briefly, but his innocence stayed with her, as did the fact that there was so much cruelty in the world. She glanced at Marcy and Allison.

"I bribed the cleaning woman, and she'll unlock Svetlana's office tonight at nine." Celia cleared her throat.

"We need to get Justin's computer back," Allison said. "There has to be something to prove his innocence."

"Let me come with you to make sure this isn't a trap," Marcy said.

"No. It might freak the cleaning woman out." Celia cleared her throat again. "I'm going to meet Stanton who I'll sneak in with me. He's going to try to insert spyware into Svetlana's computer."

"Geez," Marcy shouted. "Won't they'll be able to detect it?"

"Stanton has state-of-the-art spyware that prevents that."

Allie pivoted to her laptop. "You'll need her password. This won't work."

"We'll see." Celia kept a close watch on the time. At five of nine, she took the emergency stairs, stopping on the third floor. Sure enough, there was Svetlana talking to Vladimir in front of his office. *What are they up to at this hour?*

She prepared to run, but they walked away in the other direction. Celia tapped on the door to the walk-in closet. The housekeeper led her down the hall, opened Svetlana's office, and indicated she'd wait in the utility closet. "Thank you," whispered Celia, and she slipped inside.

In a short time, Stanton knocked three times and entered. "Did anyone see you?"

"Don't think so."

"We don't want her spooked, seeing a strange man."

"It's so simple if you have the password. Fingers crossed." He tried the password Celia gave him. It worked. "Hooray." He inserted a thumb drive. "I'm inserting spyware into her computer which gives me access, as I told you."

He had a guideline of several steps and he went through them quickly. "This system avoids her anti-spyware detecting my software." Ten minutes elapsed. "Finished. Let's get the hell out of here."

Celia balled her hands and waved them in glee. Stanton grabbed her and kissed her hard. She loved it. They had to leave.

Her forensic high-tech skills were certainly growing. *It's time I start my own detective agency.* She smiled at her nonsense.

Very early the next morning, Celia looked at Stanton's laptop as she sat next to him. The software Stanton loaded into Svetlana's computer was doing its job. Page after page of their emails showed up. Svetlana, or an assistant, was hard at work.

She leaned closer to Stanton's computer as though the device whispered sweet music in her ear. Marcy watched over her shoulder. Stanton sat on a stool in front of his computer. Allison hid out with Justin who called in an obstetrician friend to examine her. He felt she needed a lot more care than he could give.

Stanton pointed to the monitor. Every purchase order had two sets of receipts. A little further on Celia saw a list: an ultrasound, a MRI machine, a CT scanner, a case of pacemakers, four ventilators, a large box of stethoscopes, boxes upon boxes of fentanyl, oxycodone, methadone, morphine, and assorted other controlled substances.

They agreed that the monies that poured into Vladimir's foundation came from sex trafficking and this hospital theft business. It seemed Vladimir had created ways to make illegal multimillions and then needed ways to launder the bucks. His donations turned out to be chump change. It was clear to Celia now.

Stanton said, "It's working smoothly."

Celia smiled. "I'm forever grateful. Look at this." She turned to Marcy. "We're getting everything from Svetlana's computer."

"All those wares are making me weary," Marcy said.

For the next hour she and Stanton scrutinized emails and texts. One spreadsheet noted electronic payments from Vladimir's charitable foundation to the hospital at three million, plus an additional two million from another charity that Vladimir operated.

"I have to interrupt. How in the world did you get emails exchanged between Ramon, Barry, Vladimir, and Svetlana? Is it magic?" Marcy asked.

"Trade secret," he said, bringing his eyebrow together in a frown. "That's the forensic stuff I do." He smiled.

"Well, isn't this the proof we need?" Marcy said, shifting her reading glasses. "I'm not such a dumb head."

"This is illegal. Celia is my partner in crime. Hacking another computer in Pennsylvania without permission is a third-class felony, punishable by up to seven years in prison." He looked at Celia. "Wouldn't she look great in orange?"

"Stop your silliness and look at this. There was an email from Justin, asking Barry for permission to order a large number of state-of-the-art medical devices and equipment. Barry wrote back to Justin that Ramon had cut the order drastically. Justin sent a smaller revised order. We know Barry kept both the receipts and that's probably why they confiscated Justin's computer. He no longer has the proof that they put through both orders."

"The big order was sent to rented hangers at the pier in Justin's name," Stanton said, his lips pulled pencil-thin. "They made it look as though Justin was stealing the larger order that the hospital paid for."

"All of these messages that didn't go directly to Svetlana were cc'd to her. It almost looks like Vladimir uses her computer as his personal database," Celia mused.

"Justin had done what he was asked. He reduced the order and sent it to Barry for approval and purchase," Stanton said. "The smaller order came directly to the hospital."

"Okay," Celia said. "I'm following it."

Stanton cleared his throat and said, "Both purchase orders were written with Justin's signature who signed off on both. I'm sure the owners, V & S Industries, are unbeknownst to Justin. The smaller order went to Rudrow. Rudrow paid for both orders. Three years of that brought them down financially. Those scumbags made Justin the fall guy."

Stanton kept his focus on the keyboard that he attacked with an intensity that Celia hadn't seen before. He worked faster as pages flipped on the monitor. He stopped and looked up.

"Here it is. Justin is named CEO of a sham corporation where they sent the large order and called it Shaker Hangar. After that, they used sham corporations in Justin's name to send a small amount of money to offshore banks to make it look like he sent and was hiding his windfall. Their name, V & S Industries, never showed up.

"Wow," Stanton said, "Not only did Ramon detour items from Justin's big order to V & S, the order got sold and shipped to foreign customers." Stanton worked the keys. "That made witnesses to the crime almost impossible and costly to find for authorities."

"I get it," Marcy said. "The bottom line is they pulled off a crime that was sinking the hospital and blamed it on Justin."

"Bravo my dear friend. You are brilliant." Celia hugged Marcy. Marcy stepped back and tapped her chest with her hand.

"We'll break it down some more later," Stanton said. "I've got more work to do. There were large pharmacy orders for opioids as well. All on Svetlana's computer."

Celia's shoulders drooped. "Poor Justin."

"I wish we could use this. It's stunning to come up with what we need," Marcy said.

"At least we've got some answers. I'm hoping we can use the information somehow."

Celia focused on a page Stanton had brought up. Next to each item was a different Eastern European address and price for each piece of equipment. "The ostensible buyers paid more than the retail price in the USA for the stolen goods."

Celia put the data into her own flash drive. It was outrageous how they'd fooled a smart guy like Justin and still no exoneration.

"We're stuck," Marcy said in nearly a whisper. "We'll never get out."

"Were they laundering money through the hospital? Just stealing? Both?" Celia asked Stanton later that night. Allison and Marcy were asleep.

"It's a vast scheme," Stanton said. "Vladimir sells in foreign countries, not here. Money goes from sham corporation to sham corporation and finally, hard-to-trace accounts in offshore banks. It takes work to launder big sums. He might run cash through casinos or restaurants where fake bills are printed to show inflated revenues. Vladimir's foundation donations come from mysterious sources. Given all this information, I suspect the donor list is phony—part of a scheme to float illicit money through the system undetected."

"Setting Justin up as the fall guy meant Vladimir has found another scheme to deflect the money made here," Celia said.

"Justin could be charged, arrested. Criminal attorneys, forensic accountants, and a long court trial costing hundreds of thousands of dollars. Not to mention, the IRS. The debt will be massive for monies he never received. If, by some miracle, Justin is vindicated and the scheme thrown back at them, Vladimir and company will know how to slip away out of the country. On the other hand, if Justin is taken down, Vladimir becomes the hero."

"They beat the hell out of us every time we get somewhere," Celia said, anger turning her voice into a growl. "They've created a fake paper trail to open an investigation against Justin. They've buttressed themselves very well," Celia said. "What a fucking shit show."

Please, please, Svetlana. Give me something so we can expose this fiasco in real time. Help us draw a solid line connecting all these dots, a way to use this material.

Another site produced, Foundation Directory Online. Celia located the names of donors to the Stompovich Foundation. She then googled the names, one by one. About half were dead and there was little available on the others.

"This is the definition of phony donor list." *Her fingers itched to make the call to authorities. But they can then point the finger at Stanton, Justin, and herself opening a hornet's nest they didn't need.*

Late in the evening, Celia called Justin.

"Man, am I glad to hear your voice." He sounded as though someone had punched him in the stomach. "I got an official letter two hours ago from the FBI saying I was a target of an investigation for theft of hospital drugs and diagnostic devices. They mentioned me as the CEO of a company I never heard of. Offshore banks? Hangars at piers?" He was breathing fast. The words tumbled out. "Talk to me."

"It's totally phony," Celia said. "Stanton found that out. We can't use the info because he hacked it."

"I contacted that lawyer Stanton recommended, and he said I could be charged with RICO because it went across state lines and I had co-conspirators. That's the racketeering charge—much, uh, much worse. The higher ups and the board put me in the middle of this. I hope they don't drag Allie in."

"Where are you? In your office?"

"Yes. What is going on, for fuck's sake?"

"They've doctored documents that point to you. Stanton will call you and fill you in. Just keep on working as if nothing happened. We'll figure this out."

Marcy stood with a questioning look on her face. "Let's see if something came in from the pier," she said. "I know we took for granted they were useless."

Celia turned on the mini-receiver. There was mostly static, and when it stopped, the line went dead.

Allison looked fatigued. She sat across from Marcy and Celia. "We should just throw in the towel and contact the FBI," Allison said. "We somehow have to prove his innocense."

Celia could almost smell Vladimir's expensive musky cologne. Just imagining it burned her nose. "We'll be fodder for them."

"I can't leave my children again," Marcy said. "We're going in whole hog to take these fuckwits down or we're goners."

Celia smiled gloomily at Allison. "You already know what I'm about to ask."

"I know. After you told me how this operates, I did some research about when containers arrive, but that doesn't matter unless we catch a container with the women."

"Let's do a quick once over to see if we can locate a fatal flaw in their armor," Celia said. "We have the *what* and the *how*, but not the *where* and *when*. When do the women and girls arrive? Where do they live here in the United States? How do we expose them when almost every major city is involved? Where do they hide these women? That is key to getting proof if no one will testify."

Allison shrugged in a helpless gesture. She stood and pointed to her cubby then leaned toward Celia. "Justin is willing to leave the country. Between us, we have enough money to go abroad. Justin can get a job in Europe. He speaks French and Spanish. We'd all go."

Marcy stood.

"Sit down, both of you," Celia said in a determined tone. "Allie, Europe is a no-go. These organizations reach throughout the world. If anything, his grip is stronger there than it is here. No country is off-limits to them. Obviously, there is a sick demand they are happy to meet. "Let's start from the beginning." Both Marcy and Allison groaned.

Chapter 32

Thursday at 4 a.m. the sound of static awakened Celia. She saw that the noise came from the mini-receiver, boot steps thumping on the floor. She sat in front of the receiver waiting for the next sound. At 5 a.m., she heard unintelligible voices, maybe three or four people. Hard to make out, but she thought she heard one voice above the others shouting, "Looks like we have an arrival due at 7 a.m.." As she listened, she saw a shadow at the entrance. She jumped up. It was Stanton.

"You nearly scared me to death. Why are you up so early?"

"Why do you think so? I knew you'd be trying to do something foolish. You shouldn't go." He stood, legs apart as though blocking her.

"Please," Celia whispered as though she'd be heard by the port people. "I've got to go."

"I'm coming with you," Stanton said.

"No. They know Marcy and me. You'll arouse suspicion."

"I'll stay in the parking lot again. Any sign of trouble, I call the police." He handed her another signal button to ring for help as well as the gun.

Her stomach clenched. "I hate the idea of using this." She held it gingerly on the frame of the trigger as it dangled.

"I hope you don't ever have to use the gun. But you've got the skills. I was impressed with your ability when we were taking lessons at the shooting range. It's horrible to think, but if you're in serious danger I say use it."

"I was a sharpshooter back then. I've never wanted to use a gun, but after the mess at Boca Pelicano Palms…" *Oh, what's happened to me?*

While Stanton went into his cubicle to change clothes, Celia stuffed the gun in the pocket of the jacket she wore over her usual scrubs and lab coat. Stanton was dressed in jeans, a T-shirt, windbreaker, and baseball cap. "You set?"

"Let's wait until the morning shift comes on at about six. There'll be less foot traffic outside while they clock in and have coffee. I want to give Marcy a break and not wake her."

Marcy joined them. "I heard you two. And I'm ready. And I smelled the coffee."

No one protested. After breakfast, they headed for the pier. The guard at the gate recognized them and waved them in.

Marcy trailed behind Celia as they approached the gate. A voice in Celia's head repeated Stanton's warning. *Release, aim first, and quickly pull back the safety. I know that but repetition doesn't help when my nerves are jangling.*

Thoughts of Rasheed came to her. "There is no rhyme or reason, is there?"

"What?" Marcy asked.

"Nothing. Just trying to calm myself. Are you okay? You can back out right now before we go in."

"I'm just dandy."

"I really miss our old life," Celia said. "I will never complain about anything again, if we get out of this."

"You'll still complain. And I'll love it."

"Last chance, Marcy. Go back to the car."

"Shush."

Her last thought before going through the gate surprised her. *I wish we were back in our special hidden world in the basement. It's kind of a cocoon.*

Celia waved to Jack, and he waved back.

"How's it goin' with the hep C stuff?" he asked.

"Good," Celia said loudly above the noise of cranes. "Sending these guys to the hospital for shots was a blessing." Justin told her quite a few men showed up for exams and shots.

"Yeah, good for you, doc." He turned away and looked over the water. It was clear of any large ships carrying containers.

She and Marcy entered the makeshift office they'd used for their last lecture. Celia let out a ragged sigh. "Well, we got this far." She picked up an old newspaper from the floor and wiped the foggy window. It didn't help much. She kept at it until they could look out.

"Got my fingers crossed," Marcy announced.

Please, let this be the right shipment. We're almost out of time. Celia fingered the cold gun handle. "Here we go."

At seven, they spotted a large ship towed by two tugboats heading toward their pier. About a dozen men gathered near the apron where three container cranes stood in formation like protectors of the pier. Trucks edged forward and formed a single file line alongside the cranes. The massive ship was brought to berth and anchored. Cranes swung over its bow and began the robotics of clamping on the containers and swinging them onto the appropriate truck beds. Stevedores communicated via two-way handheld radios to direct the unloading. As each truck secured their cargo, they drove away, giving way to the next in line.

Jack stood beside a large machine on the dock. It was marked "X-ray." He stopped every fourth or fifth truck. Celia knew that X-rays were used to detect illegally shipped items: guns, drugs, and humans. When a truck marked "V & S" stopped, Jack waved him on.

"Take a look at that? No X-ray for them. Coincidence or deliberate?" Celia whispered.

Marcy bit her cuticle. "How about we use the doctor stuff. I can say I have directions from the US government to inspect the merchandise in the containers. And the crew for possible symptoms of hepatitis C?"

"If you do that, I can sneak around looking for air holes on the sides of containers." Celia said, feeling certain she'd find something today.

"It's worth a try. There might be representatives of the shipping company around, or owners of the goods in other containers. And some of Vladimir's guys are likely here. If they know some containers hold humans, they might not let us near them."

"Let's get moving and give our spiel," Marcy said.

After corralling six beefy workers, Celia and Mary spoke about the dangers of hep C while Jack stared at them. When the group dispersed, Celia and Marcy hustled to the lineup of flatbed trucks. Celia told Marcy to keep Jack busy while she checked things out. Celia remained in earshot.

Marcy edged up to Jack and engaged him. "Jack sweetie, how can we get into the containers to capture some rats? It's been shown that rats carry viruses related to hep C." Celia knew rats carried hep E, not hep C, but she figured Jack wouldn't know. "I need blood samples."

"No fucking way." He turned his back to her. "Only US Customs or owners can open doors. Besides, we have no rats. They check it out real clean."

"There are rats in containers when there is food. It's a public health hazard."

Celia kept her ear pitched in the direction of conversation while she tried to check the containers.

He spun around and narrowed his eyes. "Get a warrant. Insurance wouldn't cover you if you get hurt. Just do your yakking and then leave."

After he slammed the door to his office, Celia made a beeline to the crane supervisor.

"Look, this guy, Vladimir Stompovich, who owns a bunch of trucks, is on the board of Rudrow Hospital where I work." Celia choked on her words. "Um, the problem is he thinks one of his drivers might have hepatitis C." She flashed her ID.

"Oh, yeah. Heard about you docs. His trucks are being loaded now."

"Can you point them out to me?"

"Yeah. Those three." He pointed to an empty parking spot. "Hey, they're driving out of the here now. I'll make sure our bathrooms are off-limits to his drivers." He went back to directing and Celia ran back. She tried to get to more containers piled on the side.

Celia felt something cold on her neck and jumped. A man stood behind her with a gun pressed on her neck. She repressed a scream. "What the hell are you doing?" she shouted.

"You lookin' for Vladimir's drivers? Who are you, bitch?" Although he was a hulk of a guy with no definition of waist or neck, his voice pitched high.

The supervisor walked up to the man and brushed his hand away.

"Cut the shit, Dom. She's the doc helping with hep C problem. One of your drivers might have it. That's why she's askin'."

"Sorry, lady. We have expensive cargo and we watch out so, like, no one robs them? We don't know who the hell you are."

"Please don't interfere with our work," Celia spoke firmly, as the man gave her the fish eye. "I'm with the federal government. CDC."

"Okay, okay." He looked angry now. "We gotta be careful about criminals hijacking us. They send shills to scope us out, askin' all kinds of shit." He put his gun inside the back of his pants.

Celia bit her lip and agonized about how she might get inside the containers before the trucks hauled them away. They moved fast.

As Celia neared the car, Stanton waved to her and started to get out. Marcy straggled behind. Celia turned and saw Marcy's startled expression. Celia thought her howl was a joke and was reminded of Munch's painting, *The Scream*. Something hit Celia from behind that felt like she'd been struck by hundred pound weights, and she went down. The man who threatened her at the pier had struck her on the back of her head with the gun handle.

Stanton burst into a run, holding a canister of pepper spray in one hand. As Dom pointed his gun at Celia's head, she heard the hissing of aerosol. The man stumbled backward, pressing his eyes. He raised his gun and fired blindly in Stanton's direction. Stanton reeled back, dropping the canister. Celia crawled to where Stanton landed, blood dribbing down her forehead, scissored pain gripping her head. Dom spun around, rubbing his eyes, the gun in his hand raised upward. Droplets of pepper spray suspended in the air burned Celia's eyes.

"Stanton?" she gasped.

He grabbed her shoulder then someone kicked him. A shot rang out.

Celia screamed as her arms were yanked behind her. A second man was stuffing a cloth into her mouth. It tasted of rancid oil. He tried tying her hands, but Celia fought him.

The man who kicked Stanton was pummeling him, but he managed to kick the pepper spray toward Marcy. She grabbed the can. Dom headed toward Marcy, dragging Stanton by the neck of his jacket. Marcy doused the man's face, droplets dripping off his chin as he yowled.

Stanton rolled over and tried to stand. He fell back down. Celia yelled for help.

"Shut the fuck up, you old hags," the man shouted, eyes blinking, face reddened, and coughing. He looked at Celia. "I'll fucking kill your daughter and the baby," his cigarette-roughened voice snarled. "Where are you hiding?"

"Did you call us old hags?" Marcy sprayed his face again. The other man pounced toward her and she pressed the button toward his face. His hands were in a clawlike position aimed at her throat. He fell back as though struck in the face. He rubbed his eyes wildly.

Celia ripped the dirty cloth from her mouth. Both men were on the ground, grunting. Celia kicked the gun out of the man's hand as he pointed it toward them.

Stanton managed to stand, clutching his blood-soaked jacket around his left shoulder. "Run."

They started running toward the car.

One man grabbed Celia's ankle. She twisted around and kicked him in the ribs, feeling a sickening crunch of bone. Marcy sprayed him again.

They reached the car. Marcy jumped into the driver's seat. Neither Celia or Stanton seemed able to drive. She slammed the accelerator pedal.

"We need to get you to a doctor, Stanton" Celia said.

"No. Just a shoulder flesh wound." He raised his arm. His white shirt and windbreaker were bright with blood. "Ouch. Are my gals okay?"

Celia lifted his shirt. His abdomen was scratched and bleeding. "Do your ribs hurt?"

"Yup. But I'm sure not broken. I can breathe fine. Even if they are, they don't do anything but prescribe rest."

Tires screeched as Marcy pressed the gas pedal.

"I would have used the gun, but it all happened so fast." Celia's body throbbed.

Three blocks from the hospital, Celia yelled, "Stop the car. Stop the car!" Shocks of pain gripped her stomach. She leaned out the window and threw up. Stanton reached over with his good hand and caressed her head. "You've got a bad bruise on your scalp. You need attention."

"You need it more." She pulled a tissue out of her jeans pocket, wiping her mouth. Her stomach roiled again. "We must get help but not at Rudrow. Allie did years of nursing."

Stanton said, "I'll use some of that vodka Marcy stashed away."

"How dare you use my good stash for a measly wound?" Marcy said. "Use soap and water. Just kidding."

"We've got some medical things back at the apartment." She paused. "Now we know that bastard, Jack, is involved. He sent those men to get us."

Chapter 33

As the car approached the hospital, Marcy let up on the accelerator. Several men were wandering around the loading dock, some wearing overalls, and others with jeans and Philly baseball caps.

Something about them is off—no hustle and bustle as usual. Are they Vladimir's guys? Are they waiting for the trucks to arrive from the pier? Why here, of all places?

"They aren't the usual workers," Celia said, squinting at them.

"Let's get out of here," Marcy said, slumping.

"Right," Stanton said. "What about Allie?"

Celia tasted bile in the back of her throat. "I have to go in and make sure Allie is all right. Not to mention that we don't know how badly you're hurt, Stanton."

They parked a block away and went to the side exit. The door wouldn't budge. Had someone locked it? A janitor? Stanton used a key Allison had given him. Waiting for it to open, Celia kept hopping from foot to foot. She nearly threw up again but swallowed hard. Stanton looked worried.

"We're in," he said. "Let's go."

Celia rushed to Allison's cubby and threw her curtain aside. Allison slept. She lifted her head and blinked. "What?"

"Whew. No one came in?"

"It's been quiet."

"Never mind, honey. Go back to sleep."

Allison put her head on the pillow and shut her eyes.

Back in their quarters, Celia helped Stanton into a chair, took scissors from her medical bag, and carefully cut open the sleeve of his shirt. He grimaced.

"Wow," Celia said. "You're right. The bullet skimmed across your shoulder, leaving a shallow but long opening. You probably need stitches, but we'll do our best with butterfly bandages and dressing."

"It hurts like hell." Stanton said, grimacing. "Do what you need to do and get it done with." He opened the bag wider. "Anything for pain?"

Celia stroked his cheek. "We'll check. Marcy, can you help?"

"On it. I can't believe I peed my pants out there. Let me wash my hands."

With shaking fingers, Celia googled how to treat a glancing bullet wound. "Here's the plan. We use antiseptic at first. After that, we'll clean the wound with soap and water, followed by Vaseline. You ready?"

Stanton turned his head. "I'm not looking," he said, making light of it, but his voice dragged.

Celia poured antiseptic on a cloth and applied it gently.

"Yeow!" Stanton pinched his lips, stifling the bellow of pain. "It hurts like hell."

"Allie will check you out when she wakes up."

When Celia finished, she gave Stanton a shot of vodka. "It's the best we can do right now, but I'll see how we can get you something stronger."

"Yes, boss."

Allison stepped out. "Such noise. What's going on here?"

Celia hesitated. "Stanton hurt himself. I googled how to treat it. Hope you remember your nursing skills."

Marcy immediately launched into a rambling and colorfully embellished account of their morning. "We beat the shit out of those monsters. Stanton was wounded. Celia hit on the head. Blood covered the parking lot. Whew."

Allison looked distressed. "What is the matter with you people?" She rummaged in her own duffel bag and pulled out a medical kit. She removed an antiseptic and said it needed to be administered for a full week, twice a day. "It's more effective than what you used, Mom. And you need antibiotics. Here they are."

"Good. You won't have to use my vodka," Marcy said. "It's better in our stomachs." She poured a shot, and downed it. "I'm drinking for Stanton. He can't drink while on antibiotics"

"Like hell," Stanton said in a weaker voice.

Allison unwound the bandage that hung loosely. "This might leave a scar since we're not stitching it, but you'll do okay." Allison applied butterfly bandages. Then she rewrapped gauze over his shoulder and under his armpit, finishing the process with tape.

She went back to her duffel bag and pulled out a prescription bottle. "These are Percocets. There are thirty of them. Won't need all of them. Take one now. The wound will heal from inside out. No doubt there's going to be pain. I'm more worried about your ribs and possible injury to internal organs. Seems good now, but your body will tell you if there's damage."

"I'm on fire," said Stanton. "They kicked the shit out of me. When do I get the Percocets?"

Celia gave him one pill, putting the bottle in her pocket. She gently kissed his lips. With that shot of vodka and the drugs, she hoped he would sleep for a long while. A feeling of tenderness enveloped her. "Stanton, if it weren't for you…thanks."

"Wow, I have to find myself in the line of fire to get some attention around here."

"Stop talking." She brushed back his hair as he closed his eyes.

Celia's stomach still felt queasy and her head pounded. Allison had cleaned her wound, too. Although the cut was superficial, she had developed quite an egg where her forehead met her hairline over her right eye and one on the back of her head. "Listen Mom," Allie said. "You'll heal but you really should rest."

Celia couldn't calm herself. While everyone napped, she made her way to the hangar that led to the loading platform. She peered through a slot in a metal door. She saw Vladimir overseeing a semitrailer with a V & S logo parked near the loading zone. The motor revved up and it backed down the alley. It lumbered like a wounded soldier. Vladimir, surrounded by his bodyguards, looked smug and complacent.

"So, we are good to go," Vladimir said. "We can wait at the office since the next lot won't come for a while."

"Yeah, boss. Good work. Our new crew of pussies start work tomorrow. Maybe I'll visit tonight and, uh, interview them."

A chorus of hoots and howls burned Celia's ears.

"They are yours to fuck. Teach them good," Vladimir said.

Back in their quarters Marcy was pacing. "Where the hell did you go?" she said. "I woke everyone up when I saw you were missing."

Celia bent over, trying to catch her breath. "I saw a V & S Industries truck pulling out, and Vladimir and his men on the dock talking about receiving the women."

"Oh, my God. Why do you think they bring them here?"

"Maybe Vladimir checks them out? Who knows."

"They were a heartbeat away from seeing you."

"What's going on now?" said Allison, who was making a sandwich at the kitchen table.

"Your mom was incredibly brave today," Marcy said.

"Brave doesn't cut it, anymore. I'm afraid of what's next." Allison paused, holding the knife in the air.

"Maybe Allie and Justin should go back to his home." Marcy said.

"Absolutely not. Justin is in their sights now," Celia said. "They'll be watching him and where he goes."

"Justin called me while you three were on your suicide mission to say that Ramon's demanded a meeting right away," Allison said. "They pressured Justin about you, Mom. They want to know if you helped Justin steal the materials from the hospital. They have your name now and seem to know about your, uh, interesting accounting skills. Probably googled you about your troubles at Boca Pelicano Palms. They asked for your address so they could investigate."

Stanton exhaled loudly. "They're all in cahoots."

"Not a big surprise in view of how they got on Justin's back," Marcy said, exhaling.

"Their plan, so far, is meticulous. And I'm sorry they hurt Justin," Celia said. "Allison, Stanton, and Justin are the most innocent of bystanders."

"We're all family," Allison said, holding her belly. "This corruption thing was going on before you came, and they had Justin in the crosshairs when they gave him the job of procurement officer. Of all people, Justin is the most honest person. He cares about the patients."

Celia rubbed her cheek. "Just as the truck drove away, Vladimir and his cohorts made it clear a new cargo of women might be coming. I'm taking a guess as to why they stop here with the women. They bring them here right off the ships to check their health. They want them to work."

Marcy stared with her chin dropped.

Celia couldn't sleep. Thoughts rattled through her mind, coalescing into larger pieces of the puzzle.

She walked out to the kitchen area to see Stanton sipping a cup of tea. He looked up. "Couldn't sleep either?"

"How are you feeling?" she asked.

"Oh, I hurt, but the drugs help," he smiled.

"Stanton," she said, "this has to be their first stop. Those men talked about raping the young women on that truck. If we catch it right, we can follow a truck and see if they take us to where they house the women. It might be our only way to see."

She sat down and Stanton poured her a glass of red wine. "Thanks," she sighed, sipping slowly. "Those containers are horrible. Oh, the stench. I still smell it in my sleep." She waved her hand as though wiping a chalkboard. "I'm of the mind someone in the hospital is on Vladimir's payroll. A nurse? A doctor?"

"You hit it on the nose," Stanton said. "The longer their captives live, the more money they produce."

Celia swirled her wine glass. "Let's tune in to the bug."

No sound came from the mini-bug, not even static or background. I'm doing this all wrong. We can't get traction. Oh, Stanton looks wretched. Celia poured a glass of water, handed him a Percocet.

He sat up straight, his face pale. He took the pill quickly.

"How do you feel?" she asked.

"Shitty. I thought it was a flesh wound, not a shot through the head. Hurts like a bitch."

She undid the bandage, applied antiseptic, then Vaseline, and pulled clean bandages out of the satchel. Stanton grunted and then drew her to him. His lips brushed hers. She pulled away. "I'm not finished, dopey."

"We're clinging to each other for dear life, aren't we?"

"We are indeed," she said wistfully.

"I'll nap for a while. When I wake up we'll strategize."

"Is that what they call it now?" She leaned over and ran her hand through his hair. He closed his eyes.

Chapter 34

Celia and Marcy sat on squeaky metal chairs, sipping vodka, while Marcy told Allie about the guru she had once fallen in love with.

"We lived in an ashram for several years. It really was peaceful there and I loved the meditation," Marcy was saying. "I finally left the ashram when the kids were grown up. They wouldn't speak to me, but who could blame them? Still, it nearly did me in. But what I learned is helping me hold up.

"Dan was a good father but a rotten, nasty, husband. I couldn't take the mental abuse anymore, and I didn't know how to tell anyone. My father was the opposite. He loved my mother but hated me. He once tossed me down the stairs." She pointed to a long, pink scar on her knee. "But my lover, the guru, I loved him madly until I found out he was uh, messing with funds. When he left the country, well, that was that." Marcy laid her chin on her fists. "Now my kids are back in my life—I think—I hope."

"Sometimes we make bad decisions. Lord knows, I did. Who hasn't made a decision they didn't regret later in life?" Celia said, interrupting to keep Marcy from wallowing in guilt.

Celia hoped she had made up for her own missteps with Allison. *Somehow Allie and I are closer, more accepting. I guess some good has to come from all of this crap.*

Stanton's computer beeped. Svetlana was sending a message to Vladimir. Celia read it aloud. "Barry is not in good mood. Meeting with him tonight at nine."

Is Barry feeling the heat? He is in it up to his eyeballs.

"Whoa…another message. A series of names and amounts of money next to them. Could they be loan sharking deals? If the list had given a high percentage rate, like fifteen or more percent, and we were able to get one or more borrowers to turn them in, that would be a step."

"The pattern is right in our faces," Stanton said.

"Vladimir is a renaissance man of criminality," Celia said. *They have their own code words and are careful in certain communications.*

A third message came in. Svetlana said she'd look into a bar Vladimir owned. It involved an employee, Irina, who had given the manager a hard time. A seemingly business-as-usual message—unless you knew their dealings and could break the code. *Does this mean Svetlana, a kidnapping victim herself, is now a madam for these women?*

"Don't even tell me," Stanton said. "Vladimir's convoluted maze gives him a free ride on the backs of ordinary people. He makes money from sex slavery and creates a world of fake donors to cover his illegal revenues. The health of people struggling to get by is jeopardized when they get too close to him. It's a smorgasbord of crime."

Celia noticed the name of his charitable foundation, Hospital Aid. She accessed its financial statement. No question that it was designed to launder undeclared millions of dollars from criminal enterprises. Net worth: $200 million plus what they steal, and only about $1.6 million a year to Rudrow Hospital. Still, he made millions. With a hefty endowment at the charity, Vladimir received seven hundred and fifty thousand a year in salary, plus bonuses. Ramon and Barry were on the board of the foundation and listed as consultants with hefty salaries. Svetlana? Two hundred and fifty thousand a year. Several other high-paid employees. Fake? Consultants? Conflict of interest? No one was watching the store. For Vladimir, it had become a convenient way to dodge the law and launder money.

"Is there enough information to report the foundation to the IRS?" Celia asked Stanton.

"Vladimir and his cohorts covered their tracks very well. So far, I don't see any holes in the structure of his foundations that he can't counter. A few dead donors? Excusable. Vladimir could claim it came from their estates. The government would be reluctant to chase down donors in other countries. Costly, labor-intensive job."

I can't imagine such a terrible life of dire poverty. I even understand why Svetlana would pursue riches over enslavement. But causing abuse to other humans? No excuse.

Chapter 35

She changed out of her scrubs into sweats. Then she began the process of reading through the newly discovered file—all names of businesses owned by Vladimir. She found names and addresses of strip joints, bars, restaurants, massage parlors, and hotels. Surely, all had rooms for women to service male customers. On the outside, the places needed to appear legit.

Oil and Spice Spa caught her eye. Pasted next to it was a picture of a man receiving a massage from an attractive woman. The text of the ad crooned that their professional women gave shiatsu, hot stone, and Swedish massages. A heavenly touch to drive your woes and stresses away.

She felt a hand on her back and bolted off her seat. Marcy stood there peering over her shoulder at the documents.

"It's just me. And look what Goldilocks found at Grandma's house," Marcy said with a smirk and pointing a finger. "Going to let me in on it?"

"I'm going to try the Oil and Spice Spa to see if I can get information from women who work there. If you want to join me, I have an important job for you."

"And where do you think you two are going?" said Stanton as Celia put on her coat.

"We can't tell you, but we're on a mission." Celia grabbed Marcy's arm and jerked her along.

Stanton stood in their way. "Again, you're rolling the dice with Vladimir on the lookout for you. I know I can't stop you but I can set up a new phone for you."

"That's a deal. I'd rather roll the dice than sit here doing nothing."

Marcy shrugged. "I follow the chief."

"Okay, but you have to promise to call me along the way."

"Will do, Stanton. Promise."

In the car, Celia pursed her lips. "It'll look weird if both of us go to the same 'spa,'" she said, irony filling her voice. "Let's do different ones and report back what we've learned."

Celia found Oil and Spice Spa on Race Street. The hallway was decorated to look like a scene out of the movie *Indochine*. Green paper lanterns covered dim bulbs and red paper lanterns hung above the hostess desk. The scent of strong incense filled the waiting room, which featured an elaborate fountain trickling water into a bowl containing fake lotus flowers. "WAIT FOR HOSTESS," said a sign behind a wooden desk.

Ten minutes later, a young Asian woman appeared from behind a curtain. "May I help you?" she said in perfect English.

"You may. I want a massage."

The woman looked at her. "Are you sure you're in the right place?"

"I've got a pinched nerve. Your ad listed healing techniques. I'm open to anything that'll help."

The woman stared stone-faced for several seconds.

"Please. I can't walk without pain."

"All right. Do you want a half hour—that's only twenty-five minutes—or a full hour, which is fifty-five minutes? It's two hundred dollars in advance for the longer time." The woman eyed her.

She wants to get rid of me. "Okay, I'll take the hour slot. I want a deep muscle massage."

"Do you want any other services?" she said in a sugary voice.

Celia handed her the money. "Nope."

"You sure?"

"Yep. I'm sure. Just my back, please."

The woman gave Celia one last hard stare then checked her clipboard. A man in jeans and a yellow T-shirt came slithering in the front door. He kept his head down and pulled his knitted cap low.

"How are you, sir? Have a seat. Be right with you." The hostess's voice was soft and seductive. Not the same businesslike voice she used for Celia.

The woman led Celia up a flight of darkened stairs and knocked on a door labeled with the name Yan. The door swung wide and a short, thin woman in a kimono stood there smiling.

The hostess nodded at Celia. "Her back is in distress and she needs a deep massage."

Yan blinked rapidly.

"A deep tissue massage." The boss woman tapped Yan on the shoulder as though whispering a secret. "For an hour."

Celia interpreted the tap as if it were a wink and Yan should dispense the massage, ignoring the woman.

"Come, come," Yan said, and stepped back for Celia to walk in.

She hung a red robe on the door. "This for when I finish. Undress and climb under the sheet. I will come back." Yan walked out.

Celia had plotted out how she would approach the conversation and now felt helpless. What if Yan called the boss?

She undressed and slid under the sheet on the massage table, facing up. She looked at the room and saw only one bottle of oil, several hand towels, a pile of paper towels, and no music. Humming tunelessly, she waited. The door opened and Yan lifted the sheet to expose Celia's leg and started pushing her fingers into her muscles.

"I'd like to talk."

Yan took a step back. "You cop?" Yan asked in a whisper.

"No." Celia sat up, covered with the sheet. Her legs dangled off the edge of the table.

Yan handed Celia the robe and pointed to the door.

Celia put the robe on. If she left now, the suspicious manager would surely know something went wrong. "Just talk to me."

Yan pointed to a tiny black box stuck on the ceiling and then stuck a finger in her ear.

A listening device. Celia had to think fast. "All I want is for you to talk dirty to me. I have this thing…" She spoke in a strong voice.

"Oh, yes. I can do."

"Whisper in my ear." Celia said, patting her hand. "I like that. Don't touch me until I tell you to touch."

Yan's voice was nearly inaudible. "What you want?"

"Oh, that's good," purred Celia. "Keep going." Then, she whispered, "Please believe me. I'm here to help you. Do they force you to have sex?"

Yan looked away.

"Oh yes," said Celia. "Yes, turn me on."

"You like what I say?" Yan asked aloud. "Ah, nice breasts."

"Uh, huh. Do more."

Yan put her finger to her lips and went back to whispering. "How you help?"

"Tell me how you got here, who is in charge, and where the women live."

"You want to fuck," Yan said aloud. Then leaned toward Celia's ear. "We live in place worse than what I live in Thailand. It smells and has bugs. They say fancy job in US, become citizen. Lies and take my money."

"What about others who work here?"

"Same. Some at clubs, some here and some send places I don't know. They make us do all stuff—groups even." Yan opened her robe, and Celia went weak. Multiple scars like a roadmap all over her chest and abdomen. "Men take and scare us. They killers. We worry about home and safe of family."

"Will you tell the police all of this if I get you out?"

Yan's head jolted but stayed close to Celia's ear. "Where I go? No money. No papers. They deport me." Yan lifted her head a couple of inches, looking as though she'd come out of an ice bath. "They will kill mother and my baby back home."

Celia strained to hear her. "We can free you but you must talk to police."

"No. They kill us." Her words flew like daggers slicing the air.

"The police will help."

"No," Yan said, nearly shouting.

Hurried footsteps resonated outside the door. Yan whipped the sheet off the table. Celia grabbed it. In big black letters in a corner of the sheet, she saw "Rudrow Hospital."

The door burst open. The hostess marched across the small room and grabbed Celia by the hair and yanked. "Just a massage, huh? I knew there was something phony about you."

What a stupid ploy I've concocted. Would they kill her?

"She want dirty words here," Yan shouted. "Nutcase you. Don't come back."

Celia's wobbly knees nearly gave out, but a straight line of relief shot through her from toes to scalp. *All my suspicions are justified.* Yan pushed her off the table. Celia grabbed her clothes and dressed.

Yan looked at her boss. "Lady no good. She reporter."

This woman might have saved my life. As soon as Celia dressed, the manager grabbed her arm, pulled her downstairs and to the front door.

"Get the hell out."

Dizzy, she zigzagged to her car and peeled out. She rushed to meet up with Marcy. She could only hope Marcy had more luck.

Chapter 36

Celia turned off the Vine Street Expressway and waited for Marcy on 4th Street. She had dropped her off at a massage parlor just off of the Vine Street Expressway, and they were to meet at a designated spot at 8 p.m. It was now 8:30.

"Where are you, Marcy?" Celia muttered, thumping her fist on the steering wheel.

She thought about driving around the block in case they'd miscommunicated. From the corner of her eye, she saw two women running in her direction. One was Marcy. The other was a woman with flaming red hair, wearing a blue and yellow kimono that flung out behind her and revealed her bra and panties.

Celia blinked hard, hoping she interpreted the scene correctly. Had Marcy gotten her masseuse out? Marcy slowed down and bent over, her chest heaving. The woman in the kimono pulled her along. Celia stepped out and flung the doors open.

The woman's cheeks had rivulets of black eye makeup dripping under her wide-open eyes and smeared red lipstick. Her face powder was clownishly white. She is way too conspicuous. Is she a plant? Is this some kind of setup?

"Why were you so late?" Celia asked, accelerating around a corner.

"I had to go through the whole damn massage to make it look real."

The woman wiped her mascara-stained cheeks. "I'm Danielle."

Celia adjusted the rearview mirror to get a better look. "Do I know you?"

"You bet your sweet ass," she said in a husky voice. "I couldn't say anything in the massage room—wired."

Marcy sucked in her breath. "Damn, I had a feeling I'd met you before. You were in the container with us."

"Yeah. You set us free with that gun of yours, but the bastards got a bunch of us. They cruise highways and local streets where girls might hide. They found me in some small town and shipped me to Philadelphia. Some of us are gonna be moved to Florida."

"Danielle, would you go to the police and report what they did to you?" Celia asked.

Danielle looked around, seeming distracted. "I might. Got to think on it. I'm eighteen, no money. I know this Marcy ain't no innocent. I can smell 'em."

"I've been around the block a few times," Marcy said, "and I'm good."

"Tell your story later," Celia said, trying to keep exasperation out of her voice.

They pulled up to the curb a block away from the hospital.

"Where are you hiding?"

Celia's heart went into high gear as she swung around and looked directly at Danielle. "How do you know that?"

"I'm not a dummy, lady. You guys are on the lam from the same guys who kidnapped me."

"I told Danielle we'd help get her out." Marcy said.

"Been waitin' a long time, but ratting them out means death if they catch me. Don't have a dime. You got some dough for me?"

"We'll help, for sure," Celia said. "You sound Cockney. Where are you from?"

"Australia. You're close."

"You probably need help as a noncitizen. If you go to the authorities and turn the perps in, they'll give you a T nonimmigrant status that allows you to work and get services for up to four years. It gets you a green card and a way to get permanent status. Think about it."

They were near the side entrance to the hospital when Danielle said, "Hey, what's up with the hospital? You hiding here?"

"How do you know this place?" Marcy asked, her eyes half-open.

"They took me and the women here after we got to Philly. They checked us out for diseases, pregnancies, and other shit."

Celia realized how close they were to being found out if even this kid could figure it out so quickly. "Do you know if anyone else knows where we're hiding?"

"Shit, I heard one of the bozos say they're making a giant search of this place. You'd better get the hell out of there. I ain't goin' in."

Celia jumped out of the car. *What if they got Allie and Stanton?*

"Celia, she says she's willing to go to the police," Marcy said, shouting.

Dread screamed in Celia's ears. She ran as fast as she could, through the service door, down the hall into their communal space, each intake of air felt like her body being ripped apart.

Their quarters seemed deserted. Her throat constricted and she couldn't even call out a name. At that moment, Allie came out from the small bathroom.

"Mom, what is wrong with you? Are you okay?"

Celia gripped Allison's hand. "Just pack. Two minutes. We have to leave immediately."

"What? Are we found out?"

"They are looking intensely. Where's Stanton?"

"He went to get supplies."

"I've got to reach him. Go now."

"They've got a tail on him."

"Best not to have him out all of us. It's better I, once safe, tell him to try to avoid his tail and meet up with us."

Trying to speed-dial Stanton, Celia's fingers trembled and slid off. She did it again and his phone rang. Voicemail picked up.

"Stanton, do not come back to the hospital. I'll call later to let you know where we are." She and Allie packed a few things for each of them.

Where to go? As Celia navigated the long hallway to the exit, she saw shadows on the other side of the wall. She grabbed Allison and stopped her. They waited as the footsteps passed.

"You should know before where bitches are hiding, you dumb jackasses," Vladimir's voice shouted.

Celia and Allie held hands and ran until they reached the service entrance and their car. Celia got into the driver's seat and Allison slid into the passenger side. In the back, Marcy and Danielle stared as Celia started the motor, and they sped away.

"Allie, that's Danielle in the back," said Celia, maneuvering onto Pine Street. She's going to help us."

Allison turned around briefly, looking baffled. "I am so confused," she said, holding tight to her stomach. "How did they…how did you know they were coming for us?"

"Danielle," said Marcy, "and Detective Celia got into high gear by what Danielle told us."

Celia saw in the rearview mirror a green car a block away coming toward them.

"Oh, shit. Go, go," Marcy shouted. Celia made a sharp turn.

"I had just warmed some water for tea," Allison said. "The hot kettle told them we just left."

"Get your asses in gear and lose them," Danielle shouted. The green car made the turn and began gaining on them. Celia took another sharp turn and immediately another.

They lost the car. Celia no longer knew who was a friend and who was an enemy.

Soon, they were in West Philadelphia where the University of Pennsylvania and Drexel University dominated the streets.

"We'll stay on Walnut," Celia said almost to herself. "There's lots of noise, restaurants, and hundreds of students roaming the campus and streets. I'm going to look for a hotel in this area. I still have cash."

Young adults filled the sidewalks, carrying heavy backpacks and, despite the cool air, in all manner of dress from ripped jeans with hanging strands, shorts, muscle shirts, long skirts, and jean jackets.

"Well, Danielle, you'll be sleeping on clean sheets and showering in a clean bathroom." Marcy ruffled her wild, poofy hair.

"Man, oh man. That filthy apartment they lock us in. Sometimes they don't call a plumber for days on end."

Celia saw Allison shiver.

"You are going to help us, right?" Celia asked to assure herself. "And we'll help you."

"You bet your sweet ass, sister."

"What will you do once you're free?" Marcy asked.

"Well, I got a GED because they wanted me to service some rich guys. The only good thing that came out of all this. Maybe community college?"

"I'll help you financially with that," Celia said. "But we've got a lot to do first."

"Yeah. I want to whup their asses." Danielle ripped a ragged fingernail with her teeth.

Celia checked into one of the hotel chains that dotted West Philadelphia. The lobby smelled of jasmine, and a large bouquet of pale pink roses sat on a teak table. Parents with college-age kids stood in clusters near a snack bar. They'd sneak Stanton in. Right now, she and Allison would share a room. Marcy would stay with Danielle next door. Stanton and Justin would make do with a sofa bed.

Celia went to the room bar and removed an unsweetened tea for Allison and three miniature vodka bottles. She didn't wait and took a slug from one of them, and handed the other two to Danielle and Marcy.

"You guys are damned nice," Danielle said.

"Well, it's about to get better, thanks to you." Marcy said.

Danielle picked up a martini glass and filled it with her small bottle of vodka. "Nice to use a real glass for a change."

The three sat on the dark brown sofa in a corner, while Allison sat across from them on a bulky chair that looked like a big, gray cloud.

"Hope we're safe here," Allison said. "I left a message for Justin."

"They have to look through an awful lot of hotels across the city to find us," Celia said in a hushed tone, hoping her words were accurate. "This is an ideal location. There's security from the colleges and parents visiting kids who might be quick to report a disturbance."

"We've got to arrange for Danielle to tell her story," Allison said.

"I just realized," Celia said, as if coming out of a stupor, "Stanton hasn't called me back." She called again.

This time he answered. "Where are you?" Celia nearly shouted.

"I'm at Best Buy. Needed some tech supplies." He sounded sluggish and hoarse.

"Don't go to the hospital. They're onto us. Take the most circuitous route you can, but get here." She gave him the address and room number.

"I'll be there in twenty minutes."

Celia lunged toward the door when she heard a knock. "Stanton, thank goodness you're here."

She opened the door and tried to hug him but he backed away.

"Sorry. My shoulder really hurts and on top of that I have a cold. I took a pill that knocked me out. Must sit." He heavily lowered himself onto the sofa.

"Let me take a look," Allison said. She unwound the bandage as Celia looked over her shoulder.

"It doesn't look infected, but your shoulder is still swollen and the wound is not healing." She pulled out her medical kit from her canvas bag and redressed the wound. "Still taking your antibiotics?"

"Yup." He winced as Allison finished bandaging.

He looked at Celia. "So, fill me in. What happened?"

They introduced him to Danielle who sat in a far corner of the room as though the sight of a man frightened her. Celia and Marcy took turns bringing him up-to-date.

"So, you're really going to spill the beans?" Stanton asked Danielle.

"You betcha. My family moved God knows where. I was an orphan in Australia. Got buried in the foster care system. When I aged out, a guy romanced me and next thing I'm a sex slave. Nikki tried to get us out. Couldn't. Threw the towel in."

"Who treats you at the hospital?" Celia took a shot in the dark.

"Some ER nurse treats us. Cleans out our pipes." She giggled. "Don't know her name."

Celia urged Stanton to rest on the open sleeper sofa. His drooping face showed fatigue. She covered him with a blanket and felt his hot forehead. "You're feverish."

He pulled the blanket tightly around his neck. "Where's Justin?"

"I got a text earlier. He's got a bozo tailing him. He's forced to stay at the office. I told him to come straight here when has a chance, but I don't know if that's even possible," Allison said, her voice cracking.

"Let's call the police," said Celia. "Tell them about the women being treated at the hospital. We've got Danielle to verify."

Danielle interrupted, "If it's okay, I need a couple hours' sleep. Only had two hours last night. Convention in town. Can't hardly talk to cops now." Danielle's body drooped.

Allison cried for a while before falling asleep next to Celia beneath crisp white sheets. Celia stared at the ceiling, her eyes wide, rehearsing what to say to the police. Getting her hopes up scared her. With her mind streaming recent events in triple time, images flashed: the drugging, the house in Pittsburgh, the trip in the container, and the hospital sub-basement. Pictures flipping so fast, they created an entire movie, like the stereoscopes she had loved as a kid. It all transformed into a blur as new pictures appeared, overlapping. Flashbacks from her past—Florida, crazy capers, misadventures, and how they now nearly hit the end of the road if it wasn't for Danielle.

Danielle, don't back out.

Chapter 37

Celia awoke in a sweat, clammy and uncomfortable. Rolling out of bed, careful not to awaken Allison, she showered in the sparkling all-white bathroom, standing still in a brief moment of bliss under the torrent of hot water. She finished and put on the clothes she had been wearing the day before. It was 8 a.m.

From the sofa bed, Stanton snored intermittently. She brushed the front of her blouse and jeans, trying to smooth them, then gave up.

A soft knock on the door and Celia's breathing stopped. She put her mouth close to the door and asked, "Who's there?"

"It's us, Marcy and Danielle."

Celia opened the door and slipped out into the hall. Both were rumpled, uncombed, and wearing hotel terrycloth robes.

"I called the police at 5 a.m. Told them the situation," Marcy said. "Dispatcher pressed me to say it wasn't an emergency because no one was bleeding or dying. I insisted it damn well is an emergency. They said they'd send someone, and I've heard nary a word since. I called back. They said it was a violent and bloody night. Shootings. She told me we could wait." Marcy huffed. "Too damn many guns on the streets."

"No, we can't wait," Celia said.

"We have no choice. Anyway, we're starving," Marcy whispered. "Let's eat first. Won't be able to once they're here."

Celia hesitated. "No more waiting. We need to get the hell out of here now."

"Where we can get steak and eggs?" Marcy said.

"Oh, man. That sounds good," Danielle said.

"What is the matter with you both?" Celia heard her voice rising. "We're going to the nearest station. Don't you see how important it is to get Danielle's story to them? I get that we're all stressed out. But now is the time to act before we're all killed. Justin is the one most vulnerable now."

"We'll throw some clothes on," Marcy said. She took Danielle by the arm. "Got some clothes that'll fit you. Maybe tight for you. I'm so slim."

Celia followed to make sure they didn't get diverted. She found a tablet and pen and wrote a note to alert Stanton and Allie: "Don't leave! We'll be right back! I'll knock once, and then twice."

Danielle washed up and put on a simple yellow dress Marcy had handed to her. It hung loosely and Marcy rushed her to the door, making adjustments to make it fit tighter. "See? Too tight."

They took the elevator. Once in the car, Celia asked Danielle why her parents left her.

"Mom was an alkie and slept most of the day. I was five and making dinners from potatoes or noodles. A neighbor reported her when I was eleven, and I went into the fucked-up foster system while she went to jail. Went through seven homes, abuse, and crap. I ran away at sixteen and met up with the guy who was supposed to be my savior. Never saw my mom again. Heard she's out of jail."

"Did you know your dad?" Marcy asked.

"He left when I turned three. I got out of foster care and wanted someone to love me. Picked wrong."

They exited into the parking garage and found the car.

"Was it Vladimir's gang who kidnapped you?" Celia asked, her mouth in a deep frown. "The same ones who kidnapped us?"

"Vladimir and his Vlad-asses? Yes. But we get passed around the gangs. I think they trade or buy us like baseball cards." Danielle snorted. "My boyfriend said he'd get me a good job. I turned into an eighteen-year-old whore. Got my friend's thirteen-year-old sister. Man, I loved that kid. Never saw her again.

"You ladies know the drill. Big, shit-eating containers," Danielle said, then stopped and stared into space as though watching her words form into short films. "Freezing cold or hot as hell." She held her throat, her face turning parchment. "Sick or dying? You get tossed away like dirty rags."

Celia searched for the nearest police station on her GPS. They were halfway there when Danielle yelped. "Shit. Got my period. It's heavy."

"That can't wait," Celia said, parking in front of a drugstore. "Hide on the floor of the car. Marcy, don't let Danelle out of your sight. I'll get the tampons."

"Will do."

Celia went into the drugstore and pulled a box of tampons off the shelf. At the counter, she started to pay when Marcy ran in. She pulled Celia out of the store. "I went to look for a bathroom where Danielle could use tampons. When I got back, she was gone."

"Did you lock the doors? Did you look for her?"

"I thought I locked the doors. I ran up and down the block looking for her. Sorry."

"Sorry doesn't cut it."

"I'm pretty sure she lied to us. She was never really going to the police."

Celia scanned the street. She saw a black SUV turning a corner. She pulled Marcy with her into the drugstore. "Is there a back door?" she shouted to no one in particular. A man in a white jacket came up to her.

"Will you please quiet down? Do you want me to call the police?"

"Yes, and the back door, please." Celia spotted it and they moved in that direction.

He reached out to stop them. Celia and Marcy hustled through the storage room with doors wide open and boxes being delivered. They pushed past the delivery guys and took off in a run to the car.

When they returned to the hotel, Celia and Marcy burst through the door.

"We've got to get out of here. Danelle is with the mob. She'll tell where we are."

Not a word was spoken as Celia and Stanton packed some belongings and followed Allie into his rented parked car. Marcy ran behind with two canvas cases over her shoulders and a paper bag flowing over with toiletries. Marcy threw her load into the trunk and jumped into the driver's seat. Shooting pains gripped Celia's jaw.

Allison huddled in a corner of the back seat, gasping.

"I still have my medical kit," Allison said. "These are the Percocets Justin prescribed."

She rattled the pill bottle and Celia took them. "Stanton still needs some."

"I took one before we left. I'm fine right now. Where are we headed?"

Celia remembered a hotel, El Paraiso, not far from the hospital. *Maybe hiding in plain sight was the ticket. It worked before—for a while.* She said the name and address.

Allie pushed back in the seat as though she wanted to crawl inside. She looked shell-shocked.

My daughter, my baby. Her baby.

They crossed the Schuylkill, keeping on Walnut. They veered through Center City's small streets. Marcy found the hotel near the Delaware River. Stanton paid in cash for two rooms and three nights while the others huddled at the back of the lobby, not wanting to show their faces. Celia thought she'd take with her the habit of hiding her face for the rest of her life—however long that was.

In the room, Allison tried calling Justin. "It's the tenth time I'm calling him. He doesn't pick up. I can't leave a message. The animals might steal his phone."

"You need sleep, sweetie." Celia said, feeling lethargic herself. "We all need sleep."

Marcy guided Allie into the adjoining room. As soon as the door closed, Celia noticed Stanton grimacing. The ride shook up his body. It wasn't just the shoulder healing, those kicks left bruises all over his body, legs, and arms. He took a pill. Celia puffed up his pillows and settled him into bed.

"I wanted to be alert when we left. My hand lost feeling." He flexed his hand open and closed. He touched her arm. "Ah, now I can feel your silky skin. I'm good as new. It keeps me from thinking about the trouble we're in." He made a grumpy face to show he was kidding. "You're crying," he said, wiping her tears with a splice of clean gauze.

"I'm worried about Danielle. They'll harm her. We didn't protect her."

"What happened is not your fault. She left because she's brainwashed about the outside world." Stanton studied her.

"But we lost in the end." She wet a towel and wiped blood from his arm. "We moved around so much you're still bleeding." Celia bent over him. "Are you sure you're okay?"

"Whew. Not sure."

She kissed his cheek. "Stanton, if it weren't for you…thanks."

"We have to keep in the present real and be aware of the dangers, but remember what made us happy before." He held her hand, and as he drifted off to sleep he said, "The memory holds us together to our old world of love and fun… And potholes and older people driving into ponds, and taxes and…and talking to computers that hang up on you." Stanton had fallen sound asleep.

"That world is looking like bliss."

Chapter 38

Celia had fallen into a foggy dream. She was running across a hot, humid field, wasps chasing, hovering, and stinging her. When she awoke at 5 a.m. in a daze, she tried to go back to sleep. Frustrated, she got out of bed. Sweat poured off her as though she'd been stuck in a hot oven. Even her gums hurt. She put her hands in the small of her back and bent backward as pain gripped her. Stanton still slept. She poured a glass of water and drank it as though she'd been marooned on a desert island. After her third glass she gasped for air. She poured one for Stanton and put it on the night table with a painkiller.

Stanton awoke, looking at her with pain in his eyes. "I hurt."

"Take your pill, sweetie," she said. "It's important that you rest."

He started to speak, but his voice slid into silence. He popped the pill.

She bent over him and pulled the blanket up. "I think you should take the next plane back to Florida."

"I'm not going anywhere without you." His voice sounded hoarse.

"Then, we should hit the road and go far, far away."

"Marcy's a shoo-in, but what about Allie and Justin?" Stanton said.

"Maybe we can convince him to go on the run. It's terrible what they're doing to him." His look of pain touched her. "You are a good person. I love you, Stanton."

"I love you, too." He burrowed his head in the pillow. "I'm still working on who the real owner of the offshore account is, the one they put in Justin's name. I'll keep trying but it's tough. Be prepared if it doesn't work out."

"I know it's hard to trace. Got my fingers crossed." She didn't really feel hopeful.

She crawled back into bed, arms hugging him and immediately fell asleep.

Awakening just before seven, Celia felt uneasy. She slipped out of bed, leaving Stanton sleeping. Her bare feet touched the cool tile floor of the bathroom. In the shower, she let hot, stinging droplets of water fall over every inch of her. *It feels like heaven. And then I'll make coffee in the coffee machine on the bureau with its efficient pods.*

Allison and Marcy hadn't come by yet. No question, this ordeal had exhausted them.

She put on Stanton's jacket and baseball cap and walked to the door.

"Where the hell are you going?" he asked groggily.

"I'll be back soon. We need clothes, food, and toiletries."

"Don't go. It's insane. I can do it. They'll be searching the city for you."

"I won't be long. Marcy and Allie will sleep in for sure." Celia kissed his forehead and his eyes fluttered shut. The fact that Justin hadn't called Allie weighed heavily on her mind.

I hope all is okay. I can only hope. Hope is about all we have right now.

She veered around the corner toward the hospital, and circled to the back. The dock was quiet, and she parked a bit away. Stanton's warning clanged in her head. But she had to see Justin with her own eyes. That's all there was to it.

The stopper Stanton used to hold open the fire exit door remained in place. Celia took the back elevator. No longer did she have the doctor's lab coat, but she still had the ID card that she'd kept in her purse.

No one stopped her as she made her way to Radiology. At the reception desk, the janitor had plugged in his vacuum. He immediately apologized, thinking Celia worked there and said he'd come back. She signaled to the janitor to stay. She looked for a door with Justin's name on it. When she found it, she noticed a light seeping out from the bottom. A sense of relief swept over her.

Knocking softly, she waited. After no response, she tried the door and stepped inside. Justin was slumped at his desk, head down. Beside him stood an empty bottle of scotch. *Who could blame him for drinking?*

Her eyes scoured the room. Justin's computer was still not there. She walked over to wake him and saw several sheets of paper scattered near his head.

When she shook him, his head rolled to its side. Vomit was on the desk. His reddened skin looked chafed. Celia's throat closed, a vein on her neck pulsed wildly. He was unresponsive. An odor hit her— garlic—typical of arsenic poisoning. A typed note read simply: "To my love, Allison. I'm sorry, can't take the shame. I'm guilty of stealing millions of dollars and gambling it away. The hospital is investigating, and I'm about to be found out. I won't go to prison. Give our baby much love." No signature.

She took hold of Justin's dangling wrist and felt a pulse.

"Justin," she said. "Justin!"

He mumbled something and lifted his head an inch.

Celia asked the janitor to get a wheelchair. He peeked at her badge, then rushed out. No way could she let him be admitted to Rudrow. That meant death. She'd say he'd been discharged after a minor procedure if anyone asked. All patients must leave that way. Luckily, he wore civilian clothing.

"Can you get up? We need to get to a different hospital. Now! Stand up!"

She helped lift him to his feet. His knees buckled. The janitor helped seat him in the chair.

"You've got to get to the car. We can't stay here."

Somehow, he seemed to understand. She waved off a couple of nurses who tried to help. In the car, she called Pennsylvania Hospital's Emergency Room, giving a description of Justin's symptoms.

When they reached the emergency entrance, a team was waiting for them. The attending nurse immediately called a code blue and they rushed Justin inside.

Chapter 39

Stanton was waiting at the hotel. She'd called and given a cursory outline of what happened. He pulled her into the room and slammed the door. "What's going on?"

"I found Justin slumped over his desk. He was passed out. Someone made it look like a suicide."

Stanton's eyes widened with horror.

"He's alive. I was able to get him to Pennsylvania Hospital. We need to hire a security guard."

"Will he make it?"

"I hope so. He was semiconscious."

"Was there a note?"

"An unsigned confession to embezzlement. They tried to murder him and make him take the blame. I'm sure of it."

"How convenient." Stanton rubbed the stubble on his cheek, making a scratching sound.

"Justin smelled of booze, but mainly garlic."

"That tells me it's metallic arsenic. I've had a few cases like that over the years."

"How am I going to tell Allie?" Celia pressed her lips together. Her words stuck to the roof of her mouth. After several deep breaths she called the hospital and said she was his mother.

Celia shuddered when she heard the words, "In a semicoma."

Stanton had called a security company he had worked with in the past and ordered a guard to stand outside of Justin's room.

"I've made some small progress in finding out who really owns that shell corporation." Stanton cupped his injured shoulder with his hand. "I don't know who yet. I do have some insiders working on it who owe me favors. To be honest, they need more time."

Celia looked up at him. "Time is our enemy now. We don't have much. Their strategy to smoke us out might work. I've got to get answers now or combust."

"It's a two-for-one deal: Justin is scapegoated to smoke you and Allison out. Next, they have someone to blame for the theft who can't defend himself because he's gone. Maybe we shouldn't tell Allie right away. We won't be able to keep her from going to see him. They can't get into Justin's room, but they can be posted outside and all around the place."

She clasped her hands. "Allie finally caught a break in her romantic life. Now what?"

"Everything will turn out fine. We'll tell Allie that."

"Stop saying that. We don't know that. You're not her father. This is not your problem."

"You can't tell me how to feel. Take a look at this body and tell me it's not my problem."

She drew in a jagged breath. "Oh, shit. Sorry. You're right. I'm just babbling out of frustration. We'll tell Allie at the right moment or she'll walk into their trap."

"You found him early enough. He was able to stand. That's good. I know he'll make it."

"Your optimism is a good thing. I shouldn't put you down like I did, but it's lightweight saying it's all fine when you look at reality."

"Okay. I'll button my lip." He twisted his lip with fingers. "We'll keep Justin a secret for a while."

After Celia changed Stanton's bandages, she sat down in a chair. She moved her hands over the faux velvet fabric.

Need to check out the loading dock back at Rudrow. We have to see whether a container shows up. And where the women are led afterward. She took the gun from the drawer where Stanton had put it. Her head ached.

She left Stanton to work on his computer and walked into the hall past Marcy and Allie's room. She heard a soft voice call her name. "Oh, Marcy." Celia hugged her. "Oh, what are we going to do?"

"Take a deep breath, honey. Wherever you're going right now, I'm tagging along. You need me for moral support."

"No."

"Yes. I already told Allie I'd be back later. She went back to sleep. But can we get ice cream? Damn I miss comfort food. Anyway, where the hell are you going?"

"Back to Rudrow. I googled and there are lots of containers arriving at the port. We're looking in the wrong place. It was just where we lived. We can't go there again. Besides, it's been useless to try to find the right containers. One showed up at the hospital and Danielle confirmed where the women went for health checks."

Marcy linked her arm into Celia's and wouldn't let go.

Celia kept her head low as she drove near the hospital. She pulled her baseball cap down over her forehead. When they neared the loading dock she stopped. She and Marcy sat in silence.

"Okay, we've been waiting here for half an hour," Marcy finally said. "What's next?"

Without answering, Celia kept her focus on the loading platform. After another half hour, she saw an eighteen-wheeler, hauling a forty-foot container on its bed, heading through the gate. Two beefy bodyguards opened and shut the gates after the truck drove up to the platform.

"Shit," Marcy whispered. "There's Vladimir, standing on the loading platform."

The driver and Vladimir stood facing each other and appeared to argue. Celia touched the gun in her pocket and got out of the car.

"I have to get closer, so I can hear what they're saying. If I don't get back in ten minutes, keep going."

"No, way."

"If something happens to me, I'll need you to be the baby's grandmother."

Marcy frowned. "Not funny."

Staying close to the building but out of sight, Celia walked through the fire exit, ran up the steps to the hangar adjacent to the dock to the rusty, crumbled slot where she could peek through. She heard voices, and Vladimir's boomed.

"Shut the fuck up and open container. How many are sick?"

"They had to dump two in the ocean that died," the driver said nonchalantly, as though ordering lunch. "Four in there are pretty damn sick. Not my fault."

"Leaves twenty," Vladimir said, almost to himself.

A heavy-set blonde woman, dressed in a dark blue nurse's uniform, walked out of a door and stood near Vladimir. Celia shifted until she had a view of the woman. She studied her face, embedding it into her mind.

The nurse's voice got louder. "Get those women out of that suffocating box right away."

"You shut your cunt mouth," the driver sneered. "You don't have to stand the stink and crap in there like we do."

"Then clean it out more often. Buy a decent Porta Potty."

Vladimir shushed her and handed her an envelope that appeared fat with money. The woman hesitated then put it in her pocket. Celia tried to take a picture through the small, dark opening, but it came out skewed and blurry beyond recognition.

The driver tied a hankie around his nose and walked to the back of the closed container. He climbed a short ladder and yanked a thick, metal bar out of the loop that locked it. The grating sound felt like a saw against metal pipes. Celia's stomach clenched; the memory of being back in that horrible space flashing in front of her. He threw the door open, pulled out a gun, and hauled himself into the container. Vladimir followed.

She heard muffled shouting: "You, you, you, and you. Get the fuck out. Others stay."

The four went through the ER door with the nurse.

"You take good care of my workers," Vladimir snapped after them.

Now that she saw the women, the police would have what they needed. Time to make the call. She peered out and saw the driver had climbed back into the cab of the truck and seemed to be waiting. Vladimir had vanished. No one else was around.

She dialed 911. "Please, you must go to the loading dock at Rudrow Hospital," she said in a loud whisper. "There is a group of women brought here as sex slaves in a shipping container. Please come immediately."

"Do you know for sure it contains women who have been brought in illegally?"

"Yes. The top guy who imports sex slaves has gotten them into the ER right now. They're tending to some of the women who were sickened coming over."

"Do you have proof? A picture maybe…"

"No, but I saw some of them taken into the hospital with my own eyes," Celia nearly shrieked.

"I…think…this is a case for immigration."

Celia licked her lips. "No, you have to send the police out right now. They'll be gone soon. It'll be weeks, months with immigration. This is happening now!"

"Is anyone in imminent danger?"

"These women are in danger for their lives. They're half-starved, dehydrated, sick, and barely surviving."

"You know, we have had calls like this before. Never at a hospital. Always a false alarm. You have to be sure they're not delivering staples or equipment. They might just be women hurt in a brawl. Happens all the time, lady."

"I'm absolutely sure."

"Get the license number."

She craned her neck. The front license plate was just under the platform, and she had no view of the back. *I don't dare step out until the police arrive.* "Do you know what sex trafficking is?" Celia paused. "What if it were your daughter?"

"I'll have a patrol car out there."

Celia clicked off.

The truck driver jumped from the cab as Vladimir came out the door. Again, they seemed embroiled in a heated conversation. "Vladimir, what the fuck do I care what the nurse wants? I get extra for this long. I honor my deals and it didn't include waiting hours for the sick ones."

"Go to house," Vladimir said, curling his lips. "I will bring the others. Nurse hurries."

The driver jumped back into the cab and drove slowly. Celia saw his mud covered back plates. He waited for someone to open the gate. She hurried back to Marcy.

While waiting for the gatekeeper, Marcy tapped the steering wheel.

"Marcy. You wait here for the police. I've got to follow them."

"You sure you want to follow them? These are mean dudes."

"We need to know where they take the women. The police won't act if they don't see them. I called and they reluctantly agreed to send the police."

"Don't like you chasing them," Marcy said, breathing hard. "What happens when you get there? You can't do this alone."

"No. I'll have the address where they can raid and find the women," Celia said. "Those women are treated here by a nurse in the ER. They don't want a paper trail so they must treat them off the books. I'll call with the location. You can redirect the police. Hide in an alcove of the building."

"Again, I ask you to be sure."

"Positive. Go, Marcy."

Marcy got out of the car and headed for the wall where she found an alcove. The gates opened and the truck took off. She started the motor when she saw a black SUV roll into the parking lot and the four women loaded into it. The black SUV followed behind the truck. Vladimir stood on the platform watching.

Okay. Now I'm tailing armed kidnappers. Swell, how crazy is this?

But this is closer than we've ever come to finding something the police can work with.

She swerved, maintaining sight of the SUV. Keeping a three-car distance, she stayed on their tail. Suddenly, the black SUV jerked to a stop. So did Celia. A wiry man stepped out and started running toward her. Glints off the metal of a gun startled her.

Reverse. The opposite lanes were empty. Out of the corner of her eye, she saw the black SUV nosing out of line.

"Fuck," she yelled. The car appeared to be following her at a discrete distance. They were tailing her to see if she'd lead them to the others. *I must get Marcy out of there.*

She made a sudden turn into a side street. The black car barreled down on her rear. She veered into another side street. Then headed down Center City streets, Broad Street, 15th, 17th, and finally 19th. *Philly police, please stop me for speeding! Where are they when I need them?*

On 19th Street, heading south, she zigzagged across lanes. Turning on Chestnut, she found herself going in the direction of the hospital. The rising sun blinded her as she went due east, melting passersby into streaks of yellow and white paint on a canvas.

She jumped into the left lane, narrowly slamming into a car, and checked the rearview mirror. The SUV was still following her. She held her breath and veered left onto 13th where cars parked on both sides left only one lane. She heard a loud bang, and she hit the steering wheel. Her pursuers had smacked her rear bumper. Pain shot through her chest and down her spine. For a second her vision blurred. She shook her head as her car skidded in a puddle of water. She took her foot off the gas, trying to go with the skid. When she came out of it, she straightened the car and headed to the next intersection.

She kept her foot on the accelerator and blew through the stop signs on the cross streets. As the light shifted to red, she blew through it too, and said a prayer. In her rearview she saw the SUV turn a corner in the other direction. A reprieve? Maybe he needed to get the women back. She called Marcy on her cell and told her exactly where to wait for a pickup.

"The police never came," Marcy said. "Just get me the hell out of here."

"On my way."

Chapter 40

Celia leaned over and opened the passenger door and Marcy jumped in just as a police car pulled into the parking lot.

"Wait," Marcy said. "They're here."

Several men stepped out on the platform and greeted the police. Vladimir among them. The SUV must have gotten word to just beat it out of there.

Marcy gripped Celia's shoulder. "What do we do?"

"Just wait a minute." *If the police believe their lies we'll be exposing ourselves.*

A big guy stood talking to the cops, gesturing and twirling his finger at his temple, indicating the "crazy" sign. She saw them all laughing. The police got back into the patrol car. Celia started to jump out of the car to stop them when Marcy grabbed her back.

"You'll be outed, and the cops won't believe you."

"You're right." Celia sat back down and slumped. "I have to find that nurse who handled the victims. Maybe I can get a bead on where they keep them."

"She can report you."

"I have to take the chance. It might be the last hope. Can't go in while those brutes are in there. I'll go later."

"We're fucked, babe," Marcy said in a hushed voice.

"Not yet. Not as long as we're still kicking. At least we know she has the morning shift."

When Celia entered the hotel room, she saw Stanton had brought food. He didn't question where they'd been, maybe in deference to Allison. With all the adrenaline pumping through her body, she wasn't hungry. But she'd join them just to encourage Allie, who hadn't been eating much of late.

Stanton filled Celia's plate with a burger and French fries. Allison sat at the desk, her plate untouched. Marcy ate as though she hadn't eaten for a week.

"I'm starving." Marcy said, her mouth full. "And you, Allie, have a hungry baby who wants to eat whether you want to or not."

"I'm still worried about Justin. Maybe he's been hurt." She pushed her fries around on the plate. "Maybe he ghosted me."

"Never." Celia turned to Stanton and placed her hand on his arm, giving a series of squeezes like Morse code. He seemed to get the message. *We have to tell Allie very soon.*

Stanton leaned over and whispered in her ear, "I picked up a copy of the *Philadelphia Inquirer* at the Wawa. Seems Justin has made the front page. Make sure Allie doesn't see it."

Resuming his normal voice, he said, "Anyone want cold baked beans with their burgers?" He held up a can and Marcy grabbed it out of his hand.

"Did you say caviar?"

"We can pretend, can't we?" His voice seemed forced.

And, in his Stanton way, he looked good, in his jeans and a beige V-neck sweater with the bulge of bandages. He stared at Celia and

Marcy who leaned against each other. Celia saw he wanted to delay the news about Justin and so did she. But Allison had to be told.

"Ladies," he said, "you look as though you just crept out of bed with a massive hangover."

"We had, uh, a bit of a harrowing time," Marcy said and went back to shoveling food into her mouth.

Allison held her burger in the air, about to take a bite. "We thought you went out this morning for an errand. What happened?"

"A truck dropped off several women at the hospital ER," Celia said. "We called the police but the women were driven away by the time police arrived. We can talk later."

"Oh, another missed opportunity," Allison said, her face sobered. "I'm sure you ran in to see if Justin was there?"

"It was still early morning," Celia said. "Too much commotion for the new shift." *Time has nearly run out.*

When they finished brunch, Stanton nodded. Celia held her breath.

Allison looked directly at Celia. "What's going on?"

Celia realized she hadn't been breathing and now drew in a deep breath. She sat on the sofa against the wall and patted the seat for Allison who moved over slowly, wringing her hands.

"You're about to give me bad news."

"It's about Justin."

"What? Tell me."

"I am going to tell you in few words." And she did: the suicide scene, the written fake confession, the scent of arsenic, Pennsylvania Hospital, and the hired guard. "He was in a coma and he's coming out of it slowly. All his vital signs are okay."

Allison let out a howl, like a wounded animal. Tears ran down

Celia's face as Allison collapsed against her. "You should have told me," she moaned.

"We held off because we knew you'd go to see him and worried they'd be looking to get you. He's going to be all right, I'm sure."

Stanton pulled out the *Philadelphia Inquirer* with its front-page headline: "MD at Rudrow Hospital Attempts Suicide."

"I have to see him," Allison said, clutching her belly and murmuring words Celia didn't catch. She spoke in a disjointed way, each fragment a thin sliver of pain going straight through Celia's heart.

"Thank God you had the presence of mind to get him out of Rudrow," Marcy said.

"Pennsylvania Hospital's pathology department has an excellent reputation. And Stanton hired a security guard from a four-star company," Celia said.

Allison hardly spoke for the next five minutes. "Marcy," Celia whispered. "Stay with her. Keep her from going out." Marcy moved closer and lowered herself into a chair.

When the room became quiet, something hit her. Celia reached into the neck of her blouse and patted her employee placard.

Little time left. It's all or nothing.

No one spoke. She waited for them to take an afternoon nap.

She went to the Rudrow Emergency Room entrance. The ER was bustling with near chaos and she knew how easily a nurse or doctor might slip patients through without question. She was carrying Allie's clipboard and walked with authority. The ID swung with each step.

An image of the nurse on the loading dock was planted in Celia's mind and she hoped her shift hadn't ended. This was nutty, but she had to find her. Celia pushed her shoulders back and walked on, as though checking to see that the ER ran smoothly. In one of the curtained off areas a nurse worked on a patient who had a gash on his forehead and was demanding to see a doctor. She looked over the nurse's shoulder and pretended to make a note on her clipboard.

She walked toward a door that said "HOSPITAL STAFF ONLY." Through the doors came the nurse.

"I need to speak to you," Celia said, grabbing her arm. "It's about the patients from the container."

The nurse jumped back and retreated. Celia grabbed her arm.

"I don't…"

"Now."

The nurse hustled Celia into an empty examining room. Celia slammed the door shut.

"Excuse me," the nurse said, her voice shaky. "Who are you?"

"I know you're on Vladimir's payroll. You need to give me information."

"I'm going to call security." The nurse grabbed the phone.

"Go ahead if you want to go to prison for being an accomplice to sex trafficking."

"Those women were just employees of a nightclub." Her eyes scrutinized Celia. "Who the hell are you? You're not the police."

"Employees in a container? I know you are on the payroll of a bunch of criminals and murderers who import sex slaves. Do you want the hospital to find out you're getting these patients through without registering them? That does become a police matter." Celia ripped her cell out of her pocket. "Call security."

The nurse's face turned deadly white. "I'm innocent. The worst I've done is treat those women. I didn't know they were sex slaves." Her hands trembled.

"I saw you take a fat envelope of money from Vladimir." Celia scrutinized her face. "Thought so. The very least punishment is you lose your RN license. More likely it's prison time."

"You can't prove anything. What do you want? Money?"

I don't have proof, but I'll wring it out of you if I have to stay for days. "I want the address of where the women go. I won't turn your name into the police if you give it to me…um, Susan Anderson." Celia tapped the nurse's name tag. "If you don't cooperate, I'll be shouting your name from the rooftop to the authorities. You also have to swear never to do this again."

"I promise, but I don't know where they take them."

"Like hell. I'm sure you've sent medication to that address."

Susan's face turned to rage. "You have no proof I did anything wrong. Watch your step. I'm protected by these people."

"I have it on good authority that man who pays you is about to be caught. I'll turn you in without another thought."

Celia knew she'd taken the right approach by the look of horror on Susan's face. "Maybe you stole pills from the hospital for the patients you treated under the radar?" Celia gave her a smug smile. "Maybe you didn't know every detail of what Vladimir did, but will the police believe you? Will a jury? This man brings you regular shipments of women out of a shipping container and you treat them off the books? Doesn't speak to innocence."

Susan looked stricken. "Alright." She wrote down the address. As she handed the memo to Celia, she gave her a pleading look. "Please don't share my name with the police."

"Stop taking blood money from those animals. You hear me?"

Celia said through clenched teeth. "Put them through the system and call the police."

Susan looked away. "They'll kill me and my kids." She shook her head.

"You could save lives and cut a deal for yourself. Those women are ruined for the rest of their lives. Children are sex slaves. Don't you have a conscience?"

Susan looked away as though Celia had struck her. "I'm a single mom. I have three kids and an ex-husband who won't send child support. What am I supposed to do?"

"Not this. You have options as a skilled nurse. This is undeclared cash. The IRS can put a federal tax lien on everything you own. You'll need a fortune just to pay a lawyer."

Pity almost took hold of Celia. *This woman has come from a hard place. But no.* "Picture one of your children kidnapped off the street and groomed to be a sex slave."

Susan stifled a sob. When she finally caught her breath, she looked at Celia. "Now what?"

"You've helped by giving me the address." Celia gave Susan a sideways glance. "One more thing. Can you get me into Vladimir's office? Does he have a safe there?"

"Absolutely not. He'll know I did it. He knows I have access."

"It's the least you can do for me."

Luckily the offices on Vladimir's floor were either empty or their doors were closed. Susan had a key to the janitor's office. A bunch of keys hung on hooks with office numbers printed above each key. Susan wiped her forehead as she handed Celia the key and waited outside for Celia, who flicked on the lights.

Carefully, Celia went through drawers and cabinets, and found nothing. About to give up, she looked behind a printer and saw the wall panel had a very thin hinge on the side. A letter opener sat on the desk. She pushed it into a spot that looked as though it had been used for leverage before. She flipped the letter opener hard, and the section flipped open. Inside she saw three flash drives. Surprised at how easily she found them, she looked around to make sure there were no cameras. She tucked the drives inside her jacket pocket. Not all of Vladimir's business dealings they'd found from hacking into Svetlana's computer could be there. There had to be other information he had from before. She replaced the wall panel, closed the lights, and left.

Susan waited. Celia dropped the key into her trembling hand.

Susan peered back over her shoulder. "I've cooperated. You won't tell the cops?" she whispered. "I'll stop."

Celia nodded. "We have a deal."

She now could notify police once she went to the address. If it was the correct house it had to be heavily guarded. She'd have to see it for herself. She tried to devise a plan as she began heading in the direction of the address.

Celia's cell rang. "Stanton. What's wrong?"

"I'm worried about Allie. She's crying inconsolably and seems feverish. She's moaning Justin's name."

"I'll be there as soon as I can."

Celia turned back to Market Street, dotted with garish neon lights advertising every conceivable electronic and cosmetic item. She decided to call Pennsylvania Hospital, claiming to be Justin's mother once again. They told her that Justin was talking and able to get out of bed.

"Great news in this house of horrors," she said to herself.

Chapter 41

Back at the hotel, Celia found Marcy sitting on the edge of the bed, comforting Allison who sobbed.

"Allie," Celia whispered. "Justin's doing well. He's even walking."

Allison's wavy hair swirled, eyes reddened as she shook her head in disbelief. "Are you sure?"

"I just called," said Celia, her heart aching over the distress in Allie's eyes. "Dry those beautiful peepers of yours and come sit here beside your mama."

Celia made room on the couch and Allie slid in. Marcy and Stanton moved two side chairs so they all faced each other around the low-slung, wooden cocktail table.

"Look at what I found," said Celia, tossing the flash drives on the table.

"What are those?" Stanton asked, a crease forming on his forehead.

"Well, uh," Celia began. "I sneaked into Vladimir's office, and found these in a wall opening. Can't go into detail right now."

"Oh Mom," Allie said through quivering lips. "Why would you risk that?"

Celia fisted her hands. "We have to save ourselves and as many women as possible. We've been thwarted at every step. Danielle was as close as we've gotten, but…" Celia cleared her throat. "If we do nothing, they'll find us, so we may as well find them first."

"We're all dead in the water if we don't act," Marcy said.

Celia wrapped her arm over Allison's shoulder. "Honey, I hate to give your father his due, but you inherited his math brain." Celia found out after Gabe died that he secretly gave most of his money to his mistress, but kept her on a strict budget. It was math genius or Celia's naivete. "Between you and Stanton we've got a head start. Are you up to it?" Allison nodded.

Allie is a whizz at accounting. Allie, along with Stanton's skills, gives us an advantage.

Stanton understood the mechanics and structure of problems. Allie could see into problems, dig deep into numbers, and come up with a vivid picture of the heart of the issue. She could almost produce a psychological profile from how business books were kept. With a mind that was precise and organized, she could delve into the systems they used. That's what helped her go from nursing to an MBA, majoring in accounting. Only her romantic endeavors were a disaster, until Justin.

"I need quiet." Allison picked up two of the flash drives and nodded to Stanton.

Stanton picked up the third. "Let's see if we can't put this puzzle together." He got up and brought back his laptop, inserting the flash drive.

"I hope we find the proof to clear Justin," Celia said in a hushed voice.

"We have to get these people. Have to," Marcy said, stumbling out of the room.

Stanton's face grew pale. "Jail is too good for the scum."

Allison arrived at Celia's room for dinner. "I hear Stanton risked all to bring us Philly cheesesteaks, one of the reasons I love this city."

"I'm not going down without a full stomach of Philly's finest," he said, smiling.

Celia handed Allie a bottle of water. She looked like she'd been in a wrestling match, hair tousled, her blouse awry and mis-buttoned.

She gulped greedily. "Feels like I haven't had anything to drink for days." She breathed deeply as she sat down.

"You look as though you've just returned from a shaky shuttle to the moon," Marcy remarked, pouring herself a glass of red wine.

"I called Justin. He spoke to me—slowly. He sounded pretty good," Allison said. "We'll pick him up as soon as they discharge him in a few days. He thanks Mom for saving his life and putting the guard at his door." She looked up at Celia. "Good thinking."

"Thanks, sweetie."

"Now, back to business. I think I figured out something important." Allison's voice snapped out of listlessness. "One flash drive had names of hospitals where Vladimir supplied the linens. Nothing revealing except he had a big customer list."

Celia, Marcy, and Stanton immediately crowded closer around her.

"Easy," she said with a glint in her eye.

"Speak, oh mystical one," Marcy said, eyes closed and hands stretched out, pretending to conjure an imaginary crystal ball.

Allison inserted the flash drive into Stanton's laptop. "This listing of numbers on page one. I think it's an account of illegal loans." She ran her finger down a long column. "He has initials after each name with an amount paid each week. I might be off but I doubt it."

Celia leaned in closer.

"On another page titled 'trade' are initials for women and how much they brought in each week." She touched the monitor with her finger. "So, trafficking, usury, and multiple loans each woman owed for drugs is like four million a week for Philadelphia alone. Each child or woman services maybe fifteen to twenty men a day, or more.

"Not included in that title are columns that note money collected for sales and dates. Doesn't say what kind of items. Could be hospital equipment?" She tapped the monitor. "Here are companies that list unnamed big-ticket items. Guess amounts are in other books."

"It's circumstantial evidence for the police," Stanton said. "It could have been written by anyone about anything. Nothing indicates anything was stolen."

Allison nodded. "But we know, and perhaps we can trace some of it."

"How do we do that?" Marcy piped up.

"Stanton and I can figure that out," Allison said. "Maybe get one of the customers of hospital equipment to say who sold it to him."

"Not if they know it's stolen goods. They won't implicate themselves," Celia said.

"In my flash drive," said Stanton. "Vladimir shows bank accounts of several corporations that each lead to finally depositing the money in the offshore bank. All of these corporations have Justin as CEO. I need my mole at that offshore bank to find the real owner. He owes me. It's tough." Stanton studied the monitor. "This is a medium-sized bank. In big banks, people like Stompovich set up accounts with multimillions of dollars. The financial institutions combine them with other fat, questionable accounts, and they're nearly impossible for the IRS to untangle. The banks seem to look the other way while raking in big fees."

"Another way he could be doing this is through casinos," Allison said. "Casinos are a way to launder money. It's another avenue we might get police to look into." Allison rolled her eyes. "My ex bragged he could launder money in casinos when he made his windfall. I laughed at his grandiose ideas while he pissed away all of our savings at the tables."

"Irresponsible cad."

"Mom!" said Allie.

"Sorry honey, I can't help myself sometimes."

"Hold on," Marcy said. "I want to hear the answer from all this brilliance. Let's go."

"I love cyber investigations," said Stanton. "Allie and Celia can match me. And so can you, Marcy. You tend to lose focus."

"Me, lose focus?" Marcy said. "I have one goal. To get us back to Florida and find me a nice guy, like you, at the early bird special."

He tapped his hand over his heart, and puffed out his chest out. "From your lips to the goddess's ears." He pointed to Celia.

That gave everyone a laugh.

"Okay," said Allie. "Here's one scheme. Vladimir sends his crew in pairs to the casinos. One buys a small amount of chips. The other goes in with large amounts of cash and buys chips. They appear to be strangers. One gambles just a little, as does his partner. At the end of the night, the person with the big stash hands that to their partner with little money and vice versa. They cash out as though Ms. Few Chips won big and Mr. Big Chips lost all of his moola. Next, he has faked big losses he reports to the IRS. The large amount of transferred money given to his partner appears as gambling winnings that is reported to the IRS and not money from outside racketeering. Hence, laundering."

"It's the way the Mafia does it," Stanton said.

"People say the Mafia has died. Not true," Marcy said. "I've read how they've gone under the radar. Tell them Celia, 'cause we read it together."

Celia inhaled. "In addition to all the old way of doing business—extortion, drugs, and sex trafficking—they've added buying corporations with worthless stock. Once they are owners, they empty the coffers. But first, they make loans on the company assets before going bust. When they declare bankruptcy, they don't pay anyone—not the banks, not the employees, not the struggling vendors. Maybe that's Vladimir's scheme with the hospital—empty the coffers till they close. Then onto the next one. People living paycheck to paycheck are the ones who pay the price."

"See? You are very smart, Marcy," Celia finished. "You remembered the article and understood it. You hide behind your smarts with your hot sexuality. In fact, good men like smart women."

Marcy struck a playful pose. "You mean I can stop hiding my genius IQ behind this?"

"My turn," Stanton said. "I found more stuff on my flash drive. The kind of stuff I've come across before in my work."

"Give it up fast, Stanton," Marcy said.

"You hit it right, Allison. There are subtle code words I'm beginning to recognize. Vladimir appears to be using casinos for money laundering," Stanton said. "So, proof is elusive once again. Anyway, all of this was obtained illegally. It's called theft. You're good at it, Celia."

"I intend to get better. It's frustrating that we have so much information we can't use," said Celia. *I do have that address.*

"If we get one thing that sticks, we can carefully use what we found to back it up," Stanton said. "We don't want to expose ourselves."

Celia looked at him. "My question is, does Vladimir have American citizenship, Allie? Would you know that?"

"Yes, he does," said Allie. "I was at a meeting when someone objected to his being there because he was a foreigner. He laughed and declared he had dual US and Russian citizenship. What you're after is, can he escape to his native home and avoid prosecution?"

"Yes, if they don't detain him and take his passport right away."

"The upside is," Stanton looked up from lowered eyelids, "if you notify authorities with evidence that someone didn't report income and deliberately cheated the government and they collect, you might be entitled to a percentage of what is recouped. They put injunctions on the accused's property, security boxes, freeze accounts, and try to trace their bank accounts in places like Costa Rica, Panama, and the Caymans—as long as it's over two million. If my mole at the bank comes through, it might be enough evidence for an investigation. That's not theft, just good accounting."

"What are we waiting for?" Marcy shouted.

"Slow down Marcy. We're not there yet," Allison said.

"If we open an investigation and they recoup, how much can we get?" Marcy asked, eyes blinking.

"The casinos have to be subpoenaed to open their books. If it works, authorities can start looking into other criminal enterprises. If the government recoups money, fifteen to thirty percent of what they collect is given to the whistleblower. It might take a few years," Stanton said.

Marcy raised her hands over an imaginary crystal ball. "I see a beautiful farmhouse with a number of cottages, gardens, a pool, and staff. We can all live there together!"

Chapter 42

Allie tapped a pencil. "Marcy, you said the Mafias are alive and well. Do mobsters do all this?"

"Yes. Mobs still do numbers, drugs, sex trade, money laundering, paying moles for information, bribery, gambling, extortions, and usury, to name a few. Oh, and embezzling, Too much money to give up. They're quieter now so as not to agitate the FBI like Gotti did. He thumbed his nose at them for years till they got him."

"How do you know all this, Marcy?" Stanton asked.

"Once had a boyfriend who was low-level Mafia. Took a bullet to the back of his head and wound up in the trunk of a car." She made a sad face. "Made me interested in how they operated. To be frank, this windfall with the government can make up for all the trauma."

"That's out of reach right now," Celia said with a tinge of annoyance. "Allie, is there anything about the sex trade on any of those flash drives? Cost of containers, shipping?"

"Sorry, I scanned it over and over and couldn't find a thing. He used codes to identify where the money came from."

Celia touched the crumpled piece of paper in her pocket. She felt exhaustion overtaking her. "Enough information for one day. My head is bursting."

"Hold onto these, Mom." Allison handed Celia the flash drives.

"I'm off to bed." Allison rose and walked to the door. "We'll strategize in the morning. After I talk to Justin."

Celia rose and kissed Allison on the cheek. "Goodnight, honey."

"How much do you think we can get by turning in the scumbags?" Marcy asked, holding the doorknob.

"Stop asking," Celia said, gritting her teeth. She didn't have the energy to ask Stanton to say it again. Nor did he look as though he wanted to. Despite his injuries, he did a splendid job.

Stanton sat heavily on his bed and studied Celia. "Look at that beautiful face. I'm begging you, stay out of trouble. I don't want to see you hurt."

They lapsed into silence. Stanton fell back on the bed. "I hate to ask, but do you have any more Percocet? Bad day. These ribs hurt like a bitch."

"This is what they're for. Sleep well, dear Stanton." She handed him a pill and a glass of water.

He finished the glass of water and lay against the pillow. "I love you," he whispered as he closed his eyes.

Celia had just settled on the couch with a glass of wine when she heard a commotion in the hallway…then a dull thump, as though the carpet muffled the sound of someone who had fallen. She ran to the door, looked out, and saw Marcy scanning the hallway.

"I was in the bathroom and Allie went to get ice."

"What was she thinking?" Celia turned the corner and saw a canister of ice cubes scattered on the hall carpet, and a dark, wet stain spreading. The ice maker rumbled. The noise struck Celia like a hurricane. A nearby door opened, and a man stood there in a white terry cloth robe.

"Did you see what happened?" Celia demanded.

He looked sheepish. "I saw two men dragging a lady to the fire exit. I was about to call…"

Celia grabbed Marcy's hand and ran with her down the fire exit stairs.

Celia's heart beat faster than a jackhammer as she and Marcy hopped in the car and sped north on Route 95 toward the northeast neighborhood section where the house was located. They'd left in such a hurry that she'd forgotten to get the gun. She knew there'd be heavily armed guards.

Please let us find Allie at that house. It's logical they'd put her with the others. Right? Somebody tell me I'm guessing right.

They entered a neighborhood of small, tidy, brick front, one-story single homes with attached garages and small backyards. Celia had grown up in that kind of working-class neighborhood.

She parked a half-block down from and across the street of the house. As she and Marcy approached the house, she saw a mid-sized truck idling in front. Two men got out and opened the back door. They dragged a woman out. Celia recognized Allie. She made a move forward. Marcy held her back. Two armed guards stepped from the garage, the dim light outlining wiry, muscular bodies, rifles slung over their shoulders. She wondered if the neighbors had any idea about what was going on in that house.

"An Uzi can take us out in seconds," Marcy whispered. "Don't jump or get emotional."

The men tightened their hold on Allie and laughed as they hustled her inside through the garage. Celia saw a black SUV parked between stacks of unopened boxes against three walls, all the way to the ceiling.

She looked at the open truck doors and saw even larger boxes with the V & S logo sticker pasted on X-ray equipment, sterilizers, and mattresses. Only a few boxes were torn open, revealing stethoscopes hanging over the sides, surgical masks, and vials of medications.

"That's the stuff the bastards steal from the hospital," Marcy muttered. "I'm taking pictures." She took out her phone and snapped.

"We've got to get into the house and find Allie first," Celia whispered. "But we have to wait for those idiot drivers to leave." *Please, whoever listens to prayers, help us rescue Allie.*

Celia saw the fear in Marcy's face. "Understand, Marcy, you can leave if you want."

"No fucking way."

The two men appeared, laughing, joking, and elbowing each other. They motioned to one of the guards to get into the truck. "Those bitches are not going anywhere."

Okay, one guard leaving. Hope only one is left.

Their peals of laughter slashed the quiet neighborhood air. The guy on the passenger side stuck his head out the window and waved a bottle of beer. "We'll be back, ladies. So be ready."

Marcy adjusted her leotard, then her black baseball cap. "Catwoman is ready. What's the game plan?"

"We have to wing it."

They waited until a guard stepped out of the garage. He lit a cigarette and blew the smoke out, leaving the garage door open.

Celia looked around for escape routes from the stubby brick ranch house. It had no distinctive architectural features except steel shutters and padlocked doors. The backyard was encased in wire fencing and spotlights along the roof lit up the grounds. The lawn was burned-out, coffee-colored, without a bush or a tree. *I know this neighborhood.*

People are innocent of horrors like this in their midst. They probably just think of this house as the one on the block to avoid, the one that brings down the value of their own houses. The guard flipped his cigarette to the street and followed its trajectory.

Chapter 43

When Celia heard a stream of water hitting against metal, she peeked further around the edge of the house to see the guard urinating against the fender of a car, his back to her. She grabbed Marcy and they flew into the garage and through the open door that led into the house.

They stopped to get their bearings. From the corner of Celia's eye, she saw the kitchen. They inched toward it. When they entered, six women sitting around a table registered surprise on their faces. Sweat and perfume mingled with the smell of steam from the stove.

The women were dressed in shorts and filmy nightgowns. Two had cigarettes dangling from their lips. All of them looked pale to yellowish and somewhat emaciated. A woman was at the stove, stirring a small pot. She turned her head to the side.

"Nikki?" Marcy said.

Nikki spun around and waved them in. "So, you come to rescue us again. Don't you see it's useless? You'd better get out. Save yourselves."

"We're here and not leaving," Celia said in a subdued tone. "We'll all leave alive."

Nikki shrugged and pointed to the padlocked door. "All doors are locked. There's a guard outside who'd shoot his own mother for a dime. Windows are bulletproof. No escaping."

"Did you see a young woman being dragged in by two men just a few minutes ago?" Celia asked.

Nikki pointed her thumb down a long hall. "Yup, dragged her to the office. Vladimir, Svetlana, Ramon, and a guy from the docks are in there."

"Is he the supervisor named Jack?" Marcy asked.

"That's him."

"Let's call the police." Marcy grasped Nikki's arm. "You'll tell them what they've done."

"Police?" Nikki put her hand over her mouth to muffle a harsh laugh. "They get the word police are coming. We're shoved to a worse place." Nikki turned off the stove. "These women are protecting families. They're afraid of being arrested and deported. You must know that by now."

"Just briefly, there's a Trafficking Victims Act. Offers a temporary visa if you help turn these men in. In a few years you're eligible for permanent residence. They'll house and feed these women till they get on their feet."

"Look, I got to bring the big honchos their vodka. All day they drink. The only way out is the garage. It's guarded. The other guard will be back soon. You two gotta beat it out of here."

An idea hit Celia. The bottle of Percocet was in her pocket, of which she still had twenty-six pills. She knew taking between five to sixteen pills was considered an overdose. She pulled out the bottle. She laid out four pills per shot glass on the kitchen counter and crushed them with the handle of a knife. She added two more for good measure. They needed to be out for quite a while. She brushed them back into the bottle.

"Put even amounts in five glasses of vodka. The fifth is for the guard. It'll take ten to twenty minutes to take effect. It's not going to kill them. Just knocks them out pretty damn well."

Nikki took the bottle. "How do I pull this off?"

"Stir really well. Do they take ice?"

Nikki nodded.

"Perfect. Ice will hide any cloudiness. Just make sure they drink. They have my daughter."

"Oh, they will drink for sure," Nikki mumbled. "They've been looking for you. Your daughter is the prize. She'd talk sooner or later. They'll find you, kill all of you."

Celia's heart seized. "Are there other women here now?"

"Others left to work and won't come back until late morning."

"Where are the other houses?"

"All over the city—the country—the world."

"A woman's work is never done," one woman piped in, unsmiling.

"Where is the vodka?"

"Cabinet." Nikki pointed to a pine cabinet at the end of a hall-way.

"Nikki, get those drinks to them, please," Celia pleaded. "It'll work out."

Nikki scowled. "You can get us killed, but I owe you one—big time." Nikki picked up a large tray with five empty glasses with powder in each one and an ice bucket. "Whatcha think?" She looked around at the other women. All of them nodded.

"Nothing to lose except our lives." Nikki's voice was robotic. "I'll be right fucking back—maybe." She walked down the hall, balancing the tray.

"When you're free, ladies," Marcy squeaked, "please, please go to the police."

Several women backed up as though about to be struck.

The walls seemed to close in on Celia. "If you decide to go to the authorities, I swear we'll contact your families and warn them to hide." *God, is that enough?*

Ten minutes later, Nikki walked back with the empty tray. Her dead eyes revealed nothing.

Celia gripped her shoulder. "What? Oh, please…my daughter…"

"She's okay for now. Knocked her around. They were trying to get her to tell where you are now. I served them, then waited. They downed those drinks like water. By the time I left, they were a little woozy. Got the guard, too"

"I've got to go to Allie in ten minutes."

"Make sure the cocksuckers are knocked out." Nikki put the tray in the sink. Her expressionless face suddenly brightened. "We'll be out of here soon. Let's hope it's not worse on the other side."

Celia hurried along the hallway. She pressed her ear to the door but heard nothing. Then she heard a glass shatter and pushed the door open. There were fragments of glass on the floor, directly under Ramon's drooping hand. He and Svetlana were slumped in chairs across the desk from Vladimir whose head was rolled back against his chair, spittle forming at the side of his mouth. They were all breathing heavily. The remnants of Svetlana's drink had spilled on her lap.

Celia scanned the room. No Allie. She heard a sobbing sound behind the closet door. Slowly, she opened the door to see Allie huddled in the corner, shivering, her face burrowed into her arm.

"Allie, Allie," Celia cried. "It's Mom. I'm getting you out. Hang on."

Allison raised her head and Celia gasped. Allie's cheek was scarlet, blood oozed from her forehead and nose. "Can you walk, honey?"

Allison nodded.

"Here, hold onto my arms. I'll pull you up."

"I didn't tell them anything," Allison sobbed, collapsing against Celia who held her in an embrace. "They wanted you and Marcy." Allison stopped and stared at Vladimir, Ramon, and Svetlana. "How did you…?"

"Let's get out of here. I'll explain later. We can do this."

"They punched me hard, said they would shoot and bury me in the backyard, they…"

"It's okay, honey. Shush. Shush. When you're ready, we'll tell the police."

"What the fuck!" Vladimir's head jerked forward.

"Shit," Celia shouted. "Let's go, now!"

She hadn't noticed that he held a gun in his hand until now. His unfocussed eyes landed on them. He raised a gun, aiming it in their direction. Celia threw herself in front of Allison, squeezed her eyes, and waited. No shot came. She opened her eyes. Vladimir's arms dropped and he slumped forward over his desk.

"We're out of here, honey." She hurried Allison along the hallway past rooms where dirty sheets were tossed over mattresses on the floor. In the kitchen they found only Marcy.

"The women all beat it out of here when the guard dropped to the ground." Marcy said, her voice raspy. "But you have Allie, thank God. Let's get our asses out of here."

What do we need to get all this equipment investigated? Can Vladimir somehow claim all this material came from his import/export business? How do we get warrants to examine hospital records legally, so it will stick in court?

"Once we're out, we go to the police," Celia said, trying to balance Allie who clung to her.

"Maybe they'll finally listen," Marcy said. "We have the address. It has to be done before they wake up. How about we get the next crew of women to talk?"

"Problem is the men will be around. Their body language alone could intimidate the women to keep quiet."

Back at the car, Marcy settled Allie in the back seat and sat next to her. Celia started the motor but let it idle, wracking her brain about the next step. "Marcy, unless those women go to the police, we don't have any witnesses."

Their only hope was to convince the police to stake out the house. *Probably think it's a prank after receiving several calls that went nowhere.*

She called 911. The dispatcher had a terse response and put her through to a desk sergeant.

"Ma'am, calm down," the sergeant said. "Is anyone hurt?"

"These women are hurt every day of their lives and my daughter is badly bruised." Celia took deep breaths to calm herself. "We just left a house that is being used by a sex trafficking ring. You have to come and arrest the leaders."

"Are there women in the house now?"

"No. Another group is expected later tonight."

He reluctantly took the address. "Lady, you realize that we have no probable cause to come out except for what you say. Do you have names of the women?"

Celia moved the phone away from her ear as desperation fogged her brain.

"Mom," said Allie. "Give them Nikki's name."

Celia thought for a few seconds. "We don't have a last name."

She went back to the call and was told she needed last names. "Do you have substantial proof? Enough for a subpoena?"

"Only the leaders are here."

"No one to validate what you're saying?"

"Listen. I learned it firsthand. I was captured by them, but escaped. My daughter has been knocked around by them."

"Hmm. How old are you? You know they kidnap young ones only. You don't sound like you're fifteen."

"I'm not." Celia wanted to scream. "They wanted me and my friend as matrons to keep an eye on the victims and keep them in line. This is ridiculous. The ringleaders might leave. Please come." She gave the address.

"Hold on." After a thirty-second silence, he returned. "Just checked. Recently a call came in about a hospital with a truckload of these women. Did you make that?"

We're sunk. "Yes, a police car came but just missed the container that brought the women."

There was a long silence. Celia broke it. "There are loads of stolen supplies from Rudrow Hospital, too. You can look in the garage of this house. Stacks and stacks of stolen hospital supplies, machinery, and opioids."

"We'd need an official from the hospital to make a complaint. We don't have one in the computer."

"The ones responsible *are* the officials from the hospital. Why would they complain about themselves?"

There was a soft snicker. "Those are serious charges against high-ranking citizens. Do you have a history of mental illness? I can refer you to an agency for help."

"These guys don't care who they hurt or what they steal."

Celia clicked off the phone. "Shit. We're up against it. No help." She dropped the cell phone on the car's floor and smashed it with the heel of her shoe. *Leave no trace.*

I have to stop. I leave them alone and they'll leave me alone. But…

The night air cooled Celia's burning brow. Marcy slumped.

Celia felt a jolt of energy surge throug her. "We can't give up yet. We're too close. Allie, you stay in the back of the car and get some sleep."

"Mom?"

"Trust me one last time."

"I want to, but…"

"Marcy? You still have your cell phone? Allie, I'm leaving the keys with you. Lock the doors. If you see any suspicious men, drive back to the hotel fast. Come on, Marcy."

"What are we doing now?" said Marcy, rousing herself as Celia rummaged in the trunk for a tire iron.

"You'll see."

Marcy stared, stupefied.

They walked toward the house. "We're going back in," Celia said when they reached the garage. "Come on." Through the garage, into the house, down the corridor with the now empty rooms. She found Vladimir, Ramon, Svetlana, and Jack still unconscious. She searched through Vladimir's pockets and took his wallet. In Svetlana's purse she found a set of car keys. On top of the desk was a computer and two flash drives. She picked up the drives and slipped them into her pocket. Complaints from the women were scribbled on scraps of paper and even on toilet paper. They said things like, "we'll die here," "haven't seen daylight in weeks," "I'm sick and the men keep coming." Celia grabbed the notes. *Proof?*

They went around to the backyard. The lawn was littered with trash, old car parts, and empty boxes.

Marcy shook her head. "This is turning into a humdinger. Why aren't we on the road?"

"We are going to arrange for the next group of women to escape," Celia said, walking to the back door.

"The dastardly foursome will eventually wake up, and there's a guard and a fence."

"There are a couple of breaks in the fence," Celia said. She banged at one of the kitchen windows with her tire iron. "We've got to break the padlock on the back door."

"Let's smash it," said Marcy.

Celia didn't hesitate, attacking the lock with all her might. The banging rang out.

We'll wake up the neighborhood. Something came loose. *We…can… do…this.*

They took turns until the lock snapped.

"Superwomen," said Marcy, rubbing her hands together.

In the kitchen, Celia wrote across a paper towel: "Ladies! Back door is open. Run like hell."

They were leaving through the garage when the thought hit her like a speeding train. *These bastards will get away with this.* "How brave do you feel?" she asked Marcy.

"Not very. We're still screwed."

She walked past the guard sprawled across the garage floor to

Svetlana's SUV. "I don't see any cameras here. And there were none inside the house."

"Arrogant assholes," Marcy spat. "They've got everyone in their pockets and are afraid of nothing."

Celia opened the door to the SUV and wiped the key, steering wheel, and door handles with her shirt. She started the motor, holding the key with a tissue.

Mary took several steps back. "Are you doing what I think you're doing?"

"Yes. I can shut the motor if you want. Say the word."

Marcy looked at Celia with narrowed eyes. "Are you for real?"

"I'm for real."

Marcy's mouth formed a straight line. "If we don't do this, these murderers will still round up women. These bastards will hunt us down. Let's…"

Celia stopped her. "We're going to put this hose from the exhaust pipe to the open house door. Then…" Celia stopped. "Shut the garage door, and leave the motor running. Those monsters, hopefully, will be out long enough for carbon monoxide to work. Afterward, we'll take our chances and leave town."

"There'll be others like Vladimir," Marcy said.

"We are getting rid of a small group of gangsters, but maybe it will save thousands of women they have all over the city." Celia sucked in her breath and slammed the car door shut. The motor spewed out gray clouds from the exhaust pipe. They walked out of the garage and stood at the overhead garage door.

"I'm thinking about Svetlana and her mother," Celia said.

"Svetlana's an accessory to murdering those poor women," Marcy cried. "She could have gotten off by saying she was a hostage. We know she lived like a princess. When you think she could have gone to the police and she abandoned her mother to suffer at the hands of those men."

"Svetlana kept a picture of herself and her mother. Maybe she protected her mother's life by going along with Vladimir." Thumping pain in Celia's head pulled her scalp tight. "Zutka saved our lives."

Celia nodded and both of them went back to the house one more time to drag Svetlana out and lay her on the grass. "Maybe she'll recognize the human destruction she helped cause."

"And the Pope is Jewish. This is for Zutka only."

Then Celia pulled out the tube of lipstick and wrote across Svetlana's arm: "Call your mother. She needs you."

"It feels like we're in a nightmare," Marcy said.

Celia stared at Marcy without blinking. "Nothing compares to the suffering of these women. It's slavery with brutal masters. And still, the women manage to retain empathy, sacrifice themselves to save their families, and develop community."

Marcy's nostrils flared. "I hear you. It's like the brain keeps memories of the pleasantries we once knew to keep us from becoming emotional robots. Let's do it."

"On the count of three," said Celia, when they reached the garage door. "One, two, three…" And they pulled the garage door shut.

"Justice has been done, but it's a high price for us to pay," Celia said. "It's an awful thing we're doing. It will haunt us forever."

"Think of the women and children who will be set free." Marcy straightened her back and flipped her hair over her shoulder. The curls seemed to bounce a little cha-cha back and forth.

Without another word between them, they got in the car, Marcy tucking in next to Allison, who slept soundly in the back seat.

"I got some flash drives from inside. Hope it tells the story of the money trail more carefully than the other flash drives I stole," Celia said, her voice somber. "Otherwise, we'll not collect any money."

"Why not?" Marcy asked, indignant.

"Without definitive evidence we're screwed. I hoped we could use the money to help those who need it more than we do. We did this for the women." Celia's eyes welled up. "Remember the rule? Be a little bad, the kind of bad that enhances life? We're doing a bad thing but getting the creeps off the streets, enhancing a teeny, tiny sliver of life. At least we can prove Justin is innocent."

"Yes, indeed," Marcy answered. "And we don't have to worry about hiding in a wet, damp dungeon and traipsing through slime. I can't wait to call my son and tell him to take his family home." She looked down. "I hope he'll still talk to me."

"He will. After I tell him you're a hero. Just don't tell him how it ended."

Celia and Marcy looked at each other. Then Celia looked out the windshield and started the motor. Thoughts of Stanton covered her in warmth, like basking in the sun. He would need a lot of TLC. The news she'd become a killer would not be what he'd want to hear—ever.

A small dull, yellow glow on the horizon signaled a new day, this one with promise.

"I only wish we'd have even just one woman who'd talk to the police."

"It's too bad we couldn't manage that one." Marcy sighed. "How do we tell them?"

Celia thought for a second. "We say we stopped them dead in their tracks. The stolen equipment from the hospital might help convince them."

Orange streaks behind gray clouds surrounded the rising sun, a yellow dome glimmering on the horizon. She eased the car down the street, past the menacing house, and cringed. She looked for passing cars at the intersection and saw a shadow stretching across the pavement. A figure ran out in the street. Celia hit the accelerator.

"Oh, my God," Marcy gasped. "Stop."

Celia slammed the brakes and thrust a hand on the dashboard to stop her forward motion. Allison sat up.

Someone banged on the window.

"It's Nikki," Marcy shouted.

Celia opened the passenger door and Nikki got in. "Take me with. I'll tell the police everything they want to know and how they stored all the stolen stuff from the hospital. I found out a few addresses to other houses. Fuck those bastards. Got no family. Don't care if they kill me now."

Celia stared at Marcy as she backed up the street until she came to the house.

"Why the hell are we back here?" Allison shouted. "Are you crazy? Let's get Justin."

"Next on our list." Celia nudged Marcy's shoulder. They jumped out of the car and Marcy ran to the garage and opened the door. Celia shut off the motor of the SUV, leaving the door to the house open.

They looked at each other, a gleam of relief passing between them.

Celia dialed 911, telling them again what they'd find at the house. She then put Nikki on to give a brief confirmation. They agreed to come when Celia told them a new group of sex slaves would be back in about one hour.

"If Svetlana calls her mother," Marcy said, "poor Zutka won't be thrilled."

"Zutka will be happy she's alive. And, if her daughter is smart, she'll cut herself a deal by outing those bastards."

Marcy swiveled her finger in the air, making a dollar sign. "Right?"

Celia laughed. "I must confess. I apologize for cutting off your sense of humor. It gave us glimmers of hope, kept me going. Good or bad memories, they reminded us of our other lives. Of course, your outstanding, hot sexuality deserved our attention."

Marcy grinned. Celia's cell dinged. A text from Stanton: "Don't know where you all went. I hope you went out for a steak dinner to celebrate. I got busy with my mole at the offshore bank who said the true owner of the account is V & S Industries."

Celia gave the news to Marcy, Allison, and Nikki.

"I feel bad. I wanted to stay with the girls. Help them." Nikki lowered her head. "I know I have to talk to the cops now."

"You'll help all those women you love more by turning those rat asses in." Marcy sighed. "What now?"

Celia heard a police siren in the distance. "I hope that's our answer," she said, and smiled.

Women and the Sex Trade

by Frances Metzman

Federal law defines this criminal enterprise, "severe forms of trafficking in persons":

1. sex trafficking in which a commercial sex act is induced by force, fraud, or coercion, or in which the person induced to perform such an act is under 18;

2. the recruitment, harboring, transportation, provision, or obtaining of a person for labor or services, through the use of force, fraud, or coercion, for the purpose of subjecting that person to involuntary servitude, forced labor, peonage, debt bondage, or slavery.

Victims are often lured by false promises of decent jobs and better lives. The inequalities women face in opportunity and justice worldwide make women particularly vulnerable to trafficking.

When I speak about it publicly, the response is, "It happens in foreign, third-world counties only, and if it's so prevalent in the USA, why aren't the authorities doing something about it?"

For one thing, this horrendous crime seems to receive less importance in pursuing than illegal drug dealing. Perhaps it's because there is a public outcry about drugs since so many addicts or drug-related deaths are children of parents who cut through all socio-economic levels and are voters. As for the sex slaves, the women generally come from a disadvantaged class with little to no voice or clout. As a group, they don't vote.

There have been a few articles and some documentaries about the plight of women sold or kidnapped into sex slavery, but the general public seems to know little to nothing about it. The women in underdeveloped countries are more susceptible to becoming ensnared in the sex trade. The United States is a big importer of sex slaves. In recent years, laws have been instituted to be more aggressive in securing arrests. The Mann Act of 1910 and its subsequent amendment resolutions make it a felony to knowingly persuade, induce, entice, or coerce an individual to travel across state lines to engage in prostitution or attempt to do so. Other countries have introduced laws as well. The U.S. and Sweden are the leaders in this effort.

Has it helped? According to the United Nations Office on Drugs and Crime (Vienna, Austria, 2 February 2021): The share of children among detected trafficking victims has tripled, while the share of boys has increased five times in the past fifteen years. Girls are mainly trafficked for sexual exploitation, while boys are used for forced labor, according to the Global Report on Trafficking in Persons.

Research from Polaris (polarisproject.org/ourwork/), an organization whose experts analyze data from the US National Human Trafficking Hotline, shows that reports of human trafficking have increased yearly since 2015, and that the offenders are known to the victims in most child trafficking cases.

What that means in terms of worldwide profits is an approximately 99 to 150 billion-dollar business annually. It is hard to determine exact amounts because deals happen under the radar. It is the second largest global crime, second only to illegal drugs. The United Nations' International Labour Organization estimated 3.8 million adults and 1 million children around the world were victims of forced sexual exploitation in 2016. A large portion are snared close to home.

Approximately 15,000 to 50,000 women and children are trafficked into the U.S. every year. That estimate might be conservative because most of these women and children never surface to the authorities. Many are lured in by the lie that they will have good jobs and a better life. Others are kidnapped or coerced. Another vulnerable group are children aging out of foster care. This occurs in many countries, including the U.S. Not many will report their plight to the authorities. They are told that the police are the enemy and will arrest them, charge them with prostitution, and deport them. Often women fall in love and develop dependence on their captors. The major threat that keeps the women from reporting the abuse is that perpetrators will kill their families in their country of origin. They keep quiet, sacrificing their own freedom to protect vulnerable family members.

A large number of the women imprisoned as sex slaves come from third world countries and suffer from poverty and homelessness. They often lack skills or resources and stay imprisoned for fear of going back on the streets again. Although they might work fourteen or more hours every day and six or seven days a week, they are kept in squalor.

Prostitution exists in all countries, but in the sex trade it is not voluntary. The victims wind up with no money. Pimps charge the women for room and board, documents, transportation, clothing, and drugs. Captors force women into addiction so they become even more dependent. With no money, no identification (perpetrators keep their passports), the enslaved are stymied and might even think their captors are protecting them from the outside world.

Women and girls as young as eight or nine and even younger are sold and forced into prostitution. Twenty-seven is around the average top age. If any of them become too ill to work they might be killed. They work in a variety of places like strip joints, bars, massage parlors, and motels. There are about nine thousand illegal spas in the U.S. alone. The women are transported to places like sporting events, concerts, hotels, motels, and brothels. Traffickers rank women's bodies as higher-yielding income than selling drugs because the women can produce money repeatedly for years, if they survive. Many of the enslaved are also used for labor. For instance, they are forced to sew, work in factories, on farms, perform janitorial services, become domestics, and work the construction trade. This goes for boys as well.

By and large, the majority of human trafficking is dependent on women providing sexual services. They are snatched, romanced, or duped from countries all over the world. The global reach occurs because they can ship women from country to country in huge containers. It behooves Mafias, who control the majority of sex trafficking, to cooperate with one another. This enables greater profits. Many women have bar codes tattooed on the back of their necks to identify which Mafia organization owns them.

Our best defense is to learn about the plight of these women. First and foremost is awareness. Look for women and children who appear malnourished, poorly dressed, or exhibit signs of physical abuse. Many will not look you in the eye, and sound as though they rehearsed a little speech. They'll often call the older male they are with "Daddy." Truckloads of young women or young women and children who always have an older male with them wherever they go are suspect.

In 2000, Congress passed the Trafficking Victims Protection Act (TVPA), which created a special "T-visa" that enables victims of sex and labor trafficking to remain in the U.S. temporarily if they agree to assist in the investigation or prosecution of their traffickers. After three years, the attorney general can admit them for permanent residency. It is nearly impossible to convey that to those enslaved as they are guarded night and day, but notifying the authorities when the situation seems awry is in order.

These women, in most cases, are worse off than the poverty they experienced before becoming captives. In addition to aborted lives, they have the burden of worrying about families that may be murdered, and younger sisters at home who remain defenseless.

This is why I chose this theme for the Cha-Cha Babes of Pelican Way to tackle. Celia and Marcy are desperate to find justice for these women and children. Have they achieved their goal after living through all their travails? What do you think? Read the book and email me at franuc@aol.com with your thoughts.

Acknowledgments

First I want to thank the publishing team, Joy Stocke, Tim Ogline, John Timpane, Raquel, and Vincent. They helped mightily by taking extra care in the editing, design, and production of *The Cha Cha Babes Dance With the Devil*. On to the next book…

Dr. Michael Schuman gave excellent input on the psychological aspects of enslaved women, and Jill Ervais helped give advice about the the operation of shipping containers and how they are monitored in our ports. Dar Dowling inspired and cheered me on from the beginning to the end as well as providing advice. Thanks to the many others who contributed to the accuracy of the novel.

About the Author

Frances Metzman writes fiction because it affords her the ability to find closure for events and relationships that prove elusive in real life. A former sculptor, she's traded creating images with clay to images with words.

Her short story collection *The Hungry Heart Stories* was published by Wilderness House Press. She co-authored and a novel, *Ugky Cookie*s, published by Pella Publishing. She has published 24 short stories in college and university journals and speaks on panels of various writing conferences such as Philadelphia Stories and Marymount Manhattan College. She has given numerous workshops at various universities including Temple University, Bryn Mawr College, Penn State, Widener and many others. Also, she presently teaches creative writing/memoir workshops at Temple University's adult program, OLLI. At Rosemont College, she taught publishing/writing skills to graduate students. As fiction editor for a literary journal, *Schuylkill Valley Journal*, she selects and edits the submissions. Many of her articles, essays, and stories deal with all aspects of society that influences relationships for all ages, including the mature set (sometimes tongue in cheek).

Frances Metzman

If you responded positively, cheered for the characters
in this thriller, please write your response on Amazon.
It would be very much appreciated.

Thanks,
Frances

 Frances Metzman Written Work

 @FranWrites

 www.francesmetzman.com

caught up in a mystery that may cost her and her daughter their lives. The curtain goes up on a frantic call in the middle of the night. Celia's new friend Marcy is in a predicament. Marcy has been flattened, to be specific, by the hulking weight of her senior citizen boyfriend, who has died during their secret tryst. Another friend has been called in to consult. They do the only thing they can think to do, the only thing right-thinking people in such a predicament would, of course, do—swab the naked body, wrap it in blankets, and wheelchair it back to its bed."

– Beth Kephart, *The Philadelphia Inquirer*

"When 65-year-old Celia, a resident of Boca Pelicano Palms in Florida, gets a call in the middle of the night from her friend and neighbor Marcy, also 65, about a vaguely described "big problem," she wakes their 69-year-old mutual friend Deb, and heads over to help. Celia would do anything for Marcy or Deb—they recently talked her out of a suicide attempt, after all—but she doesn't yet realize how her loyalty will be tested.Metzman writes with humor and a sharp eye for characterization, as when she describes how Deb's "rheumatoid arthritis... affected every joint and muscle in her body, except for her acerbic tongue."The book is a pleasing blend of camp and procedural mystery, playing up the geriatric nature of the setting while also taking the concerns and passions of Celia and her peers seriously…Metzman has crafted a compelling and surprising whodunit whose plot likely won't end up where readers expect…The author artfully constructs each of these characters, giving them backstories full of regret and frustration that lend literary weight to their sometimes-comical present… It turns out that retirement provides plenty of opportunities to turn things around—and to solve a few murders as well. A thoroughly entertaining, lighthearted murder mystery."

– *Kirkus*

"Full of fun thrills that will make you smile and keep you on the edge of your seat."

– Chicago Tribune

"*The Cha-Cha babes of Pelican Way* is riveting! At timesyou will smile, at times you will cry but in the end you will leave with asmile from side to side. Long live the Cha-Cha babes..."

– The DailyPress

"A laugh-out-loud book that will make you take you on a whirlwind of emotion..."

– The Baltimore Sun

"A MUST Read, filled with humor, thrills and even some chills that you will love time and time over. "

– The Capital Gazette

"...filled with descriptiveness and raw grit that only a seasoned pro can pull off.

– The Virginia Gazette

"The feel good book of the summer is here; so grab the beach chairand bring the *The Cha-Cha Babes of Pelican Way* with you to your favorite reading spot.

– The Orlando Sentinel

The Potluck Murder

Celia and Marcy, are back in Boca Pelicano Palms peacefully enjoying the Florida sunshine and relieved that their friend Deb has returned after living near her son who is serving a twenty-year sentence for fraud. In the time she was away, Deb has learned more than she ever imagined about the inner workings of the legal system. And in her ardor to find peace, has become devoted to a new-found spirituality, having joined the Peace and Connection Center, modeled on the Quakers and Unitarian Universalists, whose mission is to foster friendship, unity, inclusiveness, and justice.

Within the congregation are some of the best chefs in their beach front town of Boca Pelicano. Celia and Marcy wanting to find peace of their own, good food, and in Marcy's case, a rich philanthropic husband, join Deb in their own quests for deeper spirituality. Each Sunday after the service, the community holds a potluck supper.

Marcy makes her special brisket, a favorite among the chefs, who ask "How do you keep your brisket so juicy and tender?"

"Come on over to my kitchen," she winks. "And I'll show you."

One Sunday as the group is sitting down to dinner, they hear sirens. Suddenly, three squad cars pull up, stopping at the apartment attached to the Center where the Facilitator lives with his wife. Minutes later, the police burst in and order everyone to stay for questioning. The Facilitator's wife has been murdered in an apparent robbery gone wrong.

"Not again," says Celia.

Deb goes silent. Her face turns white.

"And I was so close to finding my philanthropist," says Marcy.

They soon find that none of the pieces in this murder add up and launch their own investigatation. But the killer is on to them. As the circle tightens, the question remains: Will they survive their investigation and find the killer before the killer finds them?

9 798986 618876